EERIE RIVER PUBLISHING HORROR

MONSTERS & MAYHEM

TALES FROM THE RIVER VOLUME TWO

EERIE RIVER PUBLISHING
www.EerieRiverPublishing.com

MONSTERS & MAYHEM

Christopher Bond
Erica Ciko Campbell
Jessica Casey
Georgia Cook
Radar DeBoard
J.M. Faulkner
RJ Fuller
David Green
Chris Hewitt
Rowan Hill
Hunter LaCross
Nikki R. Leigh
Ronald Linson
Tim Mendees
E.N. Neely
Ethan Sabatella
Josh Sippie
William Sterling
Shelby Suderman
Rachel L. Tilley
Kevin Walsh
Ann Wuehler

Eerie River Publishing
www.EerieRiverPublishing.com
Hamilton, Ontario Canada

Paperback ISBN: 978-1-990245-55-8
Hardcover ISBN: 978-1-990245-56-5
Digital ISBN: 978-1-990245-54-1

Edited & Curated by Alanna Robertson-Webb & S.O. Green
Cover Art by Michelle River

CONTENTS

THE DEEPEST DARK
BY GEORGIA COOK

Sandra trailed her hand along the wall, feeling the slickness beneath her glove, searching for the spot where the natural spring gushed from the bedrock.

"Careful here," she said, turning to Clare. "Rock's slippery. We've got another puncture."

Clare nodded, headlamp bobbing in the ink-black darkness, and made a note on her little waterproof map. "How many streams does this network have?"

"God only knows."

Sandra glanced around the cavern. It was one of the larger ones—about the size of a small van, just enough room for two people to stand upright comfortably. The floor was a mass of fallen rock, through which a tiny stream gushed and flowed from a crack in the wall. One end opened into the narrow tunnel they'd descended, accessed through a three-foot squeeze gap at head height. At the other end, just visible beyond the rocks, the cave continued down through an even smaller tunnel into deep darkness.

Like a throat, Sandra thought, and suppressed a shudder. "I used to hate these caves as a kid."

"Really? Why? I thought caves were your thing."

Sandra paused. Caves were her thing; she'd loved them since she was a teenager, never bothered by tight gaps or the unknown darkness. But how to explain the childhood allure of Spin Rope Caves? A mass of low, elongated tunnels connecting tiny caverns to tiny caverns in a slow, graceful spiral deep into the earth. There were stories about this place—legends whispered by the locals—that Spin Rope was the gullet of some vast beast. Monsters lurked down here—old gods, bent on revenge. You could wander into the dark and never return.

She'd had nightmares about the place as a child—of tunnels never ending, darkness never ceasing, just an eternal climb down into the deep.

She managed a shrug. "Gave me the creeps."

"I like them..." said Clare. "You're so lucky to have grown up close by. I first read about them on the internet at college. They always reminded me of old fairy tales."

"Fairy tales?"

"You know, wood nymphs and water sprites, Titania and Oberon, things like that." Clare's smile gleamed cheerleader-bright in the torchlight. She affected a low, ominous voice: "Tunnels leading down, down to Faerie!"

Sandra tried to smile, but an image had arisen in her mind, picture-bright against the dark. As a child, she'd discovered a book of Greek myths in the town's tiny library—a building they'd passed on the drive here, empty now and boarded over, much like the rest of town—a flimsy paperback, filled with all manner of lurid illustrations: Hercules decapitating a writhing Hydra, Theseus plunging his blade into the charging minotaur, the three Moirae— sisters of Fate—weaving their tapestry of human lives...

Terrified and fascinated in equal measure, Sandra had found them each enthralling. But the picture that had stuck with her the longest was the illustration of Orpheus descending into the Underworld. In cheap ink and garish green, the artist had rendered a world of staring eyes and gaping mouths; the dead groped up from stone-choked caverns to snatch Orpheus' ankles, shadows deepening as he clambered ever downward to defy Hades.

The old gods from her stories were never so playful.

Slowly, almost unconsciously, Sandra found her gaze drawn to the tiny passageway at the back of the cavern.

"...leading down to Hades..." she murmured.

Clare glanced up. "What?"

Sandra shook herself. "Oh, nothing." She secured the safety rope around her waist, tapping her headlamp to ensure it wasn't flickering. "Let's keep going," she added, in what she hoped was a professional tone. "We need to assess another five of these caves before we head back."

And she wanted to head back. They'd been down here all of four hours already, scrambling and crawling into caves almost too small to stand. Down, down, down the winding pathways of Spin Rope Caves. She suspected the university had given her this assignment because she was a local—to pacify any dissenting voices—but what it had given them was a researcher with a local's knowledge, and a local's inherent superstition.

They approached the tunnel at the back of the cavern and peered down. It was a tight squeeze, maybe a foot, dropping straight down into sudden darkness. Clare angled her headlamp to get a better look, but the light only found more rock. "How far down do you think it goes?"

"Ten feet, maybe eleven?" guessed Sandra.

"Do the guides say anything?"

Sandra shook her head. The last attempt to map this network had been carried out in the '70s by a group of amateur cavers, following a rough map sketched in the 1800s. They'd made it to the sixth cavern before losing their bearings, splitting off as they stumbled in blind terror through the dark. Two of them—Alicia Willis and Frank Aaronovitch—had vanished in the confusion, presumably plummeting into one of the deep sinkholes puncturing the network.

Once the others had been dragged out, trembling and inconsolable, they described a winding labyrinth of unrecognizable caves, pitch black, twisting and warping into the rock. The map, they'd said, had shown them an impossible route down, looping back and over itself.

Official reports concluded that the team had been too inexperienced to handle the caves, placing their blind faith in a map drawn from memory by people with no notion of underground geography. The disappearances of Willis and Aaronovitch were put down to misadventure, and as none of the team could accurately determine where or how they had vanished, nobody returned to retrieve the bodies. The townsfolk had sealed the entrance, put up a discreet fence, and kept their distance.

Until now.

"Do you hear that?"

Sandra blinked. "Hear what?"

Clare shushed her. "Listen."

Sandra listened. There was something; hitching and falling below the splashing of distant water. A low rumbling.

"What do you think it is?" whispered Clare. "An earthquake?"

Sandra shook her head, forcing away the tendrils of dread. "It sounds like an engine..."

"What would an engine be doing down here?" Clare's headlamp swept their surroundings, watching for shivering stalactites or dislodged rocks—the tell-tale signs of a collapse. "It doesn't sound like that at all..."

Sandra opened her mouth to reply, but quickly shut it again. Clare was right; it didn't sound like that. But it sounded familiar. Not unnatural—like a car motor, or human footsteps—but constant, rhythmic...

In...out...in...out....

Breathing. It sounded like breathing.

The thought froze Sandra to the spot. She closed her eyes, struggling to ground herself in the crushing dark. She'd never been claustrophobic before—never uneasy in tight spaces or cramped cavern tunnels. It was part of what made her such a useful researcher. Only here, only now, in a place of childhood mythology, did an unfamiliar tightness grasp her lungs.

Down... Down to Hades...

God, she wanted to leave.

"We should keep going…" whispered Clare.

Sandra glanced at her. Clare's eyes gleamed in the darkness, intrigued and excited. "…you sure?" she asked. "Christ, we don't know what's down there…"

"Isn't that the whole point?"

The rumbling had already subsided, letting the subterranean silence sweep back in. Sandra shook herself. Clare was right; they had a job to do. They were qualified for this. They were assessing Spin Rope Caves, decades overdue, making sure it was safe. This was important.

Clare had already secured her rope to the nearest rock, apparently undisturbed by either their surroundings or the low, background rumble. Actually, she was smiling.

Sandra watched her turn and wiggle down into the tiny tunnel, the light from her headlamp casting jagged, violent shadows across the walls before snuffing out completely.

Sandra waited, holding her breath, half-listening for the return of the strange noise. What did she hope for? That Clare would come back? That the way would be blocked? That, despite their best efforts, they were no more able to map Spin Rope Caves than the previous expeditions?

There was a shuffling, scraping sound, followed by muffled swearing. Sandra peered down into the hole. "What's it like?" she called, hating how small her voice sounded.

"Bit tight, but workable! Come on!"

Reluctantly, Sandra attached her rope to the rock, tested her weight, and edged down into the hole after Clare.

The tunnel was tighter than she'd anticipated. After the slim entranceway, the walls narrowed again, making descent more of a downward struggle than a drop. Clare was already far below, her light occasionally flickering up towards the surface.

Sandra steeled herself, closed her eyes, and dropped.

With her eyes shut, it felt for a moment as if she were climbing upwards, then suddenly sideways. As if space had twisted in on itself for this one, painful scramble. Sandra struggled to maintain her breathing. Suddenly, crushed tight between walls of unyielding stone, she could understand the panic others described when she explained her job to them.

Down in the dark. Trapped in the bowels of the earth.

Where nobody would ever find her...

Sandra's feet struck rock. The passage opened out suddenly into a wider space. She allowed herself a gasp of relief, wiggling and twisting until the tunnel released her. She dropped gracelessly to the cave floor, landing several feet below. She stumbled, caught herself, and looked around.

They'd dropped into a long entrance chamber, curved at the ceilings to create a squat, round tube, just tall enough to stand upright. Above her head, the tunnel they'd descended spiralled upwards. Sandra tried not to picture how difficult the ascent would be; that was a problem for later.

"Clare?" she hissed.

"Over here!" Clare stood at the other end of the chamber, peering through a vast hole into the next cavern. "Look at this!" she whispered. "It just goes back and back! It's the largest entrance I've seen!"

"Thank God for that," Sandra muttered, picking her

way across the floor. It was almost completely smooth, save for a scattering of fallen stalactites here and there, creating strange, natural twists and cracks in the rock. "These tiny rooms are starting to get to me."

She paused. The cave ahead of them truly was vast. Even at full beam, their headlamps barely punctured the darkness, merely shifting shadows into clumps of grey. It was like staring into a deep, black lake.

Sandra stared. "This doesn't make sense..."

They'd studied the map left by the 1970's team—tracing the branching network of tiny spaces and cramped caverns—but none of them had indicated a cavern of this size. Nothing of this magnitude should even exist down here.

A void of this size...

"It must be huge..." Clare whispered. "How did anyone miss this?"

Sandra turned, unable to read Clare's expression in the blinding beam of her headlamp. Was that fear in Clare's voice, or excitement? Awe? Clare took a step forward, footsteps echoing out into the dark. Sandra fought the sudden urge to stop her—to grab her arm, pull her back. "Wait—"

"Come on!"

Slowly, slowly, as if she were on the verge of plunging into a deep abyss, Sandra followed.

Immediately, the air around them shifted. The temperature plummeted. Sandra shivered, her skin prickling with goosebumps. She sensed a vast, open space high above, as tall as a cathedral, leading back and back into impossible blackness.

And something else...

The rumbling was back. It rose and fell in the empty air, louder now, filling the darkness, echoing off the walls. Sandra froze, her heart pounding. Listening.

Clare had vanished up ahead, headlamp flickering against the smooth, stone floor, catching a distant wall at least 30 meters away. Suddenly, Sandra wanted nothing to do with this place, the oppressive crush of so much air, so much space, so much rock above them. She envisioned Clare's light growing smaller and smaller, deeper and deeper, until the darkness swallowed her completely. Swept away by a tide of childhood terrors...

"...Clare..." Her voice came out strange and muffled, swallowed by the distant ceiling. "Clare!"

"My God..." Clare's voice came as if from a long way off. "Sandra..."

Sandra forced herself to walk forward, guided by the distant pinprick of Clare's light, trying not to wonder how this place had sat undiscovered for so long, how nobody had ever thought to—

"Look."

Clare's voice had dropped to a whisper. She motioned ahead to the far wall.

Sandra turned, visions of Alicia Willis and Frank Aaronovitch flickering across her mind. "What the fuck—"

What she'd initially taken to be a rock formation at the back of the cavern had shifted, ever so slightly. Something glimmered in the light of Sandra's headlamp, rough as uncut diamonds. Sandra stared at it, unable to force the shape into a trick of the shadows, to merge it back into the natural scenery.

It can't be.... It can't be...

...a foot. It was a foot. A foot as long as their truck outside, attached to a long, grey leg, leading up and up...

Sandra's gaze rose to follow it, hoping against all hope that she was imagining things, that this was some terrible hallucination, another jab of madness or fear.

The leg rose to an impossible height, ending at a fold of heavy, grey cloth, the bones of a vast hip jagged beneath, then a midriff, crusted with dirt, followed by a chest, then a bunched muscular shoulder, then...

Then the face.

A man as tall as a redwood stood hunched in this vast underground chamber, his legs planted firmly on either side of the cavern floor. He was dressed in a stained and tattered winding cloth. His eyes were as vast as truck wheels and as brown as the earth, staring and wide, filled with a paralyzing madness. His hands tensed and strained, grasping the cavern roof as if he were the only thing holding it aloft.

Sandra froze, unable to rationalize what she was seeing. It was a trick of the light. A sleep-deprived hallucination. Perhaps she'd fallen down the tiny tunnel, smacked her head on the rock, and was dreaming herself awake, still fumbling through the dark.

"He's beautiful..."

Sandra turned. Clare stood a short distance away, headlamp angled upwards, expression frozen in something resembling both terror and delight. A word rose in Sandra's mind, cutting through the mists of panic and confusion: Devotion.

Orpheus gazing at his beloved Eurydice. Or maybe Persephone, realising the dark allure of Hades.

The giant hadn't moved, not even to gasp a breath or shift his grip. His gaze remained fixed on the two women, lips pressed shut, muscles straining against the weight.

"Clare..." Sandra stumbled backwards, fumbling for Clare's arm, unable to tear her eyes away. "Clare, Christ, we... We need to—"

Run. Scream. Leave and never return. Escape back to the world of normality and sense. Where this could be rationalised away into...what?

Clare didn't move. Not even when Sandra finally grasped her arm and pulled. "Look at him..." she murmured, eyes misty with wonder. "Look at him, Sandra."

Sandra let out a sob. "Yes, I can bloody see him. We have to—"

"He was down here all this time. Through all these caves. Waiting for us..."

"Not for us, not for anyone! We have to—"

But even in her panic, Sandra could see it was too late. Clare was entranced. Was this what had happened to Frank and Alicia, down here in the deep dark? Had they found this cave, stumbled upon this creature—this ancient Titan-God, holding up the world—and been filled with rapturous awe? Or had they been as terrified as Sandra was?

With a rumbling of rock and a shuddering of stones, still holding the ceiling high above his head, his eyes still fixed unblinkingly on them, the giant began to kneel.

Sandra found herself staring into a pupil as vast as a tractor wheel. Her own reflection stared back at her, small and strange in its orange jumpsuit and flickering headlamp. She saw no compassion in those eyes, no interest, no malice. They were as cold and flat as a shark's, as the eyes stitched into a taxidermy fox.

If she ran now, perhaps she would reach the entrance tunnel, then the rope leading to the upper caverns. She could scramble up, claw her way to the surface. Find somewhere to hide, someone to—

Something grabbed her arm. It was Clare. She'd removed her helmet, her hair tumbling in a matted swirl, her eyes shining in the blackness. "Sacrifice!" she whispered. Her fingers dug into Sandra's arm.

"Clare, Jesus Christ!"

"He needs a sacrifice, don't you see? He's been trapped here for so long. So, so long…"

"We have to go!"

Clare stared at her, an expression of bewilderment finally creasing her face. "Go?" she whispered. "Why on earth would I want to go anywhere?"

Behind them, the giant continued to kneel. The ground rumbled. Dust rained from the ceiling. Her mind flashed back to that old book with its garish drawings. She remembered Atlas, a creature cast from the oldest myths, the whispered legends, surviving on the fringes of human understanding. The oldest of the old gods, buried in the deepest dark, condemned to hold up the world for eternity.

What happens, whispered the quiet voice of terror, when he stops?

With a burst of strength, Sandra tore herself from Clare's grip and stumbled for the exit, tripping and falling on the uneven floor. Her headlamp juddered wildly, throwing great, black shadows across the walls.

In the midst of terror, Sandra pictured the last group to enter Spin Rope Cave. The little group of students, clambering down into the dark with their ropes and battered torches, clutching a map drawn by hands long dead. The team that had lost two of its number to the endless twisting tunnels.

What had they found down here, buried deep beneath the earth? What had found them, running blind through the twisting tunnels? Had those first explorers found it too, two centuries ago, as they clambered through this place with oil lamps and trailing rope?

Behind her came the sound of pounding footsteps; running, scrambling, stumbling after her. Clare, breathing, gasping, giggling, as she gave chase. Coming to drag her back, to yank her into the dark. Sandra didn't dare turn around. She didn't dare look.

She didn't dare—

EUGENE ANGOVE LOSES HIS MARBLES

BY TIM MENDEES

JUNE 16TH, 1933
ANGOVE HALL, HIGH BEND, CORNWALL

The stout front door of Angove hall creaked ajar, allowing the tantalising aroma of roast pheasant to escape into the early dusk. The man in the rumpled suit on the doorstep huddled against the biting wind and tried to get the kink out of his spine. The journey from London had played havoc with his ageing frame.

"Good evening, Mr Walpole." A smartly turned out valet purred from the welcoming interior. "I'm afraid we weren't expecting you until tomorrow. Can I take your coat?"

Richmond Walpole bustled inside and dropped his Gladstone bag onto the hardwood floor. "I don't know how you stand the ruddy wind over here, Hampton. I really don't. It's enough to freeze the barnacles off a whale's backside!"

Walpole had the permanent tan of the well-travelled archaeologist. This meant that, despite his Yorkshire roots, he was much more at home in warmer climates.

"Indeed, sir." Hampton took Walpole's top hat and placed it on the stand. "Perhaps a restorative brandy will do you good?"

"Aye. That'd be champion! So... Where is the old devil then?"

"Mister Angove is entertaining an old friend in the library, sir. I believe they are playing marbles." Hampton couldn't help rolling his eyes.

"What?"

"Marbles, sir... Decorative glass spheres used in a number of competitive games. I believe they are competing under championship rules."

Walpole held up his hand. "Blast it, Hampton. I know what chuffing marbles are. What I mean to say is, what is the bloody fool doing playing with them when there are important matters to be attended to?"

"I believe that Mr Angove and his guest were keen marble players at school, sir. They read about the game becoming a championship sport and decided to get in training, as it were. This quickly led to an argument over who was the Truro School King of Marbles, and a series of bets were made... They've been playing for three hours now."

Hampton directed Walpole to the lounge and fixed him a large cognac. He took a fortifying gulp and sunk into a wingback chair. "Blast that man. Championship marbles, indeed. I bet the lazy bugger has left all the cataloguing to me?"

Producing a ream of papers affixed to a board with a bulldog clip, Hampton smiled. "I think you will be pleasantly surprised, Mr Walpole. He has catalogued the entire Orkney collection and has it packed and ready for transport to the British Museum. The artefacts are laid out in neat piles over in the stables as we speak."

"Well!" Walpole looked stunned. "I'm impressed, Hampton. Is the old dog not feeling well?"

Hampton couldn't help but smirk. "I took the liberty of instructing the archaeological team to leave all the crates and equipment in the library. I'm afraid they made a bit of a mess..."

"Ha!" Walpole nearly threw his glass into the air in triumph. "Well done, Hampton. We both know that he can't stand his precious library being in disarray. I bet it drove him doolally."

"Indeed it did, sir. He even missed a charity cricket match over in Hollowhills. He was so intent on setting it straight."

"Bravo!" Walpole chuckled. "I suppose I had better go and double-check that nothing has gone missing. I know what a sticky-fingered rascal he can be when left unsupervised... I will be out in the stables, Hampton. Tell him I'm here, won't you?"

"Very good, sir. I will be upstairs preparing the guest suite if you require anything further."

Walpole snatched up the crystal decanter containing Eugene Angove's favourite tipple and followed the beleaguered valet out of the room. "I think I'll be fine, Hampton.

A couple more drops of this, and I'll be happy as a pig in sh—"

"Watch it, you dozy fopdoodle!"

The sound of a loud clatter followed by Eugene's dulcet tones echoing around Angove hall derailed Mr Walpole's train of thought. He looked at Hampton, who just shrugged and picked up Walpole's bag.

"I think it may be wisest not to ask, sir..."

Since leaving the British Army following the Great War, Eugene Angove had become the bane of the archaeological world. As a self-styled adventurer, he had neither the qualifications nor the care of his more esteemed counterparts. This didn't stop him from having a knack for stumbling over sites of extreme academic importance, much to the chagrin of museum curators and professors alike.

One such discovery was made while on a fishing holiday to the Orkney Islands. Eugene had quickly abandoned fishing in favour of the local whiskey. During a particularly messy binge with a group of fishermen, talk had turned to old island superstitions and legends.

This is where Eugene differed from the traditional archaeologist. Where most would have dismissed the tales as poppycock of the highest order, Eugene ate it up with a spoon. The more booze he imbibed, the more plausible the stories became.

One of his companions, a grizzled, old lobsterman with a beard like a rhododendron bush, spun him a yarn about a burial chamber said to contain Viking plunder along the coast of Westray Island. None of them would even go near the place. Cursed, they said. It would be death of any man who ventured inside the chamber...

Three days later, Eugene and Hampton hired a small boat and went for an exploratory jaunt.

Access to the chamber was almost exactly where the old sailor had indicated. The tricky part proved to be getting inside. The only aperture was a narrow shaft near the edge of the cliff. Hurrying back to their hotel, Eugene wired one of the few academics that would give him the time of day, Mr Richmond Walpole, for assistance. He glossed over the fishermen's tales and concocted a cock-and-bull story about Viking runes and an ancient map. Eugene was a well-practised bullshit artist.

He quickly convinced Walpole to send him a small team of undergraduates from Cambridge armed with mountaineering equipment.

Not for the first time, Eugene's gamble paid off. The chamber proved to be brimming with artefacts. On the downside, it didn't contain Viking plunder.

In fact, the chamber had nothing to do with Vikings whatsoever. It appeared to be some kind of pre-Christian place of worship. It housed an unnerving clutter of fetishistic totems, decorated animal skulls and disturbing soapstone statuettes. Eugene knew that he wasn't going to get the quick cash he would have got from jewels and trinkets, but he was happy all the same. All he had to do was play ball and collect his finder's fee.

When Walpole heard of Eugene's find, he travelled to the site along with a couple of colleagues and performed a comprehensive study. The walls of the temple were covered in strange, geometric designs that made your brain hurt if you stared at them for too long. He had seen similar plac-es in Turkey and Peru, and knew that the temple's contents would have to be treated with the utmost care. Not just for the sake of preserving history, but also for the safety of the human race.

The last thing he needed was Eugene waltzing off with some of the...more uncommon items.

Clatter!

"Watch it, you bloody fopdoodle!" Eugene bellowed, as his precious marbles vanished under bookshelves and soft furnishings. "Don't be such a sore loser!"

His guest, an old school chum by the name of Topper Trueman, had lost three of the last four rounds, and had responded by petulantly slamming a bumblebee boulder down onto an assorted pile with such force that Eugene's marbles shot off in all directions.

"You're cheating, I know it!" Topper folded his arms over his chest, sitting cross-legged on the polished wood floor. The elder of the Truro Trueman's was blessed with a bushy, silver beard, which gave him more the appearance of a petulant gnome than a shipping magnate. "You have to be cheating. Nobody is this good at marbles after thirty-odd years!"

"How can you cheat at marbles, for Christ's sake? You either knock them out of the chalk circle, or you don't." Eugene groaned as he stood up. "Now, get off your backside and help me find them."

Topper Trueman grumbled as he crawled across the floor and used a chaise longue to haul his portly frame upright. "Fine. Then one more game. What do you say to double or quits?"

A predatory smile spread across Eugene's chops. "You always were a glutton for punishment, old chap. Very well! Double or quits it is. Now get your body over here and help me shift this Chesterfield. The last time I tried to move it on my own, I damn near gave myself a hernia."

Blowing out his bewhiskered cheeks like a disgruntled pufferfish, Topper Trueman took the opposing end of the heavy sofa and started to heave it over towards the window. After a few moments of groaning, puffing and panting, the two out-of-shape gentlemen uncovered two cat's eye marbles.

"I take it you did the cleaning in here after you'd shifted those crates?" Topper asked, with a mischievous look in his eye.

"What makes you say that?"

"Well, it looks like all the dirt has just been swept under things. I can't see Hampton being so lax. This has all the hallmarks of an Angove Special."

Eugene opened his mouth to argue but quickly decided against it. It was a fair cop. All of his close friends and acquaintances knew that Mr Angove was a master at cutting corners and dodging hard work. "Shut your trap and help me move the Chesterfield back. We've got plenty more of these little devils to find before I can give you another thrashing."

For close to an hour, the two old friends bickered as they scrabbled around on their hands and knees. Due to Eugene's terrible cleaning job, most of the pesky little spheres were coated in a thick film of dust and detritus from the Orkney dig. This slowed down the commencement of their final match even more. Each marble had to be individually wiped before being added to the circle of play.

Eventually, they were ready to commence battle.

"You can go first," Eugene sniffed, flexing his shooting fingers. "You need all the help you can get."

Topper Trueman buffed his favourite aggie shooter on his sleeve, then lined it up on the starting line. He took a deep breath then they were off. It was a fast and furious contest. Glass clacked against glass. Prayers were whispered and oaths spat. Topper took an early lead. It looked like the game was his when he misfired horribly, allowing Eugene to close the gap between them. When it came down to the nitty-gritty, the two men were neck and neck. It was all to play for...and it was Topper Trueman's turn.

Trueman licked his lips and reached for a suitable shooter. There were two tiny firecrackers in play. They were close to each other, so if he could somehow ricochet them, he could clean up. Due to their diminutive size, he reached for a boulder to give him the best chance of connecting. Eugene was about to regret allowing boulders in play. The largest of all the marbles could only be included by mutual agreement, and Eugene had been the one to suggest their inclusion.

Trueman smiled. This victory was going to be sweet.

Picking it up between thumb and forefinger, Topper wiped the boulder off on his sleeve. It was an unusual design, not one he'd seen before. It was dark green, filled with lines and whorls. It was somewhere between a galaxy, a starburst, and an octopus. Placing it on the starting point, Topper Trueman leant forward, closed one eye and prepared to go in for the kill...

"What the bloody hell are you playing at, Angove?"

Just as Topper was about to take his shot, the door burst open and an irate Mr Walpole burst into the library clutching an almost empty decanter in one hand and a list of artefacts in the other.

"Oi!" Topper Trueman cried in outrage. "You nearly put me off my strike, you oaf!"

"Hello, Walpole," Eugene said, not taking his eyes off his competitor's marble. "What's the problem this time?"

Angove's nonchalance and disinterest enraged the archaeologist even further. "You know what the problem is, you blackguard. Where is it?"

"Where's what?" Eugene looked at Walpole with his hands raised and a bemused smile playing on his lips. "I have no idea what you're blithering on about, man."

"The artefact you've pinched! I must have it back. It could be dangerous if it falls into the wrong hands."

"Calm down, Walpole. I assure you, I haven't the foggiest notion what you're on about."

Walpole waved the list in the air like a flag. "The Sphere of Yog-Sothoth... Where is the Sphere of Yog-Sothoth, you bounder?"

"Silence!" Topper bellowed at the top of his lungs, stunning Eugene and Walpole. While they were dumbstruck, he leaned forward and took his shot.

Time seemed to slow to a crawl as Walpole screamed. In the last second, he'd realised that what Trueman was using as a shooter wasn't a marble at all...

It was the sphere of Yog-Sothoth.

The spinning object clattered against the other marbles, sending them flying out of the circle. Walpole dropped the decanter. It hit the floor and exploded. The library was showered in shards of cut crystal and drops of aged brandy.

Topper cheered, oblivious to the archaeologist steaming towards him. He reached down, snatched up his prize marble and leapt to his feet. "I win! Cough up, Angove!"

"Give me that!" Walpole demanded, reaching for the Sphere.

"What?" Trueman grinned. "Give up my prize shooter? Not on your nelly."

"That's not a marble, you fool!" Walpole cried. "That's the Sphere of Yog-Sothoth, believed to be part of the Outer God itself! You two idiots have been playing a children's game with a god!"

"My decanter!" Eugene growled, storming towards Walpole with his fists balled. "You smashed my decanter, you swine! And you wasted the last of the good brandy!"

Trueman backed away from Walpole, still clutching the marble. The wild look in the archaeologist's eyes was terrifying.

He was about to hand the Sphere over when the universe paused, just for a second. The artefact imploded, folding in on itself, before cracking open. A sonic wave swept across the library, shattering the windows and pulverising the other marbles.

Topper Trueman screamed. His hand had been atomised.

"Keep back!" Walpole yelled at Eugene, just as he was about to leap over to his friend.

The two men stood and watched in horror as the small, greenish ball started to swirl and expand, free-floating between them and Topper. The patterns within sped into a dizzying whirl. Its surface became iridescent and glutinous, like the skin of some kind of monstrous sea animal.

Trueman continued to scream as the impossible vortex began to suck more mass into itself. Anything it touched became assimilated. Motes of dust and sprinkles of shattered glass, pieces of furniture and books pulled from shelves. Soon, it had swollen to the size of a beachball. Then, it started to move towards Trueman.

He tried to back away, but it was no use. Two pseudopods fashioned from filth and protoplasm shot out from its body and coiled around Trueman's truncated arm, shredding and liquidising as it reeled him in.

Meat, blood and bone joined the rapidly expanding Sphere as it latched onto Trueman and engulfed his upper body. For a moment, it stopped moving, revealing the true horror of itself. Walpole gagged. Eugene couldn't help thinking that it looked like a ghastly toffee apple perched precariously on a tweed stick.

Neither man dared move. Until...

"Would anyone care for a sherry?"

Hampton's entrance, carrying a tray with a bottle and three glasses, sparked the abomination into action. It lurched towards Walpole on unsteady legs. Tendrils sprouted from its top and lashed at the ceiling.

"Out of the way, man!" Eugene bellowed, and hit Walpole with a rugby tackle that drove him away from the incoming threat and into a bookcase.

A collection of encyclopaedias clattered to the floor. Eugene snatched one up and lobbed it at Yog-Sothoth. It vanished into the maelstrom at its epicentre.

"Run for your life!" he cried, grabbed Walpole by the shoulder and dragged him towards the door.

Hampton assessed the situation. If he didn't do something, the questing fronds from the beast would snag his employer and Mr Walpole before they could escape. Placing the tray on a low table, Hampton snatched up a foot-stool and, as Eugene and Walpole went left, he belted the amalgamation as hard as he could to the right. His blow connected with the portion of the creature that was still Topper Trueman, knocking it off balance and sending it veering off towards the play circle.

As soon as Trueman's feet went within the confines of the chalk, the creature stopped. then began to vibrate, fizz and shriek.

"What the hell is going on?" Eugene asked, as he helped Walpole out of the room.

"I don't know. It must be the symbol."

Before Eugene could question further, Yog-Sothoth broke away from Trueman at the waist. The ball of twisting matter detached with a sickening rip then rose into the air. Ropes of glistening intestine dangled below it, twitching and dancing like the fronds of a jellyfish. It swung its grisly appendages at Hampton as he attempted to flee. One caught him in the back of the head with a wet smack. Hampton flew forwards and tumbled over the arm of the Chesterfield.

"Hampton!"

Eugene flew into action, grabbing the dazed valet by the waist and hauling him out of the library.

Walpole slammed the door behind them and grabbed Eugene by the lapels. "What the hell do you think you are doing?! Using a dangerous artefact as a bloody marble? You've unleashed Yog-Sothoth!"

Eugene snarled and swatted his hands away. "I didn't, you bloody idiot. It must have rolled under one of the book-cases when I sorted the crates out."

"Wait," Hampton panted, trying to scrape the foul stickiness out of his hair. "You know what that thing is?"

"Yes... yes. It's part of the Great Old One Yog-Sothoth. I had my suspicions, but I wasn't sure."

"And now?"

"Yes, Hampton. I'm afraid I was right. Yog-Sothoth is said to be comprised of thousands of spheres like the one in there. That wasn't a temple you found up in Orkney, Eugene. It was a prison. Somehow, they managed to imprison a portion of the Opener of the Way. For their own nefarious purposes, no doubt."

From inside the library, they could hear furniture being smashed into atoms and sucked into Yog-Sothoth, a din like someone chewing a mouthful of gravel.

"Right." Eugene snarled, rounding on Walpole. "Why the hell didn't you tell me what it was?"

"I... I didn't want you to pinch it. I thought if you knew it was dangerous, you'd...make off with it."

"What the devil for?"

"Money! Some secret societies would pay handsomely for such a thing."

"You're an idiot, Walpole!" Eugene snapped. "I don't dabble with dangerous artefacts. For a start, the Brotherhood of Tamesis would skin me alive, and secondly, I'm not a damned fool! I've seen first-hand what dabbling with this kind of thing gets you. Dead, that's what! You should have told me, Walpole. I would have made sure it was safe."

Hampton squeezed himself between the two men. "Calm down, both of you. This isn't going to help." Turning to Walpole. "If that's only a small part of this god, where might the rest of it be?"

"I can only surmise that the rest of Yog-Sothoth is on its way."

"And that's definitely not good..." Hampton shook his head. "What were you saying about the chalk circle."

Bang!

"Bollocks!" Eugene wailed, as the door was walloped

with such force it nearly splintered. "This isn't going to hold. Into the lounge!"

The three men scrambled into the sumptuous lounge and slammed the doors, just as Yog-Sothoth burst into the entrance hall and started to devour pot plants, coats and boots.

"What do we do?" Eugene demanded, but Walpole wasn't listening. He was busy flipping through a tatty old notebook. "Walpole? What the hell do we do?"

"Yes! Look!" Walpole yelped like an excited poodle. "The designs on the walls of the prison. They contain a circle between two lines, look. Two sides of the centre of a star."

He laid the notebook on a small table next to a wing-back chair. Eugene and Hampton gathered around it and peered at the designs. The cave had been covered in a series of interlinking, five-pointed stars with a circular eye-like motif in the centre.

"This is what had it trapped. It was the geometries of the Elder Sign that trapped the Sphere of Yog-Sothoth!"

"So, what do we do now?" Hampton asked, still clawing at the bits of Topper Trueman that had adhered to his scalp.

"Do you have any chalk in here? I think we can trap it. Cut it off from the rest of Yog-Sothoth again. Make it inert."

Eugene looked around then raced over to the billiard table. "Will this do?" he asked, brandishing a chalk cube.

Walpole sighed. "It will have to."

Crash!

"Look out! Here it comes!"

Yog-Sothoth smashed through the oak doors as though they were made of tissue paper.

"Keep it busy!" Walpole cried, as he dropped to his knees and started scribbling furiously.

"How?" Eugene narrowly ducked a flailing tentacle of intestine as it swept past his head and shattered a mirror.

"Over here, you big ball of goop!" Hampton shouted, and lobbed an empty wine bottle at it.

Yog-Sothoth fizzed furiously, swinging its appendages wildly in Hampton's direction.

"Now! I'm ready!" Walpole stood on the opposite side of the Elder Sign and started to chant. "Iä Iä Yog-Sothoth!"

The ancient creature surged towards the summons, ready to devour Mr Walpole. As soon as its body hit the centre of the Elder Sign, the universe paused for another split-second. Yog-Sothoth folded in on itself and then exploded in a shower of gore.

Walpole blinked. He was covered from head to foot in oily viscera and filth. Hampton breathed a sigh of relief. Eugene walked to the centre of the room and shifted Topper's intestines aside with his foot. In the centre of the eye was what looked like a marble.

Eugene picked it up and slipped it into Walpole's gore-soaked breast pocket. "There you go, old chap. Take good care of it."

With that, he waddled out of the room in the direction of the wine cellar.
"If you need me, Hampton, I will be very, very drunk for a very long time."

NIGHTMARES
BY SHELBY SUDERMAN

The light from the smartphone dimmed, inviting the surrounding darkness to advance.

Duncan groaned before he could think better of it, holding it away from his face to visually confirm what he already knew: his phone was almost dead.

"What? What's wrong?" His kid sister's anxious voice chirped from the other end of the line.

"Nothing." He grumbled, returning it to his ear. She was still talking.

". . . saw you get lost and -"

"I'm not lost," he growled, even as his eyes scanned the endless night stretching out in every direction. The dense greenery of the forest had been beautiful in the day, but after dark not even the moonlight was granted entry through the thick foliage. It was a vastly different scene compared to the open fields he was used to. Like another planet, perhaps, or a fairy tale. "I'm taking the scenic route, is all."

"Un-like-lay." He had to restrain the urge to hurl his phone aside when she enunciated her newest favourite word; if she could find half an excuse to use it in a conversation she would. An entire ocean away, and the little witch was still a killjoy. "Mom and Dad said you're at Loch Lomond now."

"Yup, but I'm not even close to the water, so you can stop freaking out. And you're even further away than me. What time is it in New York right now, anyway?"

"But Dunny, in my dream you - "

"Would you fuck off about the dreams?" He snapped, that awful nickname shredding the last of his patience. "So you dreamed something bad was gonna happen, so what? That doesn't mean it will. Lots of people dream bad things are gonna happen, especially kids like you."

There was a momentary silence from the other end before Cathy spoke again, "We don't have time for this. Your battery's almost dead."

He frowned, "How did you - "

"I know you think my dreams are all BS." She went on, not quite saying the word; their parents must be within earshot. "But you have to stay away from the water. Nothing good happens there."

He rolled his eyes. Did she think he was about to go swimming? "Don't worry, Cath, if the Loch Ness Monster shows up - "

"Wrong loch, stupid."

" - I'm sure Bigfoot will come out of the trees and have my back."

"Unlikely," Cathy answered, deeply skeptical. "Bigfoot knows better than to pick a fight with Nessie. You'd be screwed, Dunny."

"How many times have I told you not to - "

His phone beeped, the screen going dark. He stared uncomprehendingly at it for a long moment before reluctantly stuffing it back into his pocket.

"Little witch," He grunted, blinking in the now-total darkness. He inhaled deeply, the heavy, woodsy scent lingering on his tongue.

He shifted around in the dark, searching without much hope that the path would unveil before him. How long had it been since he'd misplaced the hiking trail?

He was more aware of the night sounds of the forest without Cathy's voice to drown it all out, and birds he couldn't name called to each other from the network of branches above.

There was a definite slant to the ground, and after a moment's hesitation he decided to follow it down. With any luck it would guide him out of the forest to the loch, and from there he could follow the water back to civilization.

He froze, startled by a sudden chatter coming through the trees up ahead. The isolation and quiet must be getting to him, because his heart railed against his ribcage as time slowed to a crawl. Then he recognized the jabber of ducks. He exhaled, relieved to find he was headed the right way. Where there were ducks there was water.

A solitary hike along the beautiful Scottish countryside, he'd told himself that afternoon, shouldn't take more than a couple of hours.

Maybe he should've brought a guide.

He was dead on his feet by the time he made it out of

the wilderness to discover he'd successfully found his way back to the shores of Loch Lomond.

For an instant he stood there, pausing to catch his breath and stare out across the water. With his cell phone dead he had no idea what time it was. He spotted the ducks splashing around, the only light to see by coming from the full moon reflected off the calm water. Occasionally their chatter was interrupted by other small animals calling out, each new noise breaking through the low din. Once the birds started singing to each other he'd know he'd been out until morning.

Duncan gazed along the shoreline in both directions, trying to decide which would lead him back to civilization. He gave up with a weary sigh and picked a direction; he had to find people again eventually.

He'd been tramping along for some minutes before a break in the treeline ahead gave him a clear view of something moving. A large, dark shape stood silent on the desolate bank, easy to spot as he edged cautiously closer.

His eyes had long since adjusted to the dark, but it was only when the creature made a sound that he realized it was a horse.

The chatter of ducks abruptly stopped, startling him into casting a glance over his shoulder. The water that had been teeming with birds only moments ago now stood calm and empty, but it wasn't just them. The night ambience he'd grown used to in the passing hours had vanished.

The horse snorted, and he refocused on the creature ahead.

"Hey," he answered, hardly daring to breathe in the sudden quiet.

The creature stayed where it was, almost like it was waiting for him.

Duncan's heart leapt. He scrambled to get closer, moving as fast as he dared, but speaking softly so the creature knew he was coming and wouldn't be spooked by him.

"How did you get all the way out here?" He asked, his voice cutting through the quiet. "Do you have a name?"

He drew up short when he was only feet from it, yet the horse hadn't done more than look at him.

His breath caught now that he could see it clearly. He'd always loved horses, and the one before him was the most magnificent creature he'd ever seen. It towered over him, at least sixteen hands, with a midnight-black coat.

He hesitated, barely remembering not to make eye contact as he trembled with nervous energy. Cathy had been terrified of horses her whole life, which meant that the last time he'd been on a horse, Hell, so much as touched one, was his tenth birthday shortly before she was born a decade ago. Growing up in the country back home, he probably would've had his own horse if it weren't for her.

Horses and water - she was terrified of both, and would hate being where he was now. The thought made him smile.

The creature shifted, and for the first time he saw that it wore a bridle and saddle. He almost laughed in surprise, but it quickly died in his throat. The horse was prepared for riding, so where was the rider? He stumbled further onto the bank, but in the darkness there was no sign of another person.

Duncan glanced back toward the horse. It was still standing there waiting, following him with its eyes.

He squinted at the ground, searching the bank for footprints, but all he could make out besides his were those of the horse. The creature must have run away, or broken loose somehow.

A stupid grin broke over his face as the horse nickered quietly. Someone was missing their horse, and here he'd gone and found it. He could ride it back to town, maybe even be rewarded for bringing it back. His mind filled with fantasies of having the money to buy his own horse, maybe even this very one.

Stepping carefully, so to keep himself in clear view of the creature, Duncan closed the distance between them. The horse only watched him with calm, dark eyes.

Carefully he extended a hand like he'd been taught, letting it catch his scent. The creature snuffled against his palm, its whiskers tickling his skin. When it raised its head, Duncan allowed himself to relax.

"I'm going to climb up now." He murmured, shifting sideways and placing his hands on the empty saddle. His limbs ached from exhaustion, but he forced himself to wait and make sure the horse understood.

Finally, moving more stiff and awkward than he remembered, he manoeuvred himself atop the horse and into the saddle. He was surprised by its patience, and how still it stood for him as he scrambled clumsily.

There was a horrible moment where he pictured the creature bolting now that he'd mounted, but his panic subsided when the horse merely flicked its tail.

Okay, he was back on a horse. Now what? Duncan

worked to remember the directions for how to steer a mount. He knew people clucked their tongue...

His heart sank when he realized that everything he knew might be completely useless. He was in another country, and for all he knew they used completely different signals when training their horses.

"Home." He announced lamely. Nothing.

He tried again, this time attempting a Scottish accent that sounded God-awful even to his ears. The horse snorted, possibly offended, or maybe it was laughing at him.

Out of ideas, he tried to cluck his tongue. The sound came out completely unnatural. At first nothing happened, then the horse either got the message or simply tired of waiting. It started forward, plodding along the bank in the direction he'd been headed.

It was easy to appreciate the surrounding landscape now that his aching muscles had a chance to rest, though the way the horse's movements jostled him never let him get too comfortable. The rolling hills would be breathtaking under the sunrise now that he could enjoy the view properly.

What a turn the last few minutes had taken. Such a beautiful place, and, at long last, he was riding again. Truly, this was kismet!

He thought of Cathy and shook his head. She didn't want him near horses, and she didn't want him near water. If only his cell hadn't died; it would've been so much fun telling her about the horse he'd found on the shore of Loch Lomond. He could practically hear her screech of horror, "No, Dunny! I saw it! I dreamed it! Stay away from the horses!

Run from the water as fast as you can!"

Nonsense.

Childish bullshit!

He shoved the thought aside, choosing instead to examine the hillside on the opposite bank. Was that part of the highlands? He didn't know much about Scotland, but there would be plenty of time to learn once he'd claimed his reward and taken a good, long nap.

For the first time he noticed that the horse had drifted closer to the water's edge.

"You thirsty or something?" Duncan asked, puzzled as it plodded along the shore at a clear angle now toward the loch.

"Hey!" He reached out a hand and patted the horse's massive neck. "No drowning my shoes, I mean it! That's the worst!" Maybe he would pick a different horse with the reward money after all.

But when his hand found the horse's neck there was an unexpected coldness to it. The wet hair was almost slimy, and he could feel the stomach-churning sensation of the creature's skin pulling apart under the slightest pressure from his palm.

Duncan blinked. In the glow of the moonlight the horse's mane, which had been black moments ago, was now tinged a dark green as though it were seaweed instead of animal hair. He tried to retract his hand, only to discover that he couldn't.

With a yelp of surprise he tried yanking harder. The slimy skin rustled and broke under the slightest pressure, but his palm remained glued to the steady, shifting muscle underneath.

He started at the splash of water and caught a glimpse of the horse's hooves marching steadily into the loch.

For the first time dread pooled in his gut. He pulled on the reigns with his free hand, desperate to turn the mount around back to shore. The creature responded with a sound Duncan had never heard a horse make, something between a whinny and a banshee scream. The sound echoed back at him off the surrounding hills.

"I saw it!" His sister's voice repeated nonsensically in his head, not so funny anymore, "I dreamed it! Stay away from the horses!"

He screamed as the creature reared up, towering ominously over their reflection. He caught sight of his own face, ghastly pale, but it was the beast beneath him that drew his attention. Its eyes were vacant sockets, its ears flattened against its head. The tint of green was now undeniable - the horse-like creature had kelp for hair, and when the seconds slowed as terror exploded in his chest the creature drew its lips back to reveal a set of terrible, nettle-like teeth.

He shouldn't have been able to stay on its back. He had no experience with rearing horses, but, like his hand, he was glued to the saddle.

The creature lunged into the loch, and Duncan was submerged before he could process what was happening. The water rushed over him, swallowing him whole and silencing his terrified scream.

His free hand flailed against the surging water as he was

pulled deep beneath the surface. He struggled desperately to yank himself free. Down the creature dragged him at a terrific speed, the water from the loch battering him mercilessly.

In an instant the saddle disappeared, leaving only his hand tethered.

He couldn't see anything beyond the dark water.

His lungs screamed for air.

The force dragging him suddenly released, and his surprise was quickly dwarfed by agony that swarmed him so suddenly he nearly blacked out from it.

He raised his injured hand, blinking through the rush of blood painting the water even darker. Some part of his mind registered the water warming as it mixed with his blood.

There was no hand, only a flood of red pouring out of the remains of his wrist. He stared as a crushed piece of bone drifted past his vision.

Duncan had one moment to be baffled by the sight before the dim glow of moonlight overhead disappeared, leaving him in absolute darkness. He craned his neck to see an immense shape lurking in the water above. He caught the glean of the nettle-like teeth that ringed the creature's open maw.

The water shifted, his only warning before sharp teeth sank into his leg. It was quickly followed by a burst of pain as razor-sharp fangs sliced into his side. Then his arm. Then his back.

He choked on what little air remained in his lungs, the

fresh agony drowning out his other senses as he flailed uselessly against the gravity towing him down. He lashed out at the water as the creature toyed with him, savouring his struggle. He was swimming in his own blood. He fought to blink it out of his eyes.

All the while the creature kept tearing pieces from him, the agony and the adrenaline keeping him awake and aware for longer than he could've dreamed.

Then, between one blink and the next, the creature's face was inches from him, eyeless sockets leering malevolently. Its kelp mane tossed in the current as it exhaled, and the noxious water caressed his face.

Through it all his lungs had not stopped their scream for air, even as he lost all strength to fight for it. The kelpie stretched its jaws wide, revealing rows upon rows of sharp teeth before it lunged for his throat and silenced his starved lungs.

THE OLD OAK TREE
BY RACHEL L. TILLEY

A gnarled, old oak tree stood proudly amongst his companions. At first glance he bore no distinction to any other oak from amongst his peers; he was getting on in years, but then there were many ancient oaks in those woods.

His crowning feature was his thick trunk, healthy despite its slightly crooked leaning. From a third of the way up branches began to twirl their way out of his center, intertwining as they reached towards the sky.

Roots curled from the trunk, mostly below ground, but some of his appendages could still be seen on the muddy forest floor. In places they caressed the roots of other trees, but they did not compete for space. Some of the oak's toes were so thick that they rivalled the branches in strength.

This was a strong, tenacious tree.

There was plenty of entertainment for an oak in this particular setting. Many magical creatures came and went, along with mundane creatures too. His favorite were the faeries.

To a behemothic tree the faeries were diminutive. They

were so tiny he could barely perceive them, at least until they landed on his outstretched arms.

The might of these miniature creatures was like a drug, and he was addicted. The gentlest touch of a wing skimming him, or the pinprick of tiny feet pitter-pattering along his boughs, held so much potential in each movement.

Their faery dust, that magical residue left behind after one had passed him by, kept him fed for days. He didn't need such sustenance, but he craved it. The old oak produced his tree sap, and laid in wait.

As the years passed – mere flickers in his indeterminable lifetime – his trap was successful on many occasions.

Should anyone have examined his trunk carefully they would have seen a number of faeries within the sap, all in varying stages of decay.

His sap, the beautiful, abhorrent glue…just one touch, and they were too stuck to escape. He could feel their wings fluttering frantically whilst they tried to break free of him. The sound of their sobs was an anathema, until the tears hit his branches and the feeling was replaced by euphoria.

He was disgusted with himself, ashamed even, but he could not be satiated. His addiction was a malady.

As the faeries were caught, his trunk and branches would grow around them. Although the tree provided them enough nourishment to live, this merely slowed their demise. It prolonged their torment, and for the nameless old oak it augmented the time during which he could feed on them. Whilst the months passed they were slowly digested, and he absorbed their essence into himself.

The more he indulged himself the less guilt he felt, only really reflecting on his repugnant nature when he had no fresh catch. The elation was simply too strong to care whilst he was intoxicated – which was most of the time.

As summer drew to a close Ari and Flo had left their colony in search of water. It had been a hard, arid period, and their copse had begun to wither.

Something about the old oak tree called them. It emanated power. There was an aura of great magics being held within it, as well as a sense of familiarity about it.

As they approached they followed their true natures. Ari was cautious and stayed back, whilst Flo made straight for the largest knot on the thick trunk.

Flo found both her hands affixed instantly. As she tried to pull them away her epidermis stretched slightly, but beyond that there was no give. She shrieked. Pushing her feet to the trunk she tried to gain leverage to remove her hands. Instead, she found they were now joined to the oak too. "Help! Help me Ari, please, I'm stuck. I can't...it's too sticky."

The old oak's roots reached far. Ari may have stayed back, but she had landed on the ground to rest from their long journey. Reaching her right arm outwards towards Flo, as if it would somehow be reassuring, she tried to take flight, but it was to no avail.

Defeated, Flo slumped against the tree, and found her entire front trapped. At first her tears fell, but then her quivering eyelashes brushed against the sap and she was forced to rip them out of her eyelids just to blink.

Ari thought only of Flo. She was conscious of her own predicament, but Flo's distress was a far more pressing concern, and whilst Flo was passed out from the trauma Ari called for help. No one came. When a squirrel passed, Flo felt a momentary panic that she might be eaten; lunch for a squirrel may have been preferable to their current fate, but she could not bear the thought of leaving Flo alone.

Whether or not the beast saw Ari, the squirrel knew to be fearful of their captor, and did not approach closely enough to pose a threat.

Night had begun to fall when Flo came back to her senses. It was strange for the two of them to be surrounded by pure, absolute darkness, as their own colony was lit by thousands of enchanted lights. Perhaps there was some sliver of a crescent moon in the sky, but the leaves sat so thickly above them that they could not see it. Ari, at least, could be reassured by the stars. Flo, with her back to the world, could see almost nothing.

Despite their silence, broken only by Flo's intermittent sobs, neither faery slept. Ari's legs ached from her extensive time standing upright, but she would not sit - she was determined not to become any further attached, and she was afraid what it would mean if she did.

The following day and the ensuing sunlight brought fresh hope to the pair. This time Flo was the one calling out for assistance as loudly as possible. Ari felt sure her efforts were futile, but was pleased to see Flo's spirits renewed.

When eventide was once again reached both Ari and Flo were claimed by sleep. Ari awoke resigned; she could support her own weight no longer. In her mind she had already equated the idea of sitting down with the notion of giving up. Alas, no sooner than she thought to do as such she discovered the roots had climbed her shins, creating a cage as high as her knees.

She was no longer able to exert enough flexibility to sit.

Ari was not the only one to find her circumstances had changed. The shifting of the tree had allowed Flo enough visibility to see inside the knot, and the decomposing husk of what had once been one of her kind now partially encompassed her limited field of vision.

It was an arduous kind of agony. As the weeks passed the days were interchangeable. The old oak had begun his work on Ari, saving Flo for afterwards. Ari could feel herself being ingested, her feet throbbing as if they were being rubbed with sandpaper. She saved Flo from the knowledge, allowing her friend to remain ignorant of what awaited her. Every moment she longed to say something, to share her burden, but her ability to exercise restraint was faultless.

Ari watched the seasons change, unfeeling. She saw the leaves fall from the oak, and the winter frost spread across the ground. Flo felt the seasons change, unseeing. She shivered without respite as the temperatures plummeted.

The faeries considered themselves forgotten, both by their own kind and the world at large. No other forms of life had passed through, and they had ceased to hold out any hope. The tree may have sustained them, preventing the release of death, but they were thirsty and hollow-feeling.

As the ground began to thaw something entirely unexpected came with the warmer temperatures: a lost hiker stumbled across the old oak.

A human!

Their voices were tiny, and Ari was too far from his ears for him to hear her, but by some miracle he came close enough to hear Flo's soft cries.

He approached the tree, unaware of Ari on the ground, and he misstepped. The tiny faery produced a barely-audible crunch beneath the man's heavy boot. Flo, still facing the oak's torso, remained oblivious to her companion's fate.

Using a hunting knife the man pried the bark from the trunk such that it was loose in his hands, before delicately clearing the enclosing wood from around the faery.

Flo looked upon the face of her savior. She was weak, and could barely fly. Her wings had been torn off – perhaps she would never fly again.

Free now to make use of her own bewitchments, she blew faery dust into his face. He collapsed to the ground at once.

After feeling her own features she was aware of how gaunt she had become. Her teeth, however, remained sharp. She prepared to feast.

When her fangs first sank into the man's leg flesh all she could think about was satisfying her immediate needs. Her mouth dripped with his blood. She quickly became full, having gorged herself, and fell asleep comfortably on his stomach. She had no desire to return to the home that had abandoned her.

Awaking to screams, and a hand trying to swat her, she re-applied her charms to send him back into slumber.

This time she sank her fangs deep into his neck.

BÖLVETR

BY ETHAN SABATELLA

Though Torhild escaped the claws of the beast, its howl raked her ears. The unbound cry, carrying the bitter sharpness of winter, dug into her skull almost as deep as its black talons did her flesh. She staggered through the pines, gripping the torn cloth and skin of her left arm with her right hand; blood dripped in a damning trail behind her.

"Dead," she sighed, her breath misty in the winter night. "All dead; you remain."

She, with her band of mercenaries, had made camp in the woods beneath the shelter of pines; the snow came down heavy, but the winds lay still enough for them to start a fire. They sat around it and shared poems, dreams, and tales of their past exploits. A woman's shriek cut through Hafthor's dream-poem about warm mead. He and his brother investigated, bringing axes and their keen sight to pierce the dark. Torhild and her remaining allies looked to the edge of the firelight, hands inching towards their axes and knives.

After minutes of silence snow crunched through the trees; Hafthor's brother staggered into the firelight, blood covering his face and soaking his clothes.

"Winter's wicked wraith." His deep voice broke into a squeak and he collapsed. Eight ragged trails criss-crossed over the back of his tunic and flesh. Bone fragments glinted in the firelight.

Torhild and her allies rose; she brandished her seax knife, huddling back-to-back with the warriors. They planted themselves beside the fire, gazing hard into the dark. Shrieks and blood followed as a pale thing entered the camp from the shadows.

It moved as if it were one with the woods. The warriors' eyes sought their attacker one moment, only for them to meet their ends in the next. Black claws from withered fingers gouged unprotected flesh and tore the thickest hide, even finding space between mail-rings worn by one man. Torhild realized the carnage only once several allies were slain; she and the three remaining men scattered from the fire as the intruder darted towards them.

A man? Torhild had wondered in that moment. It walked on two legs and possessed two arms. However, it wore no graith despite the deep chill; its skin bore no color of warm blood or exposure to the sun, making the gore upon it darker. Steam from its fresh kills wafted from the remains on the ground, and upon itself, but no misted breath left its stained mouth. Shadows covered its face.

It slashed a man's throat, moving between them as if it glided inches above the snow. As they gurgled on the ground it stooped over one man and placed its mouth upon his neck. Skin and sinew snapped, blood dribbling into the snow as the thing chewed his flesh.

Torhild backed away, seax trained on the monster. Her remaining two allies charged in, axes raised and teeth clamped in snarls as they swung at the creature. Their attacks cut deep, but neither slowed it as it slunk behind one man and tore his back. Torhild advanced as her ally screamed. Her seax sank between the creature's ribs, but it did not flinch or scream. No blood welled from the wound; her fingers, as they slipped over the guard, shivered against ice-cold flesh. The creature turned its claws on her as she retreated, and she took a blow upon her upper left arm while she stumbled away.

"Go!" bellowed Suni, the last man standing. "I'll meet the others in Valhalla! Stay out of Helheim, woman!"

He charged the creature and it changed its course from Torhild; it whipped about and strode over the snow, stirring up flakes from the ground, but left no tracks. Torhild clutched her wound and ran into the dark, her eyes straining in the blue winter's pall. Suni's shouts of battle faded as she wove through the pines, low-hanging branches scratching her face. Snow dusted her short, braided hair, drifting down the back of her neck and melting against her fear-warmed skin. Her flight's speed increased when a howl broke through the air—its mournful ululation combined tones of a man in pain, a wolf's call for the hunt, and blizzard winds shrieking through the forest. Of the legends concerning trolls, ghosts, and other monstrous forest-dwellers there were none Torhild knew of like the thing chasing her.

This new land is full of terrors, she thought, further realizing the danger of the weald itself. Even if she escaped the thing, found shelter amid the trees and endured the night, the native people of the new land—called Skraelings in her tongue—outnumbered her.

No doubt they hunt in these woods too, she thought. The forest lay quiet, the trees' moans and rasps being the only things to break the stillness; the monster's howl drifted in on occasion, with the spans between its utterances lengthening.

The air raked Torhild's nostrils and her throat, clawing into her lungs. The chill, watery scent of snow rooted in the back of her throat, making her long for thin smoke from a mellow fire. Her gut churned. The very ends of her limbs and digits fought to keep warm as she moved, but the cold gnawed at them and they screamed for respite.

I cannot stop, she told her body. *I must stay out of Helheim.* Her manly allies who perished standing, with weapons in hand, would find themselves in the hall of Odin's army. There they would wait until the end of the world, fighting, feasting and drinking. However, no seat waited there for Torhild—or any woman—Odin demanded the best fighting men in their prime. Only Helheim had room for her. Though it would give respite at least, the chill of its neighboring Niflheim shrouded it in eternal winter. She could bring her wealth there, but she had none upon her person and no grave to put it with her.

Torhild had no intention of dying poor.

She grit her teeth against her screaming wound, pressing her hand over it; her arm tightening against her body.

The pain crept into her chest, but the encroaching cold did its share of numbing it. Torhild's sight adjusted as some clouds overhead parted; the spears of the crescent moon shot into the earth, bathing the forest in sparse, silvery light. She came to a clearing within the trees, staggering to a halt. The monster's howl vanished, but the way to absolute safety hid from Torhild's sight and knowledge.

Sucking in a breath her nose tingled as a new scent touched it. *Smoke!* she thought; her eyes sought its trails, or, better yet, the fire from which it stemmed. Wisps floated through one of the moonbeams shooting past the branches at the edge of the clearing. Beneath it a structure stood between two tree trunks. Without the smoke Torhild never would have seen it, for sturdy branches made up the circular walls and conical roof—at the peak of which trailed the smoke. A threshold with a buckskin flap faced the clearing. Beneath the entrance covering a fiery glow pulsed and flickered.

Torhild rushed forth and took her hand off her wound, throwing open the flap and stepped inside. A caress of heat from the little fire within melted all cold clinging to her skin. A woman with hoary hair sat beside it, bundled in heavy robes and furs. She beheld Torhild with intense, dark eyes in her wizened face. *Skraeling,* Torhild identified the occupant.

"You're hurt, Ghost-Woman," said the Skraeling in near-perfect Danish.

"You speak my tongue?" Torhild asked. She clamped her wound again as a shot of pain spiked through it.

The Skraeling rose and approached Torhild with a shivering shamble. "Your people have been here long enough for me to listen. Now come, sit. I will see to that wound."

She gently set her hands upon Torhild and coaxed her to sit on a mound of blankets and furs, Torhild sighing as the heat warmed her flesh and joints. Her host released her and shuffled over to a collection of clay urns and buckskin bags. She hummed a calming tune unfamiliar to Torhild's ears. While the Skraeling dug through the containers Torhild withdrew her seax from her belt and slipped it under excess cloth from her tunic. The Skraeling returned to Torhild with bandages in hand, along with several herbs. She knelt beside her guest and removed Torhild's hand from the wound.

"A horrible gash." She set the bandages and herbs beside her and kneaded the flesh about the wound. Torhild winced and grunted, but the movement of the woman's fingers in her skin numbed the pain. "What gave it to you?"

"I have no name for the thing that did," Torhild answered. "It looked like a man, attacked me and my companions like an animal and acted as though it were a ghost."

"And your companions?"

"All dead." Torhild looked into the embers' sputtering flames.

I remain.

The Skraeling sighed, her breath turning into a long hum as she resumed her wordless song. She continued to knead the flesh, pressing the herbs against the ragged bits and holding them in place with the bandages.

"Do you have a name for it?" Torhild asked as the bandages were wrapped around her arm.

The elder woman stopped humming. "There is no word for it in your tongue, but the name it carries is 'wendigo.' It, and others like it, haunt the woods of this land. They were not always like how you might have seen it."

"What were they?"

"People. They turned their backs on the good way to live, and they must bear the monstrous curse, forever hungry for the thing that brought them into the wrong way to live. A life of eternal cold and love of only night."

"And what do they hunger for?"

The Skraeling secured the bandages and withdrew. "The flesh of other folk."

The monster's howl split the air. It emerged on the other side of a gulf of distance, yet still brought its chill into the fire-warmed shelter. Torhild flinched, planting her feet on the ground, but her host patted her shoulder.

"Be at ease," she said. "The wendigo wouldn't dare enter this wigwam."

"You've placed spells around it?" asked Torhild.

"Your people would call them such, but in a way, yes. Please, rest. It will be safe to travel under the sun."

Weariness crept into Torhild's limbs and filled her head; it pulsated from her patched wound. She hung her head, brought her eyelids down, and slid deeper into the furs and blankets. The soft pops of the fire and the reemergence of her host's hums sank her mind into the dark sea of dreaming. Outside the small, warm realm, the wind picked up, making the snow hiss through the trees.

The wendigo wailed.

Torhild awoke with a shiver. Tightening the fur wrap around her she opened her eyes, teeth grit against the cold. Darkness filled the hut; the scent of smoke hung in the air with no heat. The buckskin flap shifted on the wind against the threshold, revealing slivers of snow outside soaking in the darkness.

It isn't dawn yet, Torhild deduced, and pulled the fur wrap tighter.

"Ghost-Woman," the Skraeling murmured behind Torhild.

Torhild exhaled through her nose. "What is it?"

"I thought I heard something walking outside, can you peer outside and tell me what you see?"

Though far from the comfort she sank into hours before, Torhild was loath to rise; weariness pervaded her body and mind. However, the wendigo's howl still echoed in her memories despite the silence of the world outside; guard duty was the least she could offer her host.

"Very well." Torhild rose, draping the fur over her shoulders. Her arm lay numb beneath the bandages, but she set her free hand upon it. Using her wounded arm she held her seax in place beneath her tunic. The weariness did not leave her body even as she stretched her legs and rolled her shoulders; her feet staggered and stuttered as she went. She came to the buckskin flap and knelt, peering out the bottom slit—nothing stood or walked in the snow, and the only prints left by Torhild were all but filled in by new snow.

"I see nothing," Torhild said.

The shifting of blankets sounded as the Skraeling spoke, "Look once more."

Torhild brought her good hand off her bandages and took a corner of the flap. She lifted it, allowing a biting sigh of air to enter the hut. The air was warm compared to the chill running through her as she beheld the creature standing a pace away from the threshold—the wendigo locked red eyes with hers. Dark gore stained its bleached skin. Its bony, webbed feet hovered above the surface of the snow. A few wispy, dark hairs tumbled off its wrinkled scalp, which writhed in the slightest gust. Necrotic flesh hung in rags where a nose should have been. Its black lips were drawn back in a permanent snarl, revealing long fangs in its grey-blue gums. A moan like a wounded wolf escaped the death-cage of its mouth.

Torhild gasped and launched herself back into the hut, releasing the flap. She landed on her backside; her head spinning as her heart pounded. Despite the blooming heat of fear the weariness pushed against it, willing her to sink into the floor and back to sleep; her wounded arm slid towards the ground.

"It's outside!" Torhild hissed, looking over her shoulder as the Skraeling's shaded form rose from the wall.

"I know," said the Skraeling. "I have known it was out there."

Torhild furrowed her brow. "How? Can you see it with your spells?"

"Not with spells." The Skraeling shambled up to Torhild and stooped, helping her stand. "I am his mother."

Torhild stumbled as she stood; her head suddenly felt as if the earth pulled it down. "You gave birth to that monster?" she retreated from her host.

The Skraeling followed Torhild. "He was not a monster at birth. He was a strong, happy boy who took care of our tribe. It all changed when your people arrived. One winter they drove us away from the rivers and coast. We could gather no fish, and it was too cold to hunt. The hunger became great. People fought with each other for food, but never did anyone dare consume another's flesh. My son gave into his rage and hunger, killing our own and feasting upon them—but I did not stop him. We were cast out into the cold, and in the womb of winter my son became a wendigo.

"I built this wigwam with the love I had for him, and so he cannot enter. Often I hear his howl, and the screams of his quarry and they chill my heart. But it is his life now, and he must feed."

A sound drifted in through the flap, another moan from the wendigo in what could have been a single word, *"Giju'..."*

"It speaks!" Torhild said.

"It does," confirmed the Skraeling. "He calls to his mother."

She turned to the flap and called out in her own tongue, speaking slow in the same register as her humming.

The wendigo moaned once more, *"Gewisin...Gewisin...Giju'..."*

"What does it say?" asked Torhild. She tightened the muscles in her back as the weariness dragged at her more. *Something isn't right,* she thought.

"He's hungry," answered the Skraeling, "and you will feed him."

"I...will not!" Torhild's tongue hung thick in her mouth.

"You will." The Skraeling approached her, extending a hand. "The herbs in your wound have made you slow, and it will be less painful."

She wrapped her bony fingers around Torhild's neck, digging her nails into the flesh.

"Insidious seer!" Torhild spat through her teeth. The fingers around her seax faltered; she grabbed it with her right hand before the paralyzation took hold. Brandishing it she thrust it into the Skraeling's gut. A wheezing gasp expelled from the elder woman; her grip on Torhild loosened. With her dwindling reserves of strength Torhild pushed the Skraeling through the flap.

The wendigo remained where Torhild first spied it. Its crimson stare followed its mother as she flew from the hut, collapsing between it and the threshold. Blood stained the snow black in the night, and it dripped off Torhild's freed seax.

Shivering, the Skraeling looked up at her monstrous child. *"Gwi's,"* she said.

Suddenly the wendigo released a new howl, lower than the one it issued during the hunt; a whine cut through it. Its face wrinkled as it knelt. Gruff sobs followed its utterance.

"Giju'..." it moaned, reaching for its mother. Its claws

dug into her shoulder, piercing garb and flesh. The Skraeling screamed.

Dizziness slammed through Torhild's head as she stumbled back into the hut. She planted herself against a wall and slumped to the floor, holding her seax in a shaking grip.

Outside the Skraeling's cries rose, as did the wendigo's—the latter made Torhild grind her teeth as the monster's sobs rose into howls harsher than the worst winter she knew.

It all faded after one long, piercing howl echoed through the woods. In the following silence Torhild drifted into a cold sleep.

Torhild awoke at dawn to a light breeze. The snow shone a rosy gold with the rising sun. No Skraeling, no wendigo, not even blood or tracks sullied the snow—buried by the new powder.

With her seax she liberated her arm from the bandages, plucking out the treacherous herbs. In a new fire she heated her blade upon its embers, and when it glowed she seared her wound shut with it.

From the hut Torhild took what she needed—food, furs, bandages, a skin for water—and set off into the woods, heading east towards the coast.

Where my own people wait.

THE HAPPENING AT TIN CAVE

BY CHRISTOPHER BOND

COLORADO, 1877

30 MILES SOUTH OF THE WYOMING TERRITORY

"**C**ome on out, Josiah! We know you're in there. Just walk out the door, nice and slow...don't give us no trouble, alright? I'm sure there's just been some kinda misunderstandin.'"

The foreman's finger trembled on the trigger of his Colt, but he held the gun straight and true, aimed at the makeshift, wooden door that led into Tin Cave and the mine shafts beyond. He wiped the sweat away from his forehead and glanced at the handful of men gathered around him. They were nervous, same as him, sweat and dirt covering their anxious faces. The screams coming from inside of the old mine had stopped a few minutes ago, but they still echoed inside each of their heads as loud and clear as the crack of a bullwhip. These were hard men, these miners, but they were shook up, and none among them would meet the foreman's hard stare. He turned back to the door, saying a silent prayer to the Virgin Mary for strength.

"There's only us now, Josiah," he barked out, "but there'll be more coming soon. Ain't no tellin' what'll happen when town-folk get here. They'll want the girl, son...and I reckon they'll want your blood."

A man named Lefty sidled up to the foreman, the barrel of his shotgun never leaving the mine's entrance. "Hey, George," he said in hushed tones, "I think we gotta go in there. That girl's dead, ain't no gettin' around it, an' if'n that posse gets out here afore Josiah comes out they might jest be crazy enough t'think we got a stake in the matter. Folks don't act right when there's blood in the air...they might think maybe we had somethin' to do with it. They'll be hollerin' to put a rope around all our necks, boss."

George winced and sighed, running his hand along the graying stubble of his chin. "He's scared, Lefty, I know it. Holed up in the dark as he is...I...I just wanna give him a chance to come out by his own reckoning."

Lefty scoffed, spitting into the dry dirt of the canyon floor. "I know that's yer kin, boss, and that ain't no easy thing, but yer puttin' these men's lives in danger. That ain't right." He turned and squinted up at the angle of the sun, then back to the horizon where the muted tones of the canyon met the vibrant greens and yellows of the prairie. "We'll be seein' the dust from them riders in no time. You gotta face it: son or no, the man inside that cave there is a killer, and there ain't nothin' worse than a killer in the eyes of God.

Let's do what we came down here to do."

George's eyes fell to the ground as he nodded, the brim of his dusty hat draping his face in shadow, and Lefty nodded too. Lefty patted the older man on the back. "Now, you can set back a ways if ya want, boss...me and the boys can take care of this. We'll be as gentle as a lamb with him...if'n he lets us."

But the foreman shook his head, waving the other man off. "No, no," he said. "I ain't gonna let other men do my work for me. He's my son...he's my responsibility." He stared back to the door of the mine, his gray eyes running over the rugged timber slats and the splashes of red on the dirt around the rusted latch. "It's my burden."

"Alright!" George yelled, taking a couple steps forward. "You're outta time, Josiah! If you won't come out here, then we got no choice but t–"

The metal latch of the door rattled in its frame.

George froze mid-stride. Behind him the men froze too, their weapons raised.

The latch rose and the door creaked open on worn hinges, just a few inches, not enough for the sunlight to break through the blackness that hid behind the frame. The scent of blood and death wafted out of that blackness like a malignant fog, settling over the miners and poisoning the air.

A grubby, pale hand poked through the gap into the sunlight, fresh blood flaked along the fingers.

"Please," a ragged voice called from behind the door, so frail that George barely recognized it as that of his own son. "Please don't shoot me! I don't...I don't remember how I got here! I don't remember what happened, honest...I just...I just woke up in here, in the dark and there's...there's so much blood, Pop, and...and there's a body in here!" The hand disappeared back into the inky black, and a sobbing wail cut through the air, tearing at the men but tearing at George most of all. "OH GOD!" the voice screamed. "OH GOD, WHAT HAVE I DONE?"

George's legs were shaking, threatening to let go like a busted dam, and he swayed in the dry wind. "Now, hold on Josiah!" he yelled, his voice hoarse. "Whatever happened, we can work it out, alright? But you need to come out here, you need...you need to make things right, son."

"Ain't nothin' gonna make that right," one of the men mumbled behind George, and George cut him an icy glare.

"Okay," the voice inside the cave called meekly. It was the voice of a broken man, hollow and pained. The pale hand peeked out again, raised high. "I'm coming out now... please don't shoot me. God, please don't shoot me. Pop? Are you there, Pop?"

George lowered his gun and walked up to the door. The others made to follow him, but he waved them off. "Yes, son, I'm here."

"Could you come here, Pop? Could ya help me? I feel awful weak...I...don't feel like myself."

The foreman holstered his Colt and stepped up next to the crack. The awful stench of the cave was overpowering, and he clutched a dirty handkerchief to his nose and mouth. He stretched his hand out towards the door. "I can help you, Josiah. You have to trust me. Just take my hand now."

He reached out and grasped his son's bloody hand.

It was cold.

Lifeless.

"Thanks, Pop," a cruel, raspy voice said, not the voice of his son any longer.

"What the Hell!" George yelled and jumped back. He was still clutching his son's bloody fingers, still holding the pale hand that ended just below the wrist, the forearm torn, mangled and dripping blood as black as tar. He stared at the hand for a split-second, his eyes wide and unseeing, then he screamed. He flung the severed thing off into the canyon. The men were all shouting at him, telling him to get away from the door, away from the mine, but the old man was dazed. He stared at them stupidly. Something flashed out of the crack, something that could have been an arm or a claw, or maybe even an antler, so fast the sunlight barely touched it before it grabbed the old man by the neck and dragged him into the darkness. The door slammed shut, clouds of dirt puffing out around the frame as muffled screams echoed from between the cracks in the wooden boards.

The men clamored forward, feet kicking up dust, their insides shaking with terror like the tail of rattlesnake. Lefty got there first and lifted the latch, yanking at the handle hard enough that the worn hinges nearly busted. He threw the door open wide to the air, the sunlight, the canyon and to God himself. The miners rushed inside and stopped, their hearts racing and their legs refusing to move another inch.

The floor of the cave that led to the mine was littered with bones and blood, along with piles of rotting meat that could only have once been living things. Scraps of blue fabric, now stained red, clung to one small pile - the remnants of the girl from town and her pretty summer dress. Next to her lay a crushed rib cage, the bones picked clean of any meat or flesh, strips of Josiah's rawhide vest shredded and strewn around it. Carcasses of wolves, horses, coyotes and buffalo lay in varying states of decomposition, naked skulls grinning madly amidst the carnage.

In the center of it all lay George, legs splayed out toward the entrance, his top half covered by a sinewy, human-like figure bent over him. Wet smacking sounds filled the silence of the cave, like a group of hogs feeding at a trough. One of the men, Pablo, gasped, "Dios Mio!" He made the sign of the cross with his hand, and the creature stopped its feeding and turned.

The men froze in horror.

It was George's face staring at them, or at least George's face if he'd lived to be a hundred and fifty years old. His skin was sunbaked and weathered, creased by lifetimes of dust and dirt. It was like the flesh had been sliced from his head, and the ragged, bloody skin stretched across a rock to dry in the desert sun before being crudely stitched back onto this creature's elongated skull. Bulging, yellow eyes stared at the men from withered eye sockets, bits of flesh and gore pasted across the papery skin of its cheeks. The thing opened its puckered mouth and a scaly tongue ran over huge, fang-like teeth, not the teeth of anything human, anything that had ever been human. Blood ran off of its chin, catching in the thick fur that grew like sheep's wool on its chest and abdomen.

The creature smiled a terrible smile, bits of the old fore-man sticking out between its massive teeth.

"Hey there, Lefty, is that any way to treat your old boss?" the thing crooned in a perfect imitation of George's voice. "Close the door, why don't ya? Were ya born in a barn?"

"God help us," Lefty said. The door slammed shut, and there was no one left in the camp or the canyon to hear the screams, the gunfire or, finally, the crunching of sinew and cartilage and bone that came from inside of the abandoned mine.

The posse had ridden hard from the small town of Briarton. They were led by Colton Grace, the father of the girl who had been kidnapped. They reached the miner's camp and Tin Cave just before sunset; a circle of empty tents was all that greeted them. Colton jumped off of his horse and went to the firepit, kneeling to touch the pile of ash.

"Cold," he said.

"You think they ran off?" one of the ranchers from town asked.

"Don't rightly know," Colton Grace said. "All of their packs are still here, and all their food." He nodded towards the tents and the canvas bags lined up beside them. "Don't make no sense to go on and leave all yer gear."

"Don't see no horses though," another rancher said, looking around the empty camp. "Don't see much of any-thing."

Another man walked his horse up with some effort.

The animal was whinnying softly, throwing his head against the reigns, and he had to fight to make it walk straight. "Something don't feel right about this, Colton."

"Ain't that the truth!"

A metallic creaking cried out from behind them. The men jumped, reaching for their guns. They hadn't even noticed the dusty door set into the side of the rocks beside the camp. The door pushed open a crack, metal protesting in the failing light.

"Please," a voice called from inside the cave. The voice of someone hurt, someone in trouble. "Please, help me," it whimpered. Colton Grace's heart sank. It was Mary, obviously in pain and scared but alive, ALIVE, against every terrible thought he had harbored since he found out she was missing. Tears welled in the corner of his eyes as he rushed forward to the door.

The rancher on his horse was looking at the ground. There were drag marks in the dirt, hoofprints and bootprints faded from the wind, but still visible, all leading towards the wooden door. None led away from it. "Colton, wait!" he yelled, his horse whinnying madly, its eyes wild. "Hold on just a minute!"

But the distraught man didn't hear him as he stumbled towards mine entrance; he could only hear his daughter, could only hear the pain in her voice.

"Mary! Mary, darling, it's Daddy! We've come for you, you're safe now, Mary, you're safe–" Colton cried as he grabbed the handle and threw open the door to the blackness that now lived inside of Tin Cave.

The wooden door to the cave creaked open in the moonlight, the silence of the canyon matching that of the silence within. A hulking shadow walked out on footsteps as silent as a whisper. The canyon had been good hunting grounds, and the creature knew that more food would be coming, but it was dangerous to stay in one place too long - even for one such as it, even for one that had no fear of death, this wild country was untamed.

There were other places the creature could hide, other places for it to feed. It lifted its muzzle to the night air and inhaled, taking in the scent of dirt, rock and old blood. It smelled smoke and whiskey on the air, along with the nervous sweat of horses. A campfire, and only a few miles to the north. That meant more Men. Saliva pooled at the corners of its cruel mouth, and its hollow stomach tore at itself, urging it forward. It needed to eat again, and soon.

Always soon.

The creature padded silently off in the direction of the smoke, black fur glistening in the waning moonlight, until it disappeared into the thick shadows that lay over the canyon like a funeral shroud.

The night exhaled.

THE SUCKLING PIG
BY TIM MENDEES

MARCH 31ST, 1717
PLYMOUTH, ENGLAND

"**Y**ou, fair strumpet, more ale! Be quick about it!" Jasper Tremayne roared over the din of the revellers of The Dun Cow. Slamming his empty tankard on the plank across two barrels that served as a bar he wiped his mouth on the sleeve of his frilled, linen shirt. His cherubic features were flushed and accented by a drunken grin, but then Jasper had cause for celebration. His uncle had recently passed away, leaving him a sizable inheritance. It was for this reason alone that he had replaced his native Truro for the bustling port, since his solicitor was based there...as were many watering holes and high-class brothels.

After a visit to his bank Jasper had withdrawn a large sum of money, then embarked on a spree of herculean proportions. His plan was simple: drink his sizable bodyweight in grog, then hire himself a filly of loose morals and flexible limbs for the evening. After all, this new inheritance meant that he could finally escape from the horrors of work. Jasper was a wastrel's wastrel, content to let life drift on by without lifting a single sausage-like finger or giving a hoot for anyone other than himself.

"There ye go, my lovely." The pretty serving wench smiled as sweetly as she could possibly manage to yet another boorish, drunken oaf.

"I accord thanks to ye, fair maid." Jasper winked and smiled wolfishly. "Now, 'ow much would it cost to get ye up those stairs and out o' them petticoats?"

The serving girl looked him up and down, then rolled her eyes and blanched. "Ugh... not on yer life, it'd be like lying with a particularly 'orrible slug!"

A nautical-looking cove next to him roared with laughter as Jasper turned several shades of red; he stumbled to come up with a witty retort. He went to tell the tall, wiry fellow to mind his own beeswax, but thought better of it. The man looked like he had seen battle with men much more skilled than he, and had the scars to prove it.

Deciding that discretion was the better part of valour, he took a gulp of his ale and started back towards his perch in the corner of the low-ceilinged establishment. He had been sinking tankards since the sun was over the yardarm and had spent an enjoyable afternoon bar-hopping, hence his balance wasn't what it should be. As he went to pass the sailor his legs went one way and his body the other: this coincided with the man taking a step towards the door, resulting in a collision and a slight spillage of his heavily-hopped beverage.

"Watch it, ye stupid son of a biscuit-eater!" The sailor scowled, his eyes flashing with anger as ale slopped onto one of his scuffed, bucket-top boots. The man grabbed Jasper by the arms to stop him colliding with a table full of off-duty Navy types and clapped him on the shoulders.

"Oh!" Jasper exclaimed as the cold finger of fear goosed his nether-regions. "Pardon me, kind sir. I appear to be three sheets to the wind."

The sailor sniggered at a landlubber attempting to use nautical terms, and his ire evaporated. "It ain't no bother, worse things 'appen at sea, lad." The man gave him a lop-sided smile that made Jasper shudder. He quickly steadied his tankard with his other hand and hurried away. When he risked a glance behind him...the sailor was nowhere to be seen.

Jasper's inexplicable unease lasted until he made it half-way across the tavern and he got an eyeful of a maid's cleavage. Quaffing his drink he settled down into his seat with his back to the bar and contemplated his next move. It was only just after dusk, so there was ample time left for drinking before finding a soft bed and a warm woman for the night. He had only just ingested a large slice of game pie and mash from a local pie shop, and that should keep him going for at least another hour...the world was his oyster.

As he took another quaff he tried to fathom what he saw that had upset him so. The grizzled sailor had seemed benign enough. After all, if he'd have wanted to he would have been perfectly justified, and more than capable of, breaking his nose. No, he had little to fear from merchant seamen; it was the Royal Navy recruiters he had to worry about. The press gangs were always on the lookout for fresh meat to throw to the sea, though he was pretty certain that no captain in his right mind would want an overweight weakling such as he aboard his vessel.

While taking another mighty swig something cold and metallic clattered against his teeth, making him splutter and showering the table in porter. He clamped his teeth down on the object as terror seized his heart in an iron grip...The king's shilling!

Spitting it into his palm he shook with fear. "Oh, God, no...Not the king's shilling." He looked around furtively at the Naval coves: none of them had moved, nor were they paying attention to anything other than the buxom wench on each lap. If they weren't a press-gang, then who was?

Jasper's eyes narrowed as he brought the coin up to the candle to get a good look at it. "Wait, this isn't the King's shilling." Indeed, it wasn't; it was a chunky medallion emblazoned with a strange kind of family crest. It depicted a bat-like dragon above two crossed scimitars. Jasper went to pitch the evil-looking trinket under the table when...

Thunk!

A heavy object collided with the top of his head, and everything went black...

Captain Angove crossed the bare planks of his lavishly-outfitted cabin and lowered himself into an ornate chair. Teasing the ends of his moustache with wax from a nearby candle he leaned forward, taking a jewelled goblet in his hand. Baring his fangs he tipped his head back and took a gulp of the viscous liquid within. He shuddered with delight: it was good, sticky and warm...as it should be.

On the table before him charts, maps and navigation equipment lay in orderly piles. The course was set; they would be leaving the dock at midnight. The vessel, The Crimson Night, was moored outside of Plymouth at Morwellham Quay on the banks of the River Tamar. It was a haven for ships of less official capacity, and people there asked few questions. The stoutly-constructed Galleon was currently disguised as a merchant ship, and the harbour-master knew enough of the captain's reputation not to ask many questions.

Angove itched to get back out to sea; they had been ashore for far longer than he liked. Unfortunately, restocking and finding a replacement crew was a necessity. Still, he pondered as he took another sip, his first mate and quartermaster were due back any moment.

An hour passed as the captain savoured his evening meal, then a sharp rapping at his door broke his reverie.

"Enter!" The captain proclaimed as he dabbed red from his lips with a silken, white handkerchief.

The door creaked open, and a large fellow covered in tattoos entered the room. "Sorry to disturb ye, Captain. We're back, sir."

"Ah, Quartermaster Twill, that is good news indeed. Me bones ache for the sea...I fear me bones will dry out if we tarry much longer. Did ye get the supplies?"

"Aye, Captain, the men are storing it below." Twill scratched the scar that ran down the side of his bewhiskered face.

"... and crew? Do we have a full complement?"

Twill nodded. "Aye, they too are being stashed below and clapped in irons until we leave port."

"Splendid!" Angove beamed, showing off his sharp fangs. "Then we are ready. Leave me, I must gather my senses afore we set sail."

"Aye, sir!" Twill turned and started to leave when Angove halted him in his tracks.

"Twill?"

"Aye, sir?"

"Did ye get one?"

"A pig, sir?

"Aye, a pig," Angove smirked.

"Aye sir, it's down below with the other cattle." Twill nodded with a sadistic grin.

"Very good, excellent!" Angove slammed his fist on his desk in triumph, spilling gloopy, red liquid over an old book of poetry. "Extra grog for the men tonight!"

"Thank you, sir!" Twill beamed and left.

Angove dabbed up the spilt substance with his handkerchief, bringing it up to his nose and inhaled its copper aroma. "A suckling pig...a treat indeed!"

"Up! Up, ye scurvy dogs!"

Jasper Tremayne's heavy eyelids snapped open as he

was kicked sharply in the rump with a bucket-top boot. He was face-down on filthy boards, the stench of stale seawater and rat urine making him wretch. As his focus returned the floor beneath him lurched. That's when the realisation came knocking like an angry debt collector.

"Come on, lad...I didn't hit ye that hard!"

Tremayne rolled onto his back and found himself gazing up at the sailor from the tavern. "You...ugh...where in Hades am I?"

"Sir." The sailor replied.

"Eh?"

"I'm the first mate on The Crimson Night, lad, and ye'll address me as sir! Now, get yer arse up on deck!" With a pitying smirk the first mate resumed rousing the rest of the new deck-hands, some of them roughly. Each one had a matching duck-egg bruise on his noggin. Clearly the press-gang had been busy.

With his mind racing in panic Jasper tried to recall what had happened. All he could remember was coming to while clapped in irons. He had been in the back of a rattling cart that stunk of sweat, excrement and fear. There were other bodies similarly kept... the rest of the crew.

Getting unsteadily to his feet, Jasper was steadied by a thin fellow in a tattered, red coat of His Majesty, The King. "Get your hands off me, you filthy swine." Jasper hissed. "Why did you take me, I'm no damn sailor!"

"Easy, friend." The other chap pleaded in a thick Irish brogue. "I'm not the one who brought you here...look." He bowed his head and revealed a knot on his scalp. It was then that Jasper recognised him, he was one of the Naval gentlemen from the tavern. "I was in the Tavern, same as you. I went to answer the call of nature, and bang! I woke up in this Hell-hole."

"My apologies. I thought I'd been press-ganged. Tremayne's the name, Jasper Tremayne."

"Finnegan, Sheamus Finnegan." He shook Jasper's offered hand. "You have been press-ganged, just not by the Navy."

"Then, by who...privateers?"

"I'm afraid not. Didn't you 'ear what 'ee said? This is The Crimson Night..." Sheamus finished as though he was expecting a fanfare or drum-roll, so when Jasper looked at him blankly he was gobsmacked. "What? Never 'eard of The Crimson Night?"

Jasper shook his head.

Sheamus did the same, followed by a sigh. "Then you're in for a real treat."

Before Jasper could question any further the first mate bellowed in their ears to move. The two men, suitably roused, hurried up the ladder to topside. Chill night air cut through Jasper's stained and tattered shirt; somewhere along the line he had been relieved of his skirted jacket and waistcoat. Hugging himself against the frigid winds and icy spray he pulled himself upright using a barrel. Finnegan was grabbed by one of the crew almost instantly and told to get up the Jacob's ladder to the topsail. As an experienced seaman he knew what he needed to do. Jasper, however, didn't have a clue.

"Excuse me, sir?" He asked the first mate meekly. "What am I supposed to do?"

The mate looked around, then clicked his fingers at the gunner and motioned for him to bring something over. The gunner was a mountain of a man with ratty locks and a pronounced limp. "'Ere." He growled and thrust a warped pole into Jasper's trembling hands. Jasper stared at it in confusion: it was almost as tall as him and had a mass of seaweed fronds tied to one end.

"Um…" Jasper asked hesitantly. "What am I supposed to do with this?"

The mate and gunner looked at each other then roared with laughter. "What do ye think ye do with it, fish brains?" The mate mocked. "Swab the bloody deck, that's what!"

Feeling foolish, Jasper did as he was told and started to mop the standing water. After an hour of backbreaking toil he stretched upright and tried to get the various knots and kinks out of his spine. It was then that he spotted what flew from the mast…a skull and crossbones.

Just before first light Captain Angove stepped away from the wheel and checked his compass. They had been lucky to have had a favourable wind and were making good progress, yet still he was uneasy. It was no secret that he was being hunted by a man-o'-war with heavy cannon. The Crimson Night was a formidable vessel, but if caught it would be blown to matchwood. They had gone out of their way by necessity and were in a stretch of the ocean not usually traversed. They were miles from the nearest trade route or shipping lane. Out of sight, out of mind.

The first mate joined him as he took the steps down to the main deck. "We're makin' good progress, Captain."

"Aye, and no sign of the hunters…All is well, for now." The captain looked pensive. He wasn't accustomed to being the hunted; it went completely against his nature.

"Do ye mean to fight them, sir?"

"In time, Mr. Mate, in time…On my own terms, let's say." At that the captain grinned widely, his fangs flashing in the moonlight.

"I likes the sound o' that, sir." The first mate chortled above the crash of the waves and the creak of timber.

"Oh, there'll be a reckonin' one o' these days, don't ye fret about that." The captain clapped him warmly on the arm. "How are the new recruits workin' out?"

The first mate sighed. "Some good men, but most are a bunch o' useless bilge-suckin' landlubbers."

"Well, ye know what to do with the deadwood…" The captain smirked.

"Aye! I do indeed, sir…poor buggers."

The captain looked wistful, "It's just the natural order of things…" His joints cracked as he stretched and looked at the horizon. "Drop the anchor and get the men below decks, then tell Twill that he has first watch."

"Aye, sir!" The first mate turned and started bellowing orders as the captain opened the door to his quarters. As he slipped inside he failed to notice the ashen-faced form of Jasper crouching behind a couple of kegs. He had heard every unsettling word…

That night Jasper went to his appointed bunk believing that he was going to have his throat slit while he slept and his body tossed to the sharks and scavengers of the deep. Each man was given a tankard of a potent grog, and no sooner had he imbibed it he was lured away into the arms of Morpheus.

Awakening by a bellow of "Avast!" from the first mate, Jasper was confused to find that it was dusk again. Looking around with bleary eyes he was shocked to find several empty bunks. Muttered conversations drifted to his ears; it was believed that they had made a break for it during the day, and had decided to take their chances with the waves rather than stay aboard.

"Bloody fools." Sheamus Finnegan grumbled bitterly. "Don't they know anything? They will be much better looked after on a pirate ship than in the service of the King. They should have just kept their 'eads down and done the work. It's the Navy captains who are the real bastards!"

At this point Jasper relayed to Sheamus what he had heard between the first mate and the captain.

Sheamus' face took on a grave aspect. "Maybe the stories about The Crimson Night are true..." He whispered almost inaudibly.

"What? What are you talking about?" Tremayne replied.

Before his friend could answer the first mate returned and hurried them topside.

Stepping onto the deck once again Jasper went to retrieve his stick and seaweed from where he had left it. Finnegan put his hand on his shoulder and directed his eyes to a mop leaning against one of the masts. "I reckon you'd do a better job with that. Snag it quickly, before some other scallywag gets it... oh, Jasper?"

"Yes?"

"Stay away from the crew. If I'm right we have worse things to worry about than just pirates."

"What's that supposed to mean? Sheamus...Sheamus?" It was no good; his friend had scaled the rigging like a spider monkey and was already high above the deck. Suddenly conscious of his unease Jasper looked around. He locked eyes with the first mate for a fleeting moment, but it was a moment that chilled his soul: the man's eyes seemed as dark as pitch in the half-light. He quickly averted his gaze and snatched the mop.

A couple of hours of ceaseless mopping later meant Jasper had worked his way towards the forward deck and was taking a sneaky breather behind a cluster of crates. The moon hung low and gibbous, casting a silver streak over the roiling waves. For a moment he forgot his plight, and could have almost enjoyed it...until the first mate appeared.

"What're ye doin' over 'ere?" The big man asked. "Not thinkin' about makin' a swim for it, are ye?"

"Um... no... sorry, I was just looking at the moon."

"Pretty ain't it?" The mate gazed out and smiled.

Jasper was terrified, he'd been caught shirking, surely this meant punishment? The mate's actions confused the devil out of him. "Uh... yeah, it certainly is."

The mate chuckled low in his throat then turned sharply to Jasper. "You hungry?"

"Um...yeah...Yes, I am."

"Come with me." The mate led him towards the captain's quarters and had him stand by the door. "Now wait here." The mate ducked inside then returned presently with a bunch of grapes and a wedge of cheese. "'Ere, and keep it quiet."

"Th...thank you?" Jasper's head was spinning. Why was the mate showing him favour?

"Now...back to work ye, scurvy dog!" The mate bellowed in Jasper's face, though it was for effect. Jasper jumped and secreted the food in his shirt. Clutching his mop, he hurried back to the rear of the galleon and resumed working, blissfully unaware that one of the men had seen him being handed the food.

A little later the crewman cornered Jasper and held a short-bladed knife to his throat. "Hand it over, ye swine!" He demanded.

Jasper stammered and stumbled with his eyes as wide as saucers, but before he could comply the first mate appeared and clubbed Jasper's assailant around the head. Jasper carried on working and managed to consume his snack without anyone else seeing him.

He later found out that his attacker had been keelhauled.

A pattern had emerged after that night. Jasper would be roused by the mate, put to work, fed and protected. Jasper couldn't understand why he, out of all the men aboard the ship, was seemingly under the mate's protective wing. He could only surmise that it was from a sense of guilt over dragging him aboard. As dawn started to rise the men would be hurried down below decks, given a tankard of strong grog then allowed to sleep until dusk. Nobody awakened during daylight hours, and Jasper assumed that the grog contained a powerful sleeping draft...not that he minded.

Conditions aboard could have been far worse. The crew treated them fairly, as long as they did their jobs. The ones who didn't, however, vanished. Their number was dwindling as the days turned into weeks. Nobody saw them go, nor had any idea what had befallen them. Accidents were common, and it was assumed that they had perished in a fall and had joined the crabs.

It was starting to look like Jasper Tremayne had a charmed life. While everyone else starved on meagre rations he was eating so much that his already considerable waistline was expanding. He had cheese, bread and even a little meat and fish. He was reasonably content, until one wet Tuesday in late April. It seemed that his favouritism hadn't gone amiss, after all.

Jasper's dreams of warm women and cold ale were violently shattered when he was seized roughly by several of his fellow hands. He tried to shout, but was silenced by a fist in the gut that doubled him over.

"Where's the food, Tremayne?" A large Scottish chap named Willie demanded. "Hand it over, ye wee shite, or I'll do ye right now."

There were three men in total: Willie and his two pals Rich and Snuff. All three men were under the command of the gunner, and were tasked with hauling cannon. They were strong as bull oxen and just as irascible. Snuff and Rich had his limbs pinned to the bunk, while Willie waved his boulder-like fist in his face.

"Come on, Tremayne... 'and over the grub." Snuff insisted, "If ye don't Big Willie 'ere will do ye a mischief, and no mistake."

"I...I, haven't..." Jasper spluttered as he tried to simultaneously catch his breath and tear his eyelids apart. Clearly his attackers hadn't partaken of their nightly booze ration.

"Codswallop!" Rich roared. "We saw ye bein' 'anded a chunk of bread and cheese. Proper mate's pet ain'tcha?"

"Wha...I...I..."

"Spit it out, maggot." Willie snarled as he shook him roughly by the hair. "Where's the damn food!?"

"I ate it!"

This wasn't at all what the three brutes wanted to hear. They swore and cursed as they slapped Jasper around. Yanking him to his feet Willie produced a knife and slit open Jasper's shirt, revealing his corpulent midriff.

"You fat pig!" He spat. "'Ow come ye get fed and we don't, huh? 'Ow come ye get to just mop the deck while we risk life an' limb up in the rigging, huh?"

Jasper shook his head. "I...I don't know."

"Well, I reckon that if the captain won't get rid of the deadwood we should do it ourselves." Snuff grinned and looked around for approval. Every man in there nodded, everyone except Sheamus, and that was only because he was still unconscious.

"Sheamus!" Jasper pleaded. "Sheamus, wake up!"

"Har, Har!" Willie crowed. "Yer pal is fond of a drop of grog. Who do ye think we gave ours to. Paid us 'andsomely too, 'ee did."

"I'm sorry, I never asked for this!"

"Aye." Said Willie as he slashed Jasper across the gut. "Nor did we..."

The ship shook as a gust of fetid wind blew through the windowless hold, snuffing out the candles. As blood seeped from the superficial wound the air seemed to shift, as though it was charged with some kind of malevolent force.

"What in blazes is 'appening, Willie?" Rich gibbered as he let go of Jasper's arm and spun around, peering into the thick, impenetrable gloom.

"Keep 'old of 'im, damn yer eyes!" Willie boomed. "Jumpin' at a bit of wind, ye yellow-bellied Kurr!"

"Sorry, Willie." Rich babbled. "It just don't feel natural!"

"There ain't nothin' to worry about. There ain't nothin' down 'ere but us 'ands and the little piggy here..." Willie readied the knife in his right hand. "Ready to meet yer maker, piggy?"

Slam!

As the blade came down towards Jasper's flesh a blur slammed into Willie, sending him crashing into one of the supporting joists head-first. His neck snapped back with a sickening crack, and he collapsed to the floor like a sack of potatoes.

Jasper screamed and pulled himself free of the other two, but Rich was grabbed sharply by the hair and dragged into a dark corner as easily as if he were a nipper. As Jasper fumbled around in the darkness all around him became a pandemonium of screams and ghastly sucking and slurping noises. One-by-one the screams became silent as Jasper cowered under a bunk.

The air was thick with the iron smell of freshly spilled blood. He could hear it dripping onto the boards as soft footsteps circled around him, getting ever closer as his heart hammered and his ears throbbed. A salty tear ran down his cheek as he said his final goodbyes to the world.

"What the bloody Hell is going on down here?" Sheamus yelled as he used his tinder box to relight the candle next to his bunk. "Can't a fellow get a bit of kip?"

"Shh." Jasper tried to warn him as his friend struck the flint over and over until...

"Holy Mary, mother of God!" Sheamus cried as he finally illuminated the candle and found himself surrounded by cadavers.

"Sheamus," Jasper whispered. "Get the Hell out of here."

"Is that you, Jasper?" Sheamus asked, sweeping the candle across the hold in his direction. "What in Heaven's name has been goin' on down 'ere?"

Jasper was on the verge of speaking when a slender shadow moved just beyond his friend's right shoulder. Moving closer to the light the handsome features and waxed moustache of the captain became visible.

Sheamus had been talking the entire time that the captain had been looming behind him, though Jasper didn't hear a word. There was something darkly mesmeric about the captain. The man moved like smoke, making no sound as he crept up behind his friend. Jasper was sure that the captain knew exactly where he was, but didn't care. He was toying with his prey like a cat with a field mouse.

Jasper couldn't stand it any longer. "Sheamus, look out!" He screamed and broke cover.

Sheamus turned, but before he made it halfway around the captain grabbed his jaw and his shoulder with opposite hands, then pulled.

Crack!

His friend's neck snapped in an instant and he dropped to the floor.

Jasper ran headlong into the gloom. He had seen a door back there, but had never been through it. It seemed as good a place to run as any. Maybe he could barricade himself in... though what good that would do in the long run was a mystery.

His stockinged feet slapped noisily in the combination

of seawater and blood that sloshed from side-to-side with the motion of the waves. He didn't know if the captain was following him, but he had to assume the worst. As Sheamus had fallen so too had the candle. All Jasper could use to navigate by were the tiny slivers of sunlight that came from between the boards of the upper deck. He couldn't see a damn thing, and inevitably ran face-first into the door - breaking his nose and making it erupt like an inverted volcano.

"Come on, open." He growled through gritted teeth as he lifted the latch and shoved.

Stumbling inside, Jasper gasped at the sight before him. The room was lit with tallow candles, the horror before him straight from a nightmare. The crew sat in comfy chairs sucking dregs of blood from the wrists of the missing crewmen. All were present, save the captain, the mate and the gunner. They were, presumably, behind him.

Jasper turned to flee, but was grabbed by the captain and thrown with such force that he left his feet, tumbling over into the corner next to another door. The crew chuckled as Jasper begged for mercy.

The captain smirked and turned to his men. "You boys might want to join the others in there...there be a bit of a feast tonight!"

With cheers and exclamations of joy they raced through the door, leaving Jasper and the captain alone. Presently, though, they were rejoined by the first mate.

Jasper looked at the men chained to the beams. They were little more than husks. Some of them had been missing for nearly two months, and the poor wretches were so gaunt that Jasper could see their hearts beating weakly in their breasts. "Lord, have mercy...What are you, monsters?

"Hah! Hear that, Mr. Mate? He thinks we are monsters."

The first mate roared with laughter.

Jasper tried to backpedal towards the door, but with preternatural speed the captain was upon him, hauling him to his feet. After brushing his curly, black locks from his face and licking his lips the captain spoke softly into Jasper's ear. "We aren't monsters, Jasper. We are just higher on the food chain...that's all. Are you a monster when you eat duck or grouse? Of course not. It's the natural way of things. You see, Mr. Tremayne, you people are cattle to us." He bared his fangs and let Jasper get a good look at his future.

"But why did you help me? Why not just eat me and be done!?"

The captain laughed and nodded towards the other door. The first mate returned the nod and walked over to it, unlocking it with a large iron key. "Because," The captain began. "Ye are the suckling pig, and ye needed fattening up fer the feast."

With a roar the captain launched him through the newly-opened portal. Jasper landed hard, choking as the wind was forced from his lungs. As he struggled to breathe he spotted the disgusting cadaver in the corner. It had once belonged to a rotund gentleman, but now its skin hung in sallow flaps, all the blood and nutrients sucked dry by the vampiric crew.

"He's done now. He lasted quite a while. Let's see if you can last any longer, shall we?" The captain winked and squatted over Jasper's chest. As his victim sobbed uncontrollably he planted a tender kiss on his forehead. "Hush, now...It's an honour to be the suckling pig...and ye shall be rewarded."

As the captain sunk his fangs into Jasper's neck the first mate lifted his shirt to show a mass of stretch-marks. "We were all suckling pigs once, lad...behold."

As Jasper lost consciousness the last thing he saw was his predecessor's eyes snap open as he revealed his new fangs to the world.

MIDNIGHT SHIFT
BY DAVID GREEN

"I guess this is it?"

Chet gave the sign a dubious second look. A flickering bulb illuminated it, giving sporadic light to a filth-encrusted logo that hadn't seen a wet cloth since John Wayne rode horses and drank milk. If it ever boasted words the years had eroded them. He checked the text the agency sent, just to make certain.

'Premium Life. Midnight shift. Get there a little early for orientation. Wear something nice, but not a suit.'

Abrupt, odd, and not too formal. It came with a GPS location too, and that had led Chet to the grime-encrusted side-street off a side-street that he never would have stumbled upon if his cell hadn't brought him there.

"It's a job, Chet," he muttered, eyeing the building. Looked deserted. He should go home, sign up for yet another agency. His last company had sent nothing but bum jobs his way though, and the new one he'd discovered—Alucard Dynasties—came through straight away; a desk job that paid bank. "Six-hundred dollars a night. Can't say no to that."

One drawback; late hours. Chet had given it a minute's thought before shrugging. He played Xbox all night and slept most of the day, then woke up for more gaming. A midnight shift wouldn't change much; six-hundred bucks a night would.

Problem was, the joint with the filth-encrusted sign above it didn't scream 'six-hundred dollars a night', nor did a job at a blood bank called Premium Life.

Chet lit a cigarette, the smoke spreading its tendrils deeper into the abandoned side-street, then a thought rang a bell in his head, sounding like a gong. He narrowed his eyes.

"No homeless. Not one, and Haven has them everywhere."

Faded flyers peeled from the walls: 'doctors' advertising their skills for those without insurance, more offering phone numbers lonely fellas could call—he shrugged off the urge to punch the digits into his cell—even a private detective called Nick Holleran saying he'd take the cases others wouldn't. The usual ads for the seedier parts of town.

He smiled. Place must have just moved here, moved the drifters along. Blood banks had to look clean; okay, this joint didn't *right now*... but they'd hired Chet from an agency. They needed staff, and fast. The high rate of pay compensated for the late hours.

It all made sense.

The dark skies opening and spilling its contents onto his head made up Chet's mind; he detested rain.

Wincing, Chet threw his half-smoked cigarette on the

ground—the downpour snuffing it out—and raced across the side-street, his boots echoing on the slick cobbles. Another thing he hated was wasting his smokes, but he couldn't go waltzing into a blood bank with a cigarette stuck to his lips. *I'd look like a badass, though.*

Grin fixed on his face, Chet drew a hand across his forehead, moving the dripping hair from his eyes, then wiped his palms on his damp denim jacket and tried the handle.

Locked.

He rattled it again. No difference. A third time didn't help matters either.

Chet knocked instead; a flurry of rapid taps as water ran down the gap between his collar and neck, making him squirm.

"Come on," he growled, trying the handle again. "Shit... maybe it's the wrong Goddamn place."

Frustration made his foot kick out, his booted toes thudding against the bottom of the door. Chet did it again, then drew his leg back to give it a harder one, blaming the stupid door for his idiotic cell taking him to the wrong place on his first night when light oozed from beneath the frame.

"About time."

He gave the glass another rattle with his knuckles and replaced the scowl on his face with a smile. The door swung open, and the grin slipped away like tears in the rain.

Chet fancied himself a good-looking guy, an unorthodox kind of handsome maybe, which explained the years he spent single, but the figure framed by Premium Life's artificial light put the reflection he admired in the mirror more times than he should each day to shame. Raven-wing hair framed unblemished porcelain, with razor-edge cheekbones on the verge of poking through the snow-white skin covering them.

Clad in a rich, maroon suit, the man loomed over Chet. Craning his neck he took in the full, ruby lips that curved downwards—almost in a petulant pout—before meeting black eyes that shone like polished obsidian stones.

Despite the sweaty, humid dampness, Chet's skin broke out into goosebumps. He wanted nothing more than to pull his stare away, but Chet's willpower deserted him. For this nameless stranger he'd do anything, say whatever he demanded.

Shit, Chet would work for free. Screw the six-hundred dollars.

"Chet Phillips?" He nodded in return, still fixed on those cold, all-seeing orbs, tongue stuck to the roof of his mouth. "Punctual. A fine trait. My name is Petr."

The maroon-clad Adonis blinked and broke the spell. Chet shifted his stare, instead finding a point in the middle-distance over Petr's shoulder of stunning interest. Easier than meeting the man's eyes again.

"Ah, yeah." He croaked. Chet tried to work some moisture in his mouth, but came up dry. "That's me, ready to start."

"Of course."

Petr spun on his heel and glided into Premium Life. Chet followed, his heavy footsteps a sharp reminder of his gracelessness compared to the perfection who lowered himself into a seat behind the room's only desk.

Wait. I'm straight! Why am I thinking like this? Nerves. First night nerves, and this place ain't what you'd call normal.

"Never heard of a blood bank that needed nighttime receptionists." A high-pitched giggle escaped Chet's mouth. Petr continued to stare, lips still in a half-pout. The door slammed shut of its own accord, and Chet almost filled his pants.

Petr cleared his throat. "The wind. Storm's brewing. Please, take a seat."

"Ah, insurance questions before I start work, right?"

A memory of a smile flickered on Petr's perfect, pale face. "Something like that. Come, sit."

Chet crossed the room, taking in the details. The room stood almost empty. Boards blocked the only window beside the front door, blocking out all natural light; a flickering, buzzing artificial one illuminated the space. A row of bargain-bucket plastic seats lined the walls, and Petr sat behind a nondescript wooden desk in a comfortable, reclining office chair. A no-thrills plastic one waited for Chet, and another door stood against the room's back wall.

He took it, staring hard at the desk's plain woodwork. A clipboard with Chet's resume sat on it, and nothing else. *Don't look into his eyes again. Don't look into his eyes!*

"Just set up here, right?" he asked. Nerves made him talkative. On the last date he went on he hadn't shut up from the minute his Tinder match arrived. She said almost nothing as Chet rambled through topics ranging from the inherent racism of the He-Man cartoon from the 1980s to the most underrated role-playing game in Xbox history.

Chet hadn't heard from her since.

"Astute." Petr sounded bored. A small sigh confirmed it. "How could you tell?"

"The old sign outside tipped me off. The fact this joint looks abandoned. The cheap chairs. I Googled Premium Life too, but couldn't find a single thing."

"Yet here you are, Chet Phillips."

"Well...six-hundred dollars a night's a deal-breaker." His laugh bounced around the room until it spluttered to an abrupt finish. Chet thought Petr might join in, even for politeness' sake. He didn't. Petr continued to watch, expressionless. "So...well..."

A fit of coughs erupted from Chet's throat. Heat reddened his cheeks.

"Look, the job is quite simple," Petr announced over the frantic sounds of Chet clearing his throat, "we pay well for the blood we take. For the most part, our clientele comprises people who need money and do not ask questions, nor do they want them asked in return. You shall fill out a questionnaire when they arrive, then instruct them to wait until I or my colleague call them through. When day breaks you shall leave, lock the door, and ensure you switch the lights off. Understand?"

"No questions, but a questionnaire?" Always a smartass. Chet couldn't help himself.

"Again, simple. Why don't we roleplay? On-the-spot training." Chet nodded, keeping his mouth shut. "Name?"

"Chet Phillips."

"Age?"

"33."

"Do you have any tattoos?"

"No."

"Good. Those things are not ideal. We do not deal with those who have tarnished themselves. Send them away. Blood type?"

Easy enough so far, but this one made Chet hesitate. "Ah...I'm not sure."

Petr raised his eyes from the clipboard. "You do not know your blood type?"

"Well—"

"You took a position in a blood bank, but you do not know your type?"

"Negative something. It's the rare one."

The clipboard clattered on the desk. Petr's tongue snaked out, licking his lips, a hungry look in those shining, black orbs. Chet shrank back in his chair, his body acting on impulse. The image of a hawk eyeing a mouse flew into his brain.

"AB negative? *You* are AB negative?"

He had surgery once, and his surgeon had raised his eyebrows and whistled before whispering those same words.

"Yeah." Chet wanted to disappear into his chair. "That's the one."

Petr licked his lips again, then flowed to his feet. "Wait here."

"Wha—"

The door in the room's rear opened before Petr reached

it, then slammed behind him, leaving Chet alone. *I should run. Something's not right about all this.*

But the promise of six-hundred dollars for filling out a bunch of simple questionnaires each night kept him rooted to the spot.

Chet didn't have to wait long. The door swung open and Petr reappeared, followed by a woman his equal in beautiful perfection. Standing a head shorter she swept towards the room's lone table, all straight-backed poise, her chin tilted so she viewed Chet from down a nose celebrities would have paid a fortune for. Her eyes, hair color and skin matched Petr's, as did the superior, enchanting look in her black eyes. She even wore a similar suit.

"I am Valenti." She had the same neutral accent as Petr, like they'd lived in so many different places alien dialects couldn't sink their teeth in. "You are sure? AB negative?"

Petr stood behind her, a lightbulb flickering above him, the shifting light casting leering shadows across his face.

"Well...yeah."

Valenti tapped a pointed fingernail against the tabletop. Cold sweat broke out across Chet's forehead. He blinked it out of his eyes, his hands refusing to move from where they sat trembling in his lap.

"Years since we've come across AB negative." Valenti twisted in her seat, her words for Petr's ears.

"It has. Too long, and nothing compares."

"I am not sure I could stop myself if we started."

Petr gripped her shoulders and squeezed. Chet tried to clear his throat, but emitted a mewling sound instead. Had they forgotten he existed? They talked about his blood as if it belonged to them. Rage gurgled in his gut; an impotent one. His fear beat it down.

"And why should we, Valenti? Don't we deserve this?"

"We would have to replace him."

"Replace me? You're firing me already?" The words tumbled off Chet's tongue before he could stop them, his desire for a paycheck overriding his unease and good sense.

Valenti and Petr turned their heads as one to study him. Don't meet their eyes!

"Come with us," Valenti murmured.

Chet's legs twitched—oh, how they wanted to move!—but he refused the urge. Run. Get out. Now!

Valenti's arm whipped out, her fingers clutching Chet's chin. A grip like iron made his teeth ache as she wrenched his head upwards. He skewed his eyelids shut.

"Open your eyes."

She squeezed, Chet's scream swallowed the sound of his jaw cracking.

"I would do as she asks," Petr drawled.

"No!"

Fingers dug into his gums. A popping sensation, soon followed by a stabbing pain, garnered another howl from Chet as a tooth shot from its socket; warm, bitter blood oozed from the cavity, filling his mouth.

"The pain shall get worse," Valenti whispered. "Open your eyes."

"Enough of this," Petr snapped. "I hunger. Just bring him."

"No. I prefer it when they offer it themselves. It is more...civilized that way."

Another tooth threatened to tear loose as Valenti applied more pressure. Chet's eyes flew open, brown meeting her black; eyes shining with malice and desire.

"Come with us."

The words flooded his mind. The pain left his face, and without thinking Chet surged to his feet. Valenti and Petr traded hawkish grins, then flowed to the rear door, disappearing into the gloom.

Chet followed.

He screamed inside his mind, telling himself to escape in the other direction while he still could, but his legs refused. They wanted, no, needed, to follow.

A darkened room greeted him. A click echoed, then the buzz of a bulb spluttering into life. It illuminated a blood-encrusted, steel table.

"Make yourself comfortable." Valenti's voice came from everywhere and nowhere all at once, commanding his limbs to move.

They did.

Chet slid onto the metal slab, the light above burning his retinas. Restraints wrapped themselves around his arms and legs; his eyes, still working in frantic darting movements, goggled as the leather straps moved of their own accord.

Like the doors.

On cue the entrance to the room slammed shut, and silence filled his ears.

"Hello?"

Petr stepped into the light from the surrounding darkness. "For what it's worth, I believe you would have made an acceptable receptionist."

Valenti appeared on the other side of the table, hungry eyes fixed on Chet's neck. His pulse throbbed like it called to her.

"But AB negative…" she purred, licking her lips. "Too rich a feast to turn down."

The pair hissed, lips curling back to reveal razor-sharp fangs amongst their perfect, white teeth.

Chet didn't have time to scream before those canines tore into his flesh, before his own precious blood filled his throat. Instead of howling for mercy Chet gurgled and choked, fat tears leaking from his eyes as the vampires sated their appetites for blood oh-so-rare.

WHAT ONCE WAS MINE
BY RJ FULLER

Sweat slid down the back of Alana's neck, over her collar bone, and pooled at the crevice between her breasts. The flimsy, colorful blouse she'd purchased at the outdoor market in Mexico City clung to her back like fly paper. She tugged at it and fanned herself with her free hand.

"Are there any questions?" Emilio, her tour guide, asked.

Alana smiled and shook her head. It amused her that the kid spoke to her as if she were part of a full group, and not a single researcher on a private tour.

"Okay, let us continue," Emilio said.

Alana followed him into the cave. Almost immediately the temperature dropped, and goosebumps popped up along her arms. She shivered and hugged herself.

"Grutas de Cacahuamilpa is one of the world's largest cave systems," Emilio began, as they stepped through the wide mouth of the cavern and headed down the tourist path.

Alana followed, though his words fell on deaf ears.

Now that she was really here, it was as if she was walking in a dream. The soft clicking sound of her sandals bounced around the heavy stalactites illuminated by colorful lights. The humidity squeezed her skin like a warm embrace.

This was the moment Alana had been waiting for. A moment that had taken nearly thirteen months to come to fruition. Thirteen months of agonizing patience and persistence.

It all began one rainy night in Toronto, the night of Professor Phillippe Rousseau's department soiree. Philippe, Alana's friend and mentor, had just returned from assisting an excavation at Templo Mayor. At the party, he'd spun passionate tales of the Mexica peoples and their bloodthirsty Aztec Gods, then passed out colorful souvenirs to his intimate group of guests. Alana's souvenir had been a necklace with a small replica of the Coyolxāuhqui Stone bearing a blood red ruby in the dismembered goddess's eye.

When Alana had returned home that night to her tiny apartment, she'd dreamt of Aztec sacrifices; dreamt of murdered captives tumbling down the stone stairs of Templo Mayor and landing in a bloody pile on the colorful stone depicting the naked and dismembered Coyolxāuhqui.

Alana had awoken in a cold sweat. She'd chalked it up to too much French champagne and an overactive imagination.

But the next night, another dream came. This time, Alana was on a massive steed and racing across a grassy knoll. The pounding hooves of the army of mounts at her side pumped like blood in her veins. Her body was not hers. The skin was darker than her creamy pale ivory, the hips were rounder and breasts fuller. She wore brightly colored, embroidered clothing, and a headdress lay heavy on her skull. Golden bells bounced on her cheeks, as she drove her horse towards the thousand men at arms she faced.

Alana could feel the fury of the men in front of her. She raced forward anyway, screaming an ancient battle cry. When she was mere inches from the man leading the army opposing her, a god of a man who glowered at her with a loathing beyond words, she woke up.

She didn't go back to sleep that night. She couldn't do anything more than hug her knees to her chest, tears streaming down her cheeks, and rock herself until dawn.

That day, Alana called off work. She spent the day researching everything she could find about the goddess with bells on her cheeks. She'd even called Phillippe when her research went dry. And, when there was no answer, Alana left a shaky message on his voicemail, begging for a return call. At half past six, Alana fell asleep at her computer.

This time, the dream was different.

She was standing on the top step of a ziggurat under the white light of a full moon. Her gown was dark as blood. She could feel the warmth of the night air and the cool stone beneath her feet.

Then she appeared. Coyolxāuhqui. She Who Wears Bells on Her Cheeks. Her beauty was unlike anything Alana had ever seen, could ever have imagined. Her eyes swam with the stars. Her skin glowed with the moon. Alana was unable to turn away.

Slowly, as if time were only a figment of human imagination, the goddess approached Alana. Coyolxāuhqui smiled softly; her full lips curved seductively. She placed her hand on Alana's cheek and held her gaze.

That was when Alana saw it.

All the secrets of the universe.

She watched every moment in time pass by her, as if it were all a memory she'd merely forgotten.

The next morning, Alana awoke sobbing.

It was the same, over the next few months. Coyolxāuhqui would visit her at the ziggurat in her dreams and show her more secrets, more memories. Their embraces, at first nothing more than a touch on the cheek, became more casual and familiar; holding hands on the stairs or sitting wrapped in each other's arms. Like old friends. Until one dreamy night when their innocent touches became something more.

The first time they made love, Alana was so overcome with emotion and ecstasy that she feigned the flu and took an entire week off work. During that week, she drank bottles of cheap wine and took over-the-counter sleep aids so she could spend more time in Coyolxāuhqui's embrace. She ignored her phone and emails. She didn't bother to shower. She barely remembered to eat.

On the ninth day of dreamy embraces, Coyolxāuhqui showed Alana the room. It was a small room. A cavern. The archway was adorned with human skulls and the walls were covered in ancient writing.

In the center of the room was a pit surrounded by

stones. And, inside that pit, were the remains of a young woman, wrapped head to toe in delicate gauze, a jeweled dagger in her right hand.

At first, Alana didn't understand the image. Why, instead of spending the evening between her legs, had Coyolxāuhqui shown her a place of death?

But then the goddess placed her fingers on Alana's temple and smiled.

Come to me, Coyolxāuhqui summoned. Free me, Alana.

When Alana awoke that day, she stayed awake. The booze and sleep aids were replaced with coffee and energy drinks. She spent hours trying to decipher the images she'd seen on the cavern walls, trying to learn the language she'd been shown.

After Alana realized she couldn't find the translations she needed, or the means to translate the strange writing herself, she drove to Phillippe's. To Alana's relief, Phillippe was more than happy to lend her his personal library for her "archeological interest", as he'd called it. When he questioned her, she skirted the subject. She didn't speak of her dreams, only said that she wanted to learn more about Coyolxāuhqui for curiosity's sake.

Alana spent the next four months poring over Phillippe's books day and night. When she finally thought she understood the words, she decided it was time to go.

"I'd like a transfer," Alana had said, after a long evening sifting through Phillippe's library. She chewed her lip and played with the necklace he'd given her. "Please, Phillippe."

Her mentor cocked a graying eyebrow at her. "A transfer? To where?"

"Mexico. I want to assist at Templo Mayor. I read in one of your books that there was once a secret cult devoted to Coyolxāuhqui. I'd like to research that theory." She struggled to keep her voice from cracking.

Phillippe sighed and stuffed his hands in his pockets. "That's quite a jump from studying the indigenous people around the Toronto area," he'd said, with a drawn brow. "Why the sudden obsession with Mexico?"

Alana shrugged and tried not to fidget. "Maybe I'm just tired of the cold." When he quirked his mouth in disbelief, she tried again. "Maybe I just need a change, Phillippe."

"Yes, I'd heard you've been struggling at work. Missing weeks at a time. Falling asleep on the job site. It's highly unprofessional, Alana."

Alana's face burned.

"But it's also highly unlike you," Phillippe continued. "You've always taken your work seriously, almost obsessively so. Far too serious for archaeology, I've always thought."

Alana felt a spark of hope at that statement. If there was one thing she knew about Phillippe, it was that he appreciated a lighthearted approach to the profession.

"But this supposed cult of Coyolxāuhqui, why that? It's just a rumor. A myth. People have been seeking it for years with no results."

She was about to lose him...

"It would certainly be an adventure. A treasure hunt, in a manner of speaking." She smiled. "I mean, isn't that what this job is about?"

And those were the magic words. Phillippe agreed to let her transfer to Templo Mayor.

Of course, there was one stipulation: She had to finish her remaining nine months in Toronto, and she had to excel. No more call-offs. No more naps.

Alana had done her duties diligently. Those nine months nearly drove her mad. She spent her days on the job site counting the minutes until she could leave. At home, she pored over anything she could find about Coyolxāuhqui and the Mexica peoples, until the moment she fell asleep and made love to her Moon Goddess.

When the time finally came for Alana to leave for Mexico, she booked the first flight out and left all her belongings behind, save for her purse and a small carry-on bag. When she arrived in Mexico City, the first thing she did was request the Archeology department set up a private tour of the caves for her.

They denied that request.

So, Alana drained the money from her savings and bribed the young tour guide to bring her in after hours.

Now, Alana smiled to herself as she stared at the back of her tour guide's head. It had taken a lot to get here, but soon it would all be worth it. Soon, she would find the cave where Coyolxāuhqui's cult had been trying to bring the goddess back to life, and she would finish the ritual.

Coyolxāuhqui, her friend—her lover—would be with her in the flesh. No longer just a dream.

Alana's body trembled with anticipation. They had been walking for nearly an hour. Emilio had talked the whole time. Occasionally, he would turn and ask her a question, and she would hide her irritation and politely respond. But her mind was elsewhere. Her focus was on locating the hidden crevice Coyolxāuhqui had shown her in the dream.

It wasn't much longer before Alana found it. Just like Coyolxāuhqui had shown her, the small opening was tucked behind a stalagmite formation that, if she squinted just right, resembled a trio of veiled ladies. The opening was so small it blended in with the shadows of the cave.

Alana's heart began to pound. She glanced from Emilio to the opening, and back to Emilio. She slowed her pace, allowing her guide to get a few feet ahead of her. Then, before he could turn around and ask her another ridiculous question, she slipped behind the veiled ladies and squeezed through the small hole.

The space was cramped. For the first few yards, Alana had to crawl on her hands and knees across the cold cavern floor. Around the fourth or fifth yard, she was sliding across the floor on her stomach; slithering like a serpent and suffocating in the thick air.

Sharp pebbles pierced her skin. She ignored them. She also ignored Emilio's voice, calling to her from the tunnel's opening, begging her to turn around and come back. After a few more yards, the tunnel widened again.

When she could stand, Alana pulled out her cell phone and used it as a flashlight to look around.

She paused. There was a fork in the cavern, opening to two different tunnels. She remembered seeing this in her dreams, but she couldn't remember which direction she was supposed to turn. She was pretty sure it was left. Or maybe it was right?

She closed her eyes. "Breathe, Alana," she command-
ed herself. She took a long breath in, then slowly let it out.
"Think." She took a few more breaths.

It was definitely left.

Alana took a step towards the left cave. A hand on her
shoulder startled her and she spun around, slipping and falling onto the cavern floor. She cracked her wrist on a large
chunk of fallen stone and yelped in pain.

"I am sorry to have startled you, Miss." Emilio said. He
offered her his outstretched hand. "Are you alright?"

She glared at him for a split second, then quickly composed herself. "I'm fine."

"You can't be in here. This is not an excavated area. It is
strictly off-limits."

She gave him a weak smile and allowed him to help her
off the ground. "I apologize. I saw the opening and couldn't
help myself. But the space was too narrow to turn around, so
I had to keep going forward."

He frowned at her. "We must go back."

"Of course," Alana said sweetly. "After you."

Emilio nodded. No sooner had he turned around than
she stooped, grasped the chunk of fallen rock, and bashed it
into the back of his head.

"Oh my god!" Alana dropped the weapon and clasped
her hands to her mouth, as he slumped to the ground. "Oh
my god!"

It had to be done...

Alana stepped back and glanced wildly around the cavern, her cell phone illuminating nothing but stone.

You know it had to be done…

"Yes," Alana said aloud to the goddess's voice inside her head. "Yes, I know."

Come to me.

Alana turned away from the sight of blood pooling from the back of Emilio's skull and, on shaky legs, headed down the left path. She continued on for nearly another hour, winding through the slippery tunnels of the caves, trekking a path that had been lost to man for hundreds of years, the light of her cell phone guiding the way.

When she reached the sacrificial cave, she stopped dead in her tracks. Her heart pounded like a war drum in her chest. Sweat soaked her hair and dripped into her eyes. She blinked it away and stared.

The circular room was barely twenty feet in diameter, its ceiling so low Alana nearly had to duck her head to enter. The arched entryway was packed with skulls; skulls that overflowed and fell like a macabre blanket onto the floor in front of her.

They were the skulls of Coyolxāuhqui's sacrifices.

Alana shivered.

Careful not to disturb the remains, Alana stepped inside and slowly flashed her cell light over the room. More skulls lay in piles against the cavern walls, eyeless sockets staring back at her. Strange writing was painted on the walls with some sort of clay red pigment.

Alana knew that writing. She'd been studying it for nearly a year now.

Her palms began to sweat. The archaeologist in her wanted to run back, grab a crew, and begin documenting every delicate detail of the room she was in. To examine it properly with studious precision and dedication.

But the woman in her longed harder. It longed for the embrace of her Moon Goddess, Coyolxāuhqui. It demanded her to bring life to her lover.

She angled her cell light down to the stone circle at her feet. Around it, skeletal bodies lay curled in fetal positions, the rocks pillows for their eternal slumber, their bodies forever protecting the treasure inside.

Alana guided the light over that treasure. It was the body of a young woman. An unfinished ritual. From what she could tell, the girl was barely out of her teens. She was enveloped in delicate strips of sheer, aged linen. Her skin, black with time, was stretched thin across her browned bones.

Clutched in the girl's right hand was a dagger. The red stone in its hilt gleamed brilliantly in the artificial light, much like the stone in Alana's necklace.

Pick up the dagger.

Alana obeyed. She gingerly withdrew the dagger from the girl's small hand, being careful not to break the dry finger bones.

Speak the words.

Alana furrowed her brow and stared at the writing on the wall. She struggled to breathe as she sounded out the images she'd studied for so many months.

Speak the words.

Coyolxāuhqui's command was stronger this time. Alana's hand shook as she held the light up to the wall and began to read. At first, the foreign words felt strange on her tongue. She tripped over the syllables and pronunciations. But the words soon took on a familiarity, as if remembering the lyrics to a song long unheard.

Alana repeated the written spell. The words turned into rhyme. The rhyme turned into chant. The air began to grow thick around her. She could feel Coyolxāuhqui there with her; feel Coyolxāuhqui's energy in the room and on her skin. Soon, her lover would awaken in the sacrificial girl at her feet, and Alana would have her beloved with her in the flesh.

Speak the words…

The chant flowed faster from Alana's lips, rhythmically pulling her into a trancelike state. She felt something slither around her ankle and crawl up her leg, but she didn't dare look. She didn't dare break the spell.

She couldn't stop.

Speak the words…

Alana felt the slither roll up her thighs and across her hips. Whatever it was, it wrapped itself around her chest and squeezed until she could barely breathe. The slithering travelled down her arms and around her fingers; up her breasts and around her throat. With every slither, came the feeling that something was taking over her, forcing its way into her body.

Speak the words…

The slithering crawled up Alana's face, covering her mouth and nose like a stale, stagnant hand. The dagger dropped and landed with a heavy thud. The cell phone slipped from Alana's other hand and fell to the floor, its light rising to the ceiling like a beacon.

Alana continued to chant.

The slithering moved Alana's cheekbones and over her eyes, filtering the room like a dusty veil. She could no longer see the words written on the cavern wall. But she no longer needed to. She knew them now.

> *By blade of blood*
> *A choice will be*
> *What once was mine*
> *Shall set her free*

Alana felt herself fall to the ground. The slithering thing wrapped tighter. Enveloping her. Binding her. She couldn't move. She couldn't breathe. Her body felt…wrong. It was too small. Too fragile.

She tore her eyes away from the wall and looked up.

"Thank you, Alana, for giving me life again."

Alana stared through the dirty linen binding into Coyolxāuhqui's eyes. Her eyes.

Her lips twisted in an unfamiliar sneer. "With your body, I shall raise my army. I shall live again. And I will rule the land my brother stole from me."

Alana watched in horror, suffocating under the dirty linen that bound her to a body not her own, as the goddess bent and retrieved the fallen dagger. Then, the goddess lifted the blade high above her head, its red jewel gleaming in the beacon of light.

"What's yours is mine."

THE END

THE WOMAN IN THE ROOM
BY E.N. NEELY

Fear was an emotion with which Kurt Richter was well-acquainted.

During his time within the Nazi SS, he had learned how to cultivate it in others. It could, with practice, come from a look, or turn of phrase. More often it came from his uniform or the Death's Head insignia on his peaked cap.

In others, he saw it as clear as a turn in the weather in the skin's pallor, the shallowness of breathing, and in the cold sweat beading on a forehead. He saw it now in the sergeant's eyes.

"Hauptsturmführer," the thin man said with a crisp salute. "I am Sergeant Amery Müller, I am here to escort you to Château de Prométhée."

Richter stepped off the train and returned the salute. He took a moment and looked around the small station.

"Sergeant, where is the town?"

"Just below the rise, you can't quite see it in the fog, sir," he said. "We'll be driving through it to the garrison."

For late afternoon, it was dark. Gun-metal gray clouds roiled with the coming storm, making a turbulent ocean of the sky. This remote region of North-Eastern France was as miserable and cold as anything he'd experienced in Germany.

A single cold drop hit the brim of his hat, then the shoulder of his uniform, leaving a dark splatter. He would have preferred snow to the October rain, which hissed as it plinked off the train's hot engine.

"Sergeant, take me to the Château."

"Sir," Müller said, clicking his muddy heels together and leading the way to the Kübelwagen. The cold deluge soon intensified, battering the two men as they approached the vehicle.

"Your luggage will be brought along shortly," Müller shouted over his shoulder, voice almost lost in the sudden downpour.

Richter said nothing as he followed. The dark brown muck sucked at his polished boots. The sergeant reached the vehicle first and opened the door. Richter slipped inside and removed his hat. He let the water pour off it onto the floor. The other man then hurried around to the driver's side and climbed in. With a cough, the vehicle started, jerked forward, and then they were moving through the storm.

Richter looked out the window as they approached Wingen. Its crooked, cobblestone streets attempted to weave between the town's weather-stained buildings.

"And there's reason to believe the resistance is operating here?" Richter asked, frowning at what he saw. He doubted the town had changed since the Middle Ages.

"There are rumors, sir," the man said, as they took a turn down another narrow road. "Some suspect spies travel from contacts in Zweibrücken and over the Vosges."

Richter doubted it, but kept the opinion to himself. He was here to look for insurgents or sympathizers, and if they were here in this decaying little village, he'd find and dig them out.

"In fact," the man said, his voice cracking with nervous tension. "We found a woman wandering the woods around the garrison early this morning. She is being held in a room for your questioning."

Richter hadn't expected this.

"What has she said for herself?"

"Nothing, sir," the sergeant said, sounding odd. "She doesn't seem to speak at all."

Richter nodded. This was an excellent opportunity to show the others what he was capable of. He never enjoyed what he did, but it was important to take pride in one's accomplishments.

"How far do we have to go?"

"The Château is twenty minutes from town, sir, in the forest."

He quelled his rising irritation. Another castle. It made sense tactically. They were naturally in key geographic locations throughout Germany and France and had hardened defenses. Not to mention, they were perfect for housing troops. The Reich had displaced or reached arrangements with the ancestral owners of many castles. They had refurbished and moved into abandoned fortresses across the region as needed.

All the same, Richter was tired of castles. They were cold, rarely had reliable electricity, and smelled of stone and dirt.

He's spent years at Wewelsburg Castle, attending Himmler's academy for SS officers. The massive, three-sided keep had also been home to the Reich's study of Nordic mysticism, and a depository for anything the small army of desperate German archeologists could claw out of the dirt regarding the paranormal. He had heard rumors of similarly desperate measures during the Great War. The Reich, it seemed, had inherited an obsession with all things occult that Richter privately found infantile.

Plus, no amount of ornate symbolism could keep a castle's wide corridors warm in the winter. He expected little from Château de Prométhée.

As the Kübel rumbled its way down a muddy track cutting through the forest, he found himself awed by the size of the trees and the density of the foliage. If they found a woman wandering through this, perhaps she was a spy after all.

"How large is this forest, Sergeant?"

"The maps say it's roughly 8,000 kilometers," the man said. "It goes some distance on both sides of the border, and essentially connects to the Black Forest on the other side of the Rhine."

It was then a sudden sense of foreboding surprised

Richter. It hit without warning and left him squirming uncomfortably in his seat. He thought of himself as a practical man, a realist, and not prone to flights of fancy. But all the same, apprehension took root in his stomach, injecting ice into his veins.

He kneaded his hands together to bring warmth into them and distracted himself by looking out the front window. It was then they neared the top of a hill, and Richter saw the château. It was worse than he'd expected.

A pile of moss-covered wet stones with several narrow towers. He was surprised it was habitable at all. One corner tower had collapsed into a pile of giant, blocky stones and rubble. The Nazi banners hanging from the ramparts did little to imbue the morbid structure with his trust.

The sergeant seemed to pick up on Richter's doubts.

"Don't worry sir, it has electricity now and is comfortable enough, once you get used to it."

"Did I say something, Sergeant?" he asked, in a conversational tone.

"No, sir," the sergeant said, all familiarity replaced once again with fear.

Richter preferred it this way.

"How long have our forces occupied the château?" he asked.

"Nearly...three months, sir."

Three months? The castle would be intolerable for more than a few days, of that he was certain.

A nervous sentry soon stopped and checked their papers, then the sergeant drove through the crumbling gatehouse and stopped near several parked military vehicles. Lights hung in the courtyard, casting a clinical illumination in the dark spaces between the ancient walls.

Several officers and the garrison's sickly-looking commander greeted him as he entered the building. Something about the demeanor of the soldiers bothered him. They were far from the front and yet they were nervous. The makeshift mess hall was quiet as men picked at their food. He knew his presence should inspire some level of anxiety, but this was too much. Richter found it concerning.

He insisted on seeing the prisoner as soon as possible. It was better to get this part over with. The sergeant and a second lieutenant led him through the castle, up a flight of stairs to the third floor, and into his room.

"It can wait until morning, can it not?" the lieutenant asked.

"Wait until morning?" Richter asked, shaking his head. "Why would I do that? No, you'll take me to see her this evening."

"Of course, sir."

The lieutenant's hand trembled slightly as he turned the door handle, a detail Richter had not missed.

The room was small, but he took the opportunity to freshen up. Distant thunder rattled the little window by the bed.

He wasted no time, the sooner he got started, the sooner he could return to Berlin. Then, a thought dawned on him and he stopped. The soldiers weren't afraid because of his arrival. Something else had them scared.

Not bothering to even change his uniform, Richter returned to the hallway, where he was escorted back through the castle to the basement level. Supplies and crates of ammunition lay in the hallway, which he pretended not to see. He loathed disorganization.

They passed an alcove made into a makeshift radio room, where an operator listened intently to the chatter through his headset.

"We're still opening up parts of the castle," the lieutenant said, seeing his look of disapproval. "Many portions were collapsed. Some areas are being cleared for the first time in, perhaps, decades."

Richter said nothing.

With the help of the sergeant, the lieutenant forced open the door to the basement. The thick wood groaned and shuddered as they forced it wide. The smell of wet and rot was overpowering. He made no outward sign of his discomfort as they followed the string of buzzing and flickering lights down the stone stairs. There were several rooms here filled with ancient boxes and equipment he could not identify.

He stopped and brushed off the dust from one crate. There was writing on it in German.

"What is this?" he asked.

"We were not the first ones here in the castle," said the lieutenant. "We believe it was used during the Great War. At least for a short time."

Richter blew more dust off and squinted at the writing.

"Von Kairo nach Berlin," he read. "What's inside the crates?"

"Clay jars topped with little sculpted animal heads,"

said Sergeant Müller.

Richter turned to the two men and raised an eyebrow.

"Worthless antiquities. Some unimportant small jars and pots dug up from an excavation in Cairo," the lieutenant said.

"What's in them?" Richter asked.

"We believe…," the lieutenant said, stepping backward and taking the lantern's light off the boxes. "That they're filled with dried human remains."

Richter frowned, wiping his hand on a pant leg.

"Organs mostly."

Dug up and left here by some half-wit archeologists during the Great War, Richter mused.

"Is there more here? More trash dug up from tombs and discarded?"

"Most of it's on this level, sir. We've been busy and haven't made an inventory of it all," the lieutenant said.

Richter turned and continued to follow as the two men led him to a wooden door, slick with mold. He noted someone had recently bolted a lock to the outside.

"She is in here, sir," the second lieutenant said.

"Is she restrained?"

"No, Hauptsturmführer."

He eyed the man, then shrugged, and unlatched the clasp on his gun holster with a practiced flick of his thumb. The sergeant then handed him the lantern.

"She sits in the dark?"

The lieutenant and sergeant made eye contact. "Yes, sir."

"Then I will speak with her. I don't plan to take long. Wait here and shut the door behind me."

The men nodded as he tugged on the stubborn door and let himself inside. He heard it close behind him with a thick, wet sound.

The lantern did little to chase away the shadows, so he let his eyes adjust to the room. There was an untouched tray of food by the door. For a moment, he entertained the thought this was some sort of double-cross which the party had become susceptible to in recent months. Had he just allowed himself to be locked up for some imaginary transgression? The room smelled of dirt, cinnamon, and something that he couldn't place. The feeling of foreboding once again wrapped around him.

Clenching his teeth, refusing to give in, he waited until his eyes grew accustomed to the gloom and he saw the silhouette of a woman standing at the far end.

He stepped closer to see her better.

"Guten Abend Fräulein," Richter said, trying to get a better look at her.

When she didn't respond, he tried again in French. There was still no response. In the silence, he could hear the rain pounding against the outside of the château's mossy walls. It was freezing in the room, and he shivered.

He continued in French.

"I'm told you were walking around the estate. Were you looking for something? Or perhaps you were lost?"

Richter stepped nearer and felt more unease wash over him. What he mistook for a trick of the light proved to be true. She was freakishly tall, perhaps more than seven feet in height. Her narrow, even gaunt body was wrapped in dirty white bandages. She was almost like something he'd once seen in a Berlin museum as a boy. Her face was in shadow.

Richter felt whatever he was about to say next catch and die in his throat. He felt the hair on the back of his arms stand as she took a step toward him, his sidearm forgotten. When she spoke, it was so faint that he thought perhaps it was a trick of his hearing or the sound of moths flittering through the room. In time, his brain processed them as whispered words, which he could not understand.

"I am a German officer," he said, finding his voice weak and brittle.

She took another long stride forward. Looking up at her, he shuffled backward. There was something unnatural in her movement, like a disjointed wooden puppet on strings. Then she spoke again in that incomprehensible whisper. It reminded him of palms, water, sands glistening under a full moon. He pointed the lantern in front of him, but the feeble light couldn't quite reach her as she swayed closer.

His heart pounded and his mouth went dry.

She said something else, and stepped into the light, grinning at him.

He turned and hurried for the door and struggled with it, trying not to scream. It wouldn't open. Richter imagined the tall thing walking across the dark room toward him, reaching out.

She spoke again in his ear and his mind filled with images of suffocation and the mindless skittering of insects.

Wide-eyed, he turned to look at her as the door opened from outside. He fell backward into the sergeant.

She was not behind him.

The three rushed to close the door and lock it.

"Sir? Are you alright?"

He felt dazed. Why had they let him go in there?

"Yes," he heard himself say, as he looked at the other two. They were pale with fear.

He knew he shared their look.

"You found her in the forest?" he asked, getting as much distance between him and the door as possible while trying to retain his dignity.

"No, sir," the sergeant said. "We said that because the explanation is...improbable."

"Improbable?"

"We did not find her in the woods," the lieutenant said. "We found her inside the castle. In the room you were just in."

The three walked swiftly to the stairs, eager to leave the basement.

"So, she somehow snuck in?" Richter said, desperate to be on familiar ground once again. To find something, anything, rational about what he'd just witnessed.

"No, sir. She was already there," the sergeant said. "When we dug the collapsed stone away from the basement door yesterday. She was already in the room."

He heard the words, but his brain couldn't make sense of them. How was this possible?

The soldiers had been in the château for three months

before they discovered her in the cellar. As he worked to process this, the sergeant interrupted his thoughts.

"Did she speak to you, sir? What did she say when you found her?"

Richter stopped and looked back the way they had come. Despite the hanging lights, the room in the back lay in darkness. He didn't know what she'd said to him, but it had felt like a threat.

Once surrounded by people, and the better-illuminated areas of the castle, Richter began to feel better. He felt the warmth return to his limbs, and his earlier reaction seemed suddenly foolish. However, the temperament of the men at the château now made sense. If indeed she'd been discovered down there, however improbable, it would certainly spook the men at the garrison. She was...abnormal.

He forced himself to have an appetite, to engage in conversation, and to look as unconcerned as possible as they watched him with sidelong glances. He wouldn't let them see how the experience had rattled him. Shaken him to his core. The way it made him feel soon grew into anger. He wouldn't be made a fool of in front of these men.

After several glasses of red wine and a long, rambling story of a half-forgotten Bavarian winter by the commandant, Richter had made up his mind. He stood and gave the order to have the crate with the jars brought up and dragged into the courtyard. The SS officer knew what he must do to conquer his fear and theirs. With some work, three men did as he asked.

Once the largest crate was moved outside, he had them take off the lid.

In the electric light and drizzle of the courtyard, the men stood watching as Richter reached into the ancient straw used for packing and removed a simple, clay jar with the head of a dog. In front of everyone, he placed it against the far courtyard wall, took twenty paces, stopped, turned, removed his pistol, and fired. The gun jerked back in his hand and the jar exploded. There was a tense silence after the demonstration. He would not let the thing in the room scare him. He didn't know how, but he felt these items were important to her.

He removed another jar, set it down by the original, aimed and fired. It shattered, spreading its contents like sawdust. Even as the ringing in his ears died, he could make out the shouts of encouragement from his audience.

He ordered the men to bring up the remaining boxes and do the same. Convinced his job was done, the tension of the garrison broken, he then quietly excused himself. Richter returned to his room as the sounds of pistol fire echoed from the courtyard.

That night, while he lay in his small bed, looking up at the stone ceiling, he forced himself not to think about the tall woman. His success at dispelling his own anxiety faded as she seemed to creep again and again back into his mind. The odd, disjointed way she walked continued to plague his thoughts. For a moment, down there in the dark room, he'd seen her smile as she stepped toward him.

But it hadn't been a smile at all. He knew it was the grin of a dried corpse.

Once surrounded by others, he'd dismissed it as being

only a trick of the light. But his mind went in tormented directions that eventually led him into a fitful and restless sleep.

He wasn't sure how long he'd been asleep when a noise startled him awake.

There had been a gunshot.

He listened in the dark as he heard another. Then a burst of automatic fire. Were they still using the contents of those boxes for target practice? Then, somewhere, a man screamed like a wounded animal. It was long, mindless and bestial, before it was cut abruptly short.

There was yelling, movement, more gunfire. All the while, Richter stared at his gun belt draped across the chair at the far end of the room, unable to move. He felt frozen in place as the sounds of violence came nearer.

Then, without warning, there was silence. It lasted long enough that he could almost convince himself that it hadn't happened. That it was a nightmare, and only now was he fully awake. He closed his eyes, telling himself over and over that it wasn't real. Like a child, he pulled the sheets over his head, hoping that whatever horror gripped the castle would wash past, leaving him unharmed.

Then he heard his door open and close. Someone had entered. He stopped breathing.

He was being foolish. No one could have come into his room. It was all in his mind, some part of a waking dream. As soon as his heart stopped pounding, he would fall back asleep and wake and everything would be as it was.

He waited in the darkness, the bed sheets his only protection. An impossible period seemed to pass as he stared into their dark recesses. Then he heard a leathery creek. Sinews and joints, dry as centuries forgotten, moving. They brought something near. He heard what he thought was the scrape of dry bone on the rough stone floor.

Richter lay in the dark, listening to the sounds of his own breathing and the rain as it tapped at the window. The rain continued to tap, and he stayed where he was until the fear lessened in him. His mind explaining away what he thought he heard as imagination.

He allowed himself to exhale and slowly pulled down the sheets to survey the room. It was dark and nothing stirred. His eyes bored into the far shadows, finding nothing. There was just the ticking of the rain on the window next to his bed.

He turned and saw a dried, skeletal finger tapping on the glass. He looked up at its owner.

The dead woman leaned forward out of the dark and wrapped her long, icy fingers around his throat, and squeezed with horrific strength. She was still grinning.

And Kurt Richter knew fear.

THE END

IF YOU DON'T LAUGH, YOU CRY

BY ERICA CIKO CAMPBELL

He came to her alone in the night with wide, gleaming eyes. It had been ten Halloweens since Nora last saw him. When she answered the door, her hair nearly stood on end at the sight.

"The years were kind to you, sister."

She didn't want to say it out loud, but they hadn't been kind to him.

It was two in the morning when she offered him a chair in the living room, silently praying that whatever was all over his shoes wouldn't stain the carpet. She didn't say a word until they both sat down, not even a 'hello'.

This was no surprise. After all, it had been exactly ten years since they'd parted ways. And he was back, just like he'd said.

Finally she spoke, folding her hands in her lap. "Part of me didn't think you would come, Martin." She glared at him. "I hoped it was over. But here you are."

"Here I am!"

His purple and red jester hat hung down over his face. There were little bells on the tips that jingled every time he moved his head. The tips of the hat reminded her of tentacles, and she shuddered.

"It's been so long I can hardly remember," she said. "Where are we supposed to go?"

Inside, she already knew the answer. She just wanted to hear him repeat it, to make sure it wasn't a dream.

Martin's face was covered in black and white makeup. There were little triangles under both eyes that looked like tears. She cringed, realizing that it looked more 'worn-in' than makeup should. It blended perfectly to his skin. There was no color on his face, except for the thin, red line traced around his lips. His mouth was painted into a permanent smile, and the creases were almost sinister.

The rest of his outfit clashed horribly with the tendrils of the jester hat. His shirt was ruffled and green, with yellow triangles across the chest. All his clothes were covered in dirt, and there were plenty of holes. He looked like he'd fallen out of a circus clothes reject bin.

"We're going to see Melinda. How could you forget?" His sick smile gaped open in awe. "She's been waiting for us for a long time."

"Melinda isn't waiting for you," she said. "You're the last person she wants to see."

"I doubt you wanted to see me either," he said, "but you were still expecting me."

Nora gulped. The jester's ear twitched from under the

hat, picking up the sound.

"Let's not make this any worse than it has to be," she said.

The bells on his pointed shoes jingled as he climbed to his feet. He offered her a hand.

"I'm sure we'll have a wonderful time, sister."

She grabbed his skeletal hand and stood. She was ready to go, but suddenly she remembered: It was improper to leave the house in a nightgown. Hers was long and white, with little bows down the front.

"Let me get dressed."

"There's no time," he said. "Besides, no one will see us where we're going."

If Martin wore a jester's outfit covered in dirt, then surely she could get away with wearing a nightgown. She sighed and headed for the door. "Fine. I guess fashion is the least of our worries."

She put her hand on the doorknob, and the cold metal seemed to jolt her back to reality. For the first time, she was overcome by fear. Her hand shivered and for a moment she wanted nothing more than to run away and never look back. But she looked back to Martin, and knew there was no escape.

There was no point trying to reason with him, but she tried anyway. "Are you sure we have to do this?"

"You made the deal ten years ago. You knew the consequences, but you said you would give anything," he said.

Nora didn't bother responding. She tried not to look at him as she threw open the door. Martin followed her out into the night, and they began their long walk. A tainted yellow moon watched over them as they made their way silently through the streets.

As they walked along the winding, cracked sidewalks, Nora wished they would run into someone. She'd never hoped for anything more in her life. Someone, anyone, must be out at this hour. But it was getting close to 3 AM, and no one in this neighborhood stayed up past ten. They walked in silence for what seemed like eternity, and time began to blend together. Every once in a while, Martin would mutter something under his breath. Everything he said made the hair on the back of Nora's neck stand up.

"We're getting closer. I can almost taste her."

An hour must have passed, along with a hundred houses that all looked the same. Finally they reached a fork in the road, and they followed a broken sign that read 'Allen Street'. Nora knew the house the moment she saw it. And Martin did too, judging by the way he trotted excitedly to the door. It was a little red house with green shutters. Christmas colors, she thought.

She stood on the steps, keeping her distance. Her brother was bolder than her, and wasted no time heading for the door.

It flew open. There was an unwelcoming hiss, and the air was filled with a stinging cloud. Nora coughed and almost tripped down the steps, fleeing. She shielded her eyes, and heard a voice screaming.

"Stay back! Stay the hell away from my house, you monster!"

Nora's throat burned a little from the mace, but luckily she'd stayed out of the blast radius. Martin wasn't so lucky. Melinda didn't want any visitors. She'd sprayed him mercilessly in the face. She threw the can on the porch and reached into the pocket of her bathrobe. Nora gasped when she saw her pull out a pistol.

Martin coughed relentlessly for a moment, but appeared unscathed. The attack didn't seem to have much effect on him.

"Melinda! Is that any way to treat a guest? Clearly you were expecting us!"

His voice was raspy, probably from being sprayed with mace.

Melinda stood in the doorway, waving the pistol around like a maniac. "Nora, is that you?! You've got to be kidding me! You brought him to my house?"

Tears were running down Melinda's face now. Her long blond hair was pulled back in a ponytail. She wore a pink bathrobe, and red cat-eye glasses.

Nora said nothing. There was no point; Martin would do all the talking regardless.

"We made this deal a long time ago, Melinda. There's no use fighting. Now shut your pretty little mouth," he said. "You'll wake the neighbors."

"Melinda, I think you should just let us in. He's right. We can't hide any longer . . ."

Nora's voice trailed off. Her sister stared at her with such contempt that she couldn't bear to say anything else.

Melinda aimed her pistol at the jester's heart. Finally, she backed down, stepping aside so they could come in. Martin trotted through the door, shoes jangling. Nora wasn't so eager. She stood outside in silence for a moment, looking up at the moon. Then, she followed him into the house, shutting the door behind them.

This is an awful house, Nora thought.

She'd always hated it here. Peeling, yellow wallpaper smothered them from all sides. All the furniture looked like it was from the 1940s. A musty smell lingered in the air; the same one that had haunted her for her entire childhood. Her eyes were fixated on the portraits on the wall. There was her grandfather, frowning in black and white. Her parents' wedding photo hung next to it. But the one that made her squirm was of three children, two girls with a little boy in the middle. Both the girls were smiling, but the boy scowled.

"What do you want from me?! Haven't you taken enough?" Melinda's screams were frantic now. She was still crying as she pointed the gun at the jester. "Why can't you go back to hell where you belong?"

"Because you made a deal, sister." He laughed mockingly, unconcerned by the gun. "You wanted this, remember?"

"I didn't make a deal! I was a goddamn kid; I had no clue what I was doing!" Melinda was breathing heavily. There were beads of sweat on her forehead as she yelled. "You're a devil! You're nothing but a devil!"

Nora stared back to the portrait of the three kids. None of them looked like they had a care in the world. It was hard to believe that one of the happy little girls was her, back when she could still smile, back before the nightmare. If only those portrait kids knew what the future had in store.

Melinda's voice was desperate now. "What do you want from me?!"

"It's your turn to go in the basement," he said. "Don't worry. It's not so bad. I was there long before you were born."

Melinda's eyes turned wide and glassy. "N-no! Why me? Why do I have to go next? Why not her?" She trembled uncontrollably and looked to Nora for an answer. She said nothing.

"That was the order we agreed on, remember? First your brother goes in the basement, then it's your turn! And sweet, quiet Nora goes last." His bony hands moved wildly, tracing a circle in the air over and over. "It's a beautiful cycle, isn't it? All of you take turns!"

He said it like it was the simplest thing in the world.

Nora could hear her heart pounding in her ears as she stared at the jester. He'd really done a job on her brother's body. She was starting to think that the awful, white makeup really was permanent. It looked like his skin was withered and cracked. She wondered if he'd burned it on. And that creepy, red outline around the lips...

It almost looked like real blood.

"No, I can't do this! I don't want to go! I can't!" Melinda screamed. "Take her instead, I'd rather die than rot in that basement for a decade!"

The jester grabbed her by the hand, leading her towards the cellar door. He was almost polite. He held her gently, carefully. "I'm afraid it doesn't work that way, darling. It's your turn. We all have to go through it."

Melinda's face was almost as pale as Martin's now. Her pistol clattered to the floor, and she surrendered to his will. He opened up the basement door and led her down the stairs. Nora trailed slowly behind them, standing at the top of the staircase and watching them descend. She followed regretfully, flicking the light switch at the top of the stairs.

Nora heard her sister weeping somewhere up ahead. It looked like nobody had been in the basement for years. There was an old mannequin at the bottom of the steps. Old clothes in dusty bags hung from the rafters. She walked past stacks of boxes, and recognized some of her childhood toys. There was her rocking horse, tucked away. It tilted back and forth, creaking ominously.

They walked until they reached the furthest corner. Long before they saw it, she could see it in her mind's eye. She knew what awaited them in that dark, musty recess. An old, wooden toy chest was the only thing left in that spot. Melinda let out a bloodcurdling scream when she saw it, falling to her knees.

"Are you ready, Melinda?"

The jester wasted no time. He threw back the lid of the oak chest and grinned like a psychopath. His smile was horribly accentuated by the blood around his lips. Nora was drawn to the chest. A purple light emanated from it, and she peered inside.

Ten years had passed since Nora had seen her brother. And there he was.

Inside the chest, there was a lifelike jester doll. It wore a purple and red hat, and had little bells on its pointy shoes.

Its skin was ghastly pale, and the black paint under its eyes made it look like it was crying. The doll's face was permanently fixed into a frown. The most striking thing about it was the pair of terrified blue eyes. They almost seemed to move as Nora gazed into them. She recognized those eyes. Martin, her beloved brother. In the naivety of childhood, she had condemned him to the worst of fates.

The real jester's hands were glowing with the same eerie purple light that came from the chest. His smile stretched so wide it threatened to tear his face in half. Maybe that's why it was so red around the edges, Nora thought. Because he contorted his smile so gruesomely that he made it bleed.

After all, it was good to be alive.

Melinda kneeled on the floor, bowing her head. She didn't even bother to look in the chest. It was too much for her. After all, it would be her tomb for the next ten years.

"It's your turn, Melinda. You'll be stuck in the chest for a while, but there's good news! Your brother gets his body back," the jester said. "And I get yours! How exciting! I've never been a girl before. Usually only little boys are stupid enough to make a deal with me." He giggled. "You'll get your body back eventually, of course. In ten years! But I hope you don't mind if I make some modifications."

Nora gazed at the monster. She couldn't believe that body once belonged to her brother. It didn't look a thing like him. The jester had desecrated it, making him into a fool. Melinda wept on the floor, but she could offer no comfort. She stroked her sister's hair absentmindedly, but felt nothing. In ten years, they would be back here again, and this would be her.

Her memories drifted back to childhood. They'd spent countless hours playing in this basement, and their favorite toy was the sad jester doll. They often fought over who got to play with it. They acted out elaborate scenes, and even built a whole circus once. They built tents from sheets, and used toy dinosaurs in place of elephants. They loved that doll more than they loved each other. How they wished it could be real...

They devoted so much time and love to the doll that no one was surprised when, one day, it returned the sentiment. Nora remembered it like it was yesterday. Their dream had come true! The jester had talked, and he had a deal for them.

The doll could finally be real, but there was a catch. It had to trade bodies with someone who was already alive. But that was a small price to pay, right? After all, they were only 8 years old. The girls had ganged up on Martin and decided that he would go first.

Don't worry, Martin! You'll get to play with the real jester in ten years when it's your turn!

Children don't have much foresight, Nora thought.

Melinda's squeals snapped her back to reality. "No! Please! Please just kill me! I don't want to go in the chest! I don't deserve this! We were only kids. We didn't know what we were doing... Please!"

Her pleas fell on deaf ears. She stared helplessly at Nora with her piercing green eyes.

"Well, let's get on with it!"

The jester was cheery as he laid a hand on Melinda's shoulder. He reached for the doll, and held it in his other hand. Both hands were glowing intensely now, emanating that wicked purple light. He chanted under his breath and the air began to churn. The room spun like a vortex, and Melinda shrieked so loud that Nora's ears felt like they would bleed.

But soon her scream died off. The jester's body collapsed to the floor in a heap.

Melinda's head rose slowly, and the fear was gone from her eyes. Her lips slowly curled into a smile, so tight the corners of her mouth started to split. Her eyes had changed. They weren't green anymore, but a cold shade of grey. The same as the jester's.

The jester's body was curled up lifelessly on the floor. The doll, a miniature version of the man who held it, lay close by.

Nora picked up the doll with shaking hands. Its green eyes spun wildly with horror. They were Melinda's eyes. A tear ran down the doll's face as Nora placed it in the chest where it belonged.

THE END.

FOSTER DOLL
BY J. M. FAULKNER

Angelica exclusively wore pre-teen pink but spent summer evenings ripping the wings off injured greenbottles. I can estimate the year by the Spice Girls and Marilyn Manson CDs she shifted between on the stereo. A kaleidoscopic flittering of emotions, vented by a child who kept two faces: one effervescent, the other monstrous. When the metal music came on, I ducked under the cupboard.

A week before Mabel fostered Angelica, she came to my room and assessed me coolly while dabbing her mouth with a napkin. Burnt oil from a fried lunch wafted from the kitchen.

She settled me on her knee with a hairbrush and said, "You have a sister coming, Catherine. You'll have to mind her temper." The bristles touched my scalp, and she brushed, careless of the knots that snagged and my silent wincing. "Her dad was prone to violent outbursts. The apple doesn't fall far from the tree, but you'd know all about that. Remember your daddy?" She pinched my shoulder. "I've told her all about you, Cathy. And she is ever so eager to play."

I could but look up at her.

In the autumn of 1996, Mabel ushered Angelica into my bedroom and encouraged her to lie down. There was only one bed. A single. Angelica wheeled her luggage through the door, squinted at the sequined duvet cover and threw herself down. Mabel clapped, perhaps seeing the incautious dive as daughterly acceptance.

I endeavored to blend in with the wall.

"Oh," said Mabel, forgetting herself, and she trotted over to poke my belly. "This is Cathy. When you're sad, you can whisper all your worldly secrets to her. She never talks. Not a word. When you're mad, you can twist and pull her, and she never complains. So long as you never hurt anyone outside this room, you will have a place with me. And Cathy will love you always." She left me and kissed Angelica's cheek on the way out. "I'll cook us some pasta. Unpack your things. Make yourself at home."

I watched Angelica empty her luggage, and she returned my attentiveness with furtive glances. Clothes, CDs and a Game Boy all dumped on the bed. After some time, she appeared to have forgotten me entirely and was fully engaged in the task at hand.

Then, she pulled a photograph from her luggage and clutched it to her chest, out of sight. Her shoulders hitched. When she turned on me, her eyes came over misty and accusatory. Her mouth contorted at my voyeurism. She dropped the photograph, stomped across the bedroom, and slapped me clean.

"Don't look at me!"

I bounced against the shelves and clapped the floor, my breath knocked out. A branding of her palm seared my cheek.

Angelica loomed overhead, chest heaving, mouth wide with disbelief. But soon her panting calmed and her lips settled into something thin and wicked. The test finished, she regarded me with slit blue eyes.

"Think you're something special, don't you?" She wiped a tear from her chin. "Beautiful? I think you're the ugliest little doll that ever lived."

And from that day forward, I was her outlet. Angelica grew mad, and I became the subject of her torment.

I wasn't always like this. I was a real girl once, born in Brentwood on August 1st, 1979. Mom was a barmaid; Dad was a drunk. Mom sold herself to make ends meet; Dad stole the money to buy more booze. One could never keep up with the other. When Mom worked nights and Dad drowned his misery at home, he raked me over the coals. The bullying was verbal at first, but escalated when puberty came knocking.

A year later, Mabel fostered me. For a while, I found her disarming and considered myself lucky. She was no older than my parents, though already affected a grandma aesthetic. She wore her dark locks in a perm, was fond of knitted clothes and looked stout and frumpy. Her being a spinster was fine too. Fantastic. I didn't need another dad.

The problems started because of my shyness. I seldom spoke because I had learned chatterboxes got smacked. And, when I did speak, it was in the acerbic stabs ingrained from a previous life. See, the only thing more terrific than her embraces was my anxiety of being abandoned.

Mabel didn't take kindly to that. Misread my behavior as rejection. It wasn't a couple of months before our fights turned physical. I needn't explain how. It's not cathartic for me anymore, and catharsis is my reason for penning this. But the bit Doctor Daniels calls a delusion, that's worth another spin in the brainbox.

The fact that bitch turned me into a doll.

The year was 1991, about a month after my twelfth birthday. Mabel didn't buy me anything, though she outdid herself by remembering the date. Freddie Mercury had died of AIDS, and the nation mourned him in fits of sobbing and stunned silence. I was mopping up baked beans on toast the night Mabel bid me into the Locked Room.

The Locked Room was the only place in the house I was banned from. For a year, it was a source of speculation and teasing. To even mention the Locked Room was forbidden, and that only fueled my curiosity. To see the rustic door hanging open and Mabel leaning against the jamb, gesturing me inside with a quiet smile, gripped me with as much excitement as it did unease.

"It's time," she said.

I drew close, unable to curtail my curiosity, despite every fiber of my being warning me to do otherwise. My fringe fell into my eyes and I let it be.

Mabel looped an arm around my lower back. If it was supposed to be comforting, it was undermined by her pincer-like grip. She guided me inside and closed the door.

A long mound of cotton twill dust sheets occupied the far side of the room, leaving just a strip of twilight from the window behind it. I imagined a piled collection of antique furniture beneath. Mabel was fond of flea markets.

Before I could comment, she turned my attention to a standing mirror on my left. I went into that room a willowy girl—a sapling, really—with mousy hair and hazel eyes. Twelve years old and unscarred. Beige pajamas that fit like a blanket. To think, I hated the sight of myself in that golden frame...

There was a sturdy wardrobe beside the mirror, filled with pretty dresses and leather tomes. How I wish I'd paid more attention to the latter, but Mabel promptly had me unclothed and set up in a pleated, black and white polka dot dress. That done, she commenced pulling the dust sheets from the furniture.

Only there wasn't any furniture. Patch by patch, an intricately crafted sculpture peeked through. I thought it was a garden playhouse at first, but then it revealed itself to be a miniature. A giant, minutely crafted dollhouse.

Mabel seized my wrist and fastened a bracelet. Click. I took the purple jewel to be a piece of costume jewelry.

"Now," she said, "I want you to go around the side and enter the door there. You should be small enough to squeeze through. If you can find the front door, unclip that bracelet and hand it back to me, I'll let you keep it."

I didn't care about winning a gift from her. I'd long stopped caring about her favor. But I didn't want to face the consequences of not following along.

My foster mother shut the side door behind me, and I was left feeling around in darkness, the whiff of glue and sawdust high in my nostrils. I felt for the exit again, but I couldn't find a seam in the rough wood. I tightened my fist to bang the wall—

"Can you hear me, Cathy?"

She sounded impossibly far away. "...Yes."

"Follow my voice."

So I did, crawling on hands and knees in the cramped space until I came into a larger one. My ears popped, and I paused to knuckle them. "Am I close?"

"Can you see a light?"

Now she mentioned it, I could see something up ahead. A small, white square. "I think so."

"Hurry along. You don't want to stay in the dollhouse too long."

I made a beeline for it, my heart pumping. What if she locked me in here? The light grew into an A4-sized beacon, and it struck me suddenly that I had been crawling a long time. Too long...

When at last I came to the front door, I barely registered that the head jamb finished an inch above my eyebrows. Dots peppered my vision; nausea gave way to faintness. In my haste to escape, I tumbled over the threshold and skidded onto the carpet down on my belly.

I craned my neck. Mabel towered above, grinning. She snatched at me, but I rolled away.

Normally sized, I might have slipped away. She was a

dumpy, squat woman. But now I fled with all the grace of a maimed Ray Harryhausen figurine.

She grabbed my ankle and hoisted me skyward. She dangled me at arm's length, like I was a spitting cobra. The carpet stretched beneath me, plush and grassy.

"You'll need to catch up, Cathy, and there's a lot to tell. But I might not tell it all. Sometimes it's better if you don't know."

Angelica kept me in a display box, the plastic inside molded precisely to my frame. From this prison on the shelf, years before her arrival, I watched the police rummage through my room. Mabel spluttered I had run away, eyeing me all the while. I tried beating the packaging, but I could no more move than someone buried in sand. The police accepted Mabel at face value. She sniveled into a hanky for all to see.

And threw me a wink.

Five years later, Angelica slid right into my bed. Unreproached, her cruelty only escalated with time. Beatings became normal, though being inanimate none of my pains were mortal. It follows that her extraordinary torments, her acts of humiliation, scarred me most.

She came home from school with a lighter she had found beside a curb. Cackling, shaking it for fuel between strikes, she singed my hair until it blistered at the root, the smoke so close it scratched my throat and wrung imagined tears from my eyes. She left my temples bald and pinched what was left into a mohawk.

If she had a bad day at school—children treated her like roadkill; girls gave her a wide berth, and boys were inclined to throw stones—she strung me up on the doorknob by my thumbs. While I dangled there, she positioned a candle beneath me. If I stopped kicking, my toes would sway to a stop above the flame.

"I don't like it when you look at me, Cathy."

One day, Angelica returned from school in a particularly foul mood. She removed me from the shelf and squeezed my packaging, sighed, and drummed her fingers on the plastic.

"I know what you're thinking: What part of me is she going to cut off next." She walked over to the stereo and pressed play. Electronic noises, drums, scratchy guitar. The Beautiful People. "But I'm bored, Cathy. I might kill you today."

I didn't have a working mouth to scream.

She tossed me on the bed and left me wondering at her plan. A heavy door clattered somewhere. The fridge, maybe. Another slammed. The microwave rang out a hum.

I pressed against the plastic. It crinkled, but my effort was no good.

Angelica darted into the bedroom and yanked me from the packaging. Like Mabel, she snatched me by one foot and held me out like a snotty hanky.

"Time to go, Cathy."

I curled to swat her fingers, but I couldn't reach. She flattened me on the kitchen worktop, upturned a fruit bowl so that the contents spilled on the floor, then pinned me by the clavicle with it.

She peeked at the scissors beside me and smiled. "Now you're thinking: Is she going to snip at the webs of my fingers again? Cut off my other thumb? No, Cathy. What would I hang you by?"

She grabbed a tea towel and pulled something from the microwave. A jar of marmalade. "This will burn a little."

A butter knife flashed. She scooped a generous portion from the glass and splattered my exposed arms.

I flailed, but the marmalade hung tight, wobbly and sticky. A deep, emanating scold burrowed into my inhuman flesh. Unable to cry, unable to clench my teeth, I thought my brain would explode.

Angelica chuckled and clapped the worktop. "That's only the start. You see, Mother Mabel has an ant problem in the kitchen, and the exterminator isn't due 'til Friday." She nipped her underlip. "Do you think ants like marmalade?"

I shook my head: Please, *don't do this*. She read it to mean: *No, ants don't*.

"Well, you're about to get an education." Her scowl hovered over me, close enough that her hair curtained my vision. "How about a bet? If the ants don't come, I won't kill you today. If they do—" She glanced at the microwave. "— ants'll be the least of your problems. Ouch!"

She leapt backward and raked a blob of marmalade from her fringe. Nostrils flaring, she vanished into the hall-way and called, "Remember our wager."

Through the orange lava coating my arms, I saw discolored plastic melted beneath. I wriggled my hands under the rim of the fruit bowl, braced my legs, and pushed. My soft sternum expanded until my elbows buckled and the bowl pressed down. My chest bowed and my chin jutted forward. Dragging my body out wasn't an option.

A faucet switched on. Water sprayed the shower basin in the bathroom. Angelica was singing pop music, my torture forgotten, at least for the minute.

My insides jolted. The discarded knife was crawling with ravenous inspectors. A caravan of ants was already marching in my direction, antennae twitching. Frantic, I searched for any means of escape only to spot more ants. They poured from every crevice and cubbyhole in the kitchen.

I tried the bowl again, but it was no use. If I wasn't pinned by the clavicle, I would be pinned by the sternum or waist, and then I wouldn't be able to square my arms under it to push. An ant tickled my wrist, palps wriggling. Being this small, this close, the mandibles appeared gigantic.

But if I couldn't move my body, what about my head?

As a second and third ant sank their mandibles into the marmalade, I hefted the bowl and swung my head under and inside. Darkness. Something gnawed my forearm. I tried rolling to my knees, but the bowl snapped me downward. The rim had trapped my mohawk. I turned, kicked the bowl and ripped the hair from my scalp. An ant dangled from my arm, leeching. I shook it free and stomped its thorax until it chirped and I heard a splat.

Then I sat in the gloom, panting into the echo, head spinning. The shower's hiss was audible through the ceramic. Its stopping would herald Angelica's arrival. Winning the wager wouldn't spare me her wrath.

I found the bowl's ceiling and pushed, lifting it an inch off the worktop. Knees buckling, I struggled a few steps. Paused. Then I squatted the bowl until the edge of the worktop came into view. Light from outside leapt at my feet, and I dropped through the gap onto the kitchen tiles.

The bowl followed and shattered.

Fragments whipped across my back. I shielded my face with my hands, and the shower cut off in the bathroom. Angelica yelled, "Mabel? You home?"

The idea came to me all at once. I suppose it had been bubbling away in my imagination in the form of several ideas, but now coalesced into a whole.

I sprinted for the bedroom, careless of my pattering feet. The shower curtain screamed on its reels. "Cathy?"

I found the photograph that had caused Angelica's first fit of rage against me lying on the bedside table. It featured a woman who shared a likeness to Angelica, but there was no time to study it. I snatched her most precious belonging and raced back into the hall. Angelica came out of the bathroom in time to see me dive, bare and dripping feet stomping in the carpet. I shoved the photograph under the door of the Locked Room.

Belly-down, I peered up at her blood-red grimace. I thought she was going to crush me, but instead she tightened the towel over her non-existent breasts and grabbed me by the scruff.

"What, you think I don't know where the key is?" She smirked, and my insides tangled. "Once we're through here, you're going to wish I had killed you."

We shot down the hall, fast, with me spinning at the center of what felt like the world's greatest carousel. I punched and kicked the air, thinking we were bound for the microwave. A cupboard opened—a key jangled—and slammed.

Angelica circled back to the Locked Room and hesitated at the door. "You know, I've always wondered what she kept in here." She brought me up to eye level. "If I could squeeze it out of you... Shame you can't talk. But you can keep a secret, right?"

She unlocked the door and pushed it open, immediately forgetting the photograph. Dustsheets littered the floor, leaving the dollhouse exposed.

"Holy shit, Cathy. You and Mabel have been holding out on me."

Not taking her eyes off the dollhouse, she shut the door behind us to prevent my escape, then dropped me like a toy she no longer wanted to play with. While she went about prodding the miniature's façade, I scrambled for the wardrobe and mirror on the left of the room. If only I could get inside. One of the leather tomes was certain to contain a spell to transform me.

"What are you looking at?"

Angelica leered at me from the dollhouse. I pointed to the wardrobe.

"Something I should know about?" She sauntered over, and I dashed out of the way before she could send me flying. She peeled open the doors and gasped, "That's the prettiest dress."

The towel fell into a pile around her ankles. Nudity, another of Angelica's weapons.

"You better not be looking at me, Cathy." I fidgeted while she slipped into a pink halter neck dress fit for a Spice Girl. "Love it, Cathy. Maybe we can be friends, after all."

I stabbed my forefinger at the wardrobe again.

Her nose and lips pinched, but finally she looked inside and spotted the bracelet. "Just like yours," she said, clicking it into place.

While she twirled in front of the mirror, I retreated to the forgotten photograph and swiped it off the carpet. I sneaked around the dollhouse, found the side door, packed my fingers into the groove and pried it open. Its ancient hinges whined, and Angelica twisted to a halt.

"Cathy?"

I waited until she came around the corner. Then I stepped inside, trailing the photograph behind me.

"You want to play hide and seek, huh?" She dropped to her hands and knees and beamed toothlessly into the entrance. "But friends don't steal from each other. I'm not going in there. Stinks like sheds and cobwebs."

My heart sank. But the bluff was on my side because, if she left me here, Mabel would discover she had entered the Locked Room. Unable to speak or emote with my face, I shrugged.

Her mouth contorted. "Give it back!"

I stepped back. Her nostrils flared. I stepped—

She leapt into the dollhouse, and I bolted into the darkness.

"Bitch, I'm going to boil you alive for this. Melt you like an ice cream. You hear me?"

My ears popped, but not because of her shrieking. A change in air pressure. It was what I had experienced the first time around. I was going the right direction.

Bounding into the unknown, I continued as my tormentor scraped across the carpet, swiping at my heels.

I saw light ahead. The exit. I ran—

And whacked my head. It had reached the ceiling...

"Cathy?" Angelica skidded to a stop. Her voice sounded squeaky and far off. Fragile. "Where are you? I...don't like it here. Cathy..."

But I didn't wait for her to finish. I dove into the buzzing light and out of the dollhouse. Everything went black.

When I came to my senses, I was stretched out, fullsized, on the carpet. Crying real tears and soaked in real sweat. I stumbled to my feet, gasping for breath, and found myself in the mirror.

The polka dot dress was torn. A straggly mohawk topped my head, flanked by rumpled, pink burn scars. A thumb was missing from my left hand. Stranger still, I hadn't aged a day.

There was a patter on the carpet, and I spotted Angelica cowering under the bath towel. A doll approximation of Angelica.

My first instinct was to run, but then I remembered the humiliation she had put me through and saw how she trembled. I snatched her from the ground and hurried into my old bedroom, possessed by a fury I hadn't felt in half a decade. I took my old packaging and crammed Angelica inside, her flailing the whole time.

I thumped her on the shelf. I wanted to curse, but I hadn't spoken in so long. On second attempt, I could little more than rasp.

The front door opened. The sound of someone blowing their fringe from their face after an exerting walk. Footsteps. A silent pause at the kitchen entrance. *The fruit bowl…* Mabel shouted, "Angelica?"

I held up a maimed hand to my foster sister in farewell. Before Mabel could disturb us, I unlatched the bedroom window, dropped onto the garage and flopped onto the grass below.

There was a tremendous cry in my knee and a deafening whistle in my ears. I slapped a hand to my injury and writhed on the lawn, unable to repress a wail.

The front door opened. "Catherine?"

Head spinning, I pulled myself to a crawl with fistfuls of grass. When I heard Mabel shuffling on her shoes, I gathered what little strength I had to shut out the pain. Teeth gritted, I sprinted into the twilight, only allowing myself a glance back at the end of the street.

Mabel stood at the foot of the driveway, among the rose bushes, arms folded. Mouth tight.

She beckoned me with a forefinger.

If you're expecting this story to end with her in handcuffs, you'll be sorely disappointed. Who would believe me?

Did she foster again? Probably not. Now Angelica knew her secret, Mabel would never let her go. Two foster children up in smoke. With a track record like that, who would approve of her fostering again?

Nor did I reunite with my wayward mother to find her fit to parent me. I lived as a vagrant until I could turn things around.

Have I turned things around?

Doctor Daniels says I've created a heroic escape fantasy to cope with trauma. That I'm a victim of domestic abuse who really felt and experienced those things, but as a little girl, not a living doll.

This much is true: the house exists. Once a year, I wait until nightfall and stroll past the rose bushes out front. I keep my hood up, though the curtains of my old bedroom are drawn.

I think about Angelica. Of the humiliation she wrought, of the photograph I stole from her and now hold in my thumbless hand.

And I wonder how she feels living as a haunted doll.

THE END.

LITTLE STARS
BY CHRIS HEWITT

"Look, mom," said Elle, rushing from the garden holding up a multi-colored, glowing jam jar. "Look how they shine. I've got at least twenty now."

Sue stood on the porch, arms crossed. "That's great, hon, but it's time for bed."

She confiscated Elle's home-made butterfly net, receiving a huffy pout for her parenting efforts.

Her daughter stomped off indoors, chin resting on her clutched prize. "But it's too bright to sleep."

"I know, but it's gone midnight and you have school tomorrow."

The vibrant northern lights bathed the valley blue-green, bright enough to see the town of Pensacola nestled at the base of the distant Blue Ridge mountains. The towns-folk partied, the caution of the first night abandoned for a global Mardi Gras, as everyone reveled in the cosmic spectacle. By the second night, the cavorting aurora borealis had become a backdrop to an even more wondrous sight, as motes of neon lights floated like dandelion seeds on the wind. Tonight, there wasn't a parent in the neighborhood that could keep their children indoors.

"Can I take them to school?" yelled Elle from the bathroom, toothbrush buzzing.

"I guess. Just make sure you wash your hands."

Sue followed the trail of discarded clothes, picking up the jam jar and placing it on the bedside table before closing the curtains. The thin fabric could do little to block out the emerald glow. Sat on the bed, she scrutinized the luminous motes floating in their jar, defying gravity. The news said they were harmless, solar snowflakes, a crystallized peculiarity of the Sun's unusual mass ejection.

There was no denying they were beautiful.

"I bet no one got more than me. Not even Thomas and he caught three last night," said Elle, bounding into bed.

Sue pulled the covers up and tucked her daughter in. "We'll see. Remember, quality, not quantity. I'm sure yours will be the brightest. After all, you're my bright, little star. Sweet dreams."

She kissed Elle on the forehead and retreated, the pulsing contents of the jam jar almost too bright for a nightlight.

"Mom?"

A single word uttered a hundred times a day, so familiar that its subtle inflection communicated endless meaning. This time it spoke of procrastination.

"What?"

"They tickled."

"I'm sure they did. Now, go to sleep."

Sue returned to the porch to watch the festivities, music and laughter echoing up the valley, a glass of wine her only exuberance. A glance at her phone confirmed the cell network remained down, as it had been since the solar flare started. Thankfully, they'd not seen the power cuts reported in other countries. No internet. No phones. Part of her considered it a small price to pay to witness this once in a lifetime event in peace. What tales she'd have to tell her grandchildren.

She held out her hand to catch a floating red mote. It fizzed as it melted on the back of her hand. Elle was right; they tickled.

With a groan, Sue turned off the alarm clock and stumbled, bleary-eyed, to the bathroom. "Elle! Time to get up!"

Fifteen minutes later, feeling almost human, she peeked in on her daughter. Elle lay unmoving in her bed. "Elle! Come on."

Coffee, orange juice and a splash of milk on a bowl of Cocoa Krispies, and Sue was getting annoyed. "Elle! Come on! We're going to be late. Where's your homework?"

Silence.

She marched into her daughter's room and pulled back the curtains, eliciting a muffled moan from under the covers. "Come on. Homework. Where did you leave it?"

"Mom..."

The word oozed sickness. Often faked, but Sue knew the difference. She sat on the bed. "What's up?"

"I don't feel well."

"You're tired. Too many late nights."

Sue's hand snaked under the covers in search of Elle's forehead. Her cold and clammy forehead. "Oh! You're frozen."

She threw back the covers, feeling her daughter's icy body, frozen but for the odd patches of warmth. Closer investigation revealed dozens of angry, red welts. Many on her daughter's fingertips where she'd been catching the motes. Sue brushed aside Elle's hair and ran a trembling finger over a raised red bump over her daughter's right eye, another nestled against Elle's left earlobe, a thumbnail-sized volcano.

"Mom!"

Panicked urgency, hard-wired to trigger Sue's motherly instincts. But this time, the call came too late. Elle vomited over the side of the bed, and it was all Sue could do to hold back her daughter's hair. As the retching eased, Elle shivered into a fetal position and Sue wrapped her in the folds of the blanket. Mind racing, she replayed her daughter's last few days in her head, searching for a cause. Plant? Insect? Bacterial? Viral? Yes, viral. There was always some plague going around the school.

"Okay. No school for you today. I'll be right back."

She returned with a bucket of supplies and pushed an electronic thermometer into Elle's ear. A beep and she stared, perplexed, at the digital readout. "Thirty-three?"

"I-is that good?"

"For a popsicle, honey. Why are you so cold?"

Elle shook her head, a chill that snaked up Sue's spine.

A fever she could understand. Elle had seen her fair share of childhood illnesses. But hypothermia? She ran her fingers over the red marks, warm—almost hot—against her daughter's frigid, goosebump skin. A second reading from Elle offered only more concern.

"Thirty-two. Okay. We need to get you warmed up."

Sue pulled Elle's frozen body close, hands rubbing up and down her back, willing her body's warmth into her daughter. "It's okay. You've just got a bit of a chill is all."

"K-k-kay," Elle stuttered.

"I'm going to run a warm bath."

Sue wrapped another blanket around her daughter and snuggled Elle's favorite teddy bear beside her head. The welt above Elle's eye seemed bigger, angrier.

"Stay here. Stay warm."

Sue filled the bath, wandering to the kitchen to retrieve her cellphone. "Damn it. No signal, no messages, no internet. Typical."

She tossed the useless device aside, closed her eyes and rubbed her temples, considering her next move. The landline! She'd almost canceled it. When was the last time she used it? The purring welcome of the dial tone was music to her ears, and she dialed the only number she knew.

A woman's voice answered. Sue didn't hesitate. "My daughter is ill. Her body temperature is plummeting and I..."

"We're experiencing a high volume of calls at the moment..."

She stared at the phone in disbelief. "Please. I need an ambulance."

"...hang on the line for one of our operators. If this is an emergency..."

"Of course it's a fucking emergency!"

The line died.

"Hello? Hello!"

She tapped the receiver, desperate to hear the reassuring tone, fingers curling around the plastic handset as she fought down a rising panic. The hospital was a thirty-minute drive, the nearest neighbor fifteen. They were on their own. She returned to her daughter's room, wondering what to do.

"M-mom. T-t-they're dead," said Elle, hugging the empty jam jar.

Sue snatched the jar from Elle's hands, several small beads tinkling against the glass. "It's daytime. They've gone to sleep. Let's get you warmed up."

She scooped up her daughter and carried her to the bathroom. "Arms up. Come on, let's go."

Her daughter's skin looked almost blue, but for the angry red polka-dots. She turned off the faucet and tested the water. "Lukewarm, just how you like it. Ready?"

Elle nodded or shook. It was impossible to tell as Sue eased her daughter's shivering body into the water.

"Moommm!" cried Elle through gritted teeth.

Sue had only heard this cry once, after Elle fractured her arm falling from a tree. It was the worst sound in the world. "I know. It's okay. It'll pass. Just breathe."

Elle thrashed, water lapping over the side of the bath as

Sue pinned her daughter's shoulders under. Thrashing gave way to squirming and, finally, stillness.

"Better?"

Elle nodded, her skin flushing red as she took a long, quivering breath.

"Good. I'll get the thermometer."

She ran to the bedroom, side-stepping the sick soaking into the carpet, and returned a moment later.

"Okay, let's see what—"

The thermometer slipped from Sue's hand and rattled across the tiled floor as she stood frozen in the bathroom doorway. Elle hung in the air, back arched impossibly, tips of her fingers and toes the only parts of her touching the water. The marks on her skin glowed red, bright as the neon motes the night before, each one the tip of a burning cigarette.

"Elle!" She rushed to her daughter's side and stared into her pallid face. Elle's eyelids flickered, eyes rolling back into her head. "No. No. No. No! Elle! Can you hear me?"

Elle convulsed. "Mom?"

The hairs on Sue's neck bristled. She'd never heard this tone before. It sounded different. Alien. "It's okay. I'm right here."

"I'm floating."

Her daughter's eyelids continued to flicker even as her fingers swirled through the water in figures of eight.

"I know. Don't worry. It's going to be okay."

"I like floating."

Sue laughed, tears streaming down her face, happy

to hear her daughter's voice, even with its odd, dreamlike tone. She pulled her daughter to her—a limp, weightless rag doll—and twisted her around her torso. The red marks burned like hot embers, but it didn't stop Sue from holding her daughter close. She brushed the wet strands of hair from her Elle's face as her eyes blinked open.

"There you are."

"Peekaboo," said Elle, grinning.

Sue hugged her daughter tight until the heat of the welts became too much to bear, and she reluctantly let her daughter float free.

"Wheee!" cried Elle, hands flailing for the edge of the bath. Her foot found the floor, and she drifted towards the ceiling.

Sue grabbed her leg. "Careful now. Let's get you back into bed."

"Oh! Can't I go outside and play?"

Sue stared at her, shocked, seeing only a vision of Elle whisked away on a gust of wind. "Let me see. You're naked, you're ill and I bet you still haven't done your homework."

"I feel fine."

"You're burning up," said Sue, tugging her daughter down and toweling her off.

She still felt cold. The welts, hotter. She dabbed at a large contusion on her daughter's arm. Snaking tendrils glowed like volcanic fissures under Elle's skin.

"They don't hurt."

"I don't care. I'm not Mary Poppins and this isn't normal."

Sue dragged her daughter down the hall by the foot as Elle practiced her breaststroke, eager to explore her new-found freedom.

"Let go of the door," said Sue, swinging Elle into her bedroom. She floated to the far corner, bumping against the ceiling, giggling. Sue retrieved her daughter's favorite pink onesie out of the draw and, spinning Elle like a cartwheel, dressed her.

"Again!Again!"

"No! Bed," said Sue, pulling her daughter down to the mattress and fighting to keep her there while she tucked the blankets in place. "Stay there while I sort this out. I'm serious. Don't move."

Elle nodded; innocence incarnate.

"I mean it," said Sue, heading to the door.

When she looked back, her daughter had floated half-way to the ceiling, blanket and all.

"It wasn't me."

"Of course, it wasn't," said Sue, walking to the window and checking the locks. "At least stay away from the win-dow."

Elle performed a slow backwards somersault, the blan-ket slipping over her face as her foot kicked the light shade. "Course."

Sue closed the door behind her and listened to her daughter's sniggering efforts to right herself.

"The Wapture?" said Elle, sat in her pink onesie, cross-legged, on the living room ceiling. A length of twine dangled from her foot, the other end tied tight to her mother's wrist as she sat on the sofa flicking through news channels.

"It's the 'Rapture', and it's nonsense."

A pencil landed beside her, and not for the first time. She sighed as she held it up in the air and Elle reached down to retrieve it.

"I'm sure you can do your homework at the table."

"Where's the fun in that?"

"Whatever. Just get it done."

Homework had been Sue's way of normalizing the crazy situation while she figured out what to do next. She flicked to the next channel. Several poor people floated up into the sky as a circling helicopter attempted a desperate rescue. Sue skipped on before Elle saw the gruesome outcome. An animated figure talked about an alien invasion.

"E.T. phone home," mocked Elle, holding out her glowing index finger.

Sue groaned. "Put it away. You are home."

She flicked back to a bishop claiming this was the end of days. Flick.

"What we do know is that those infected are being dragged upwards as these creatures desperately try to escape our atmosphere and return to their natural habitat in the vacuum of space. It's important that anyone with red marks remain inside. I can assure you our top scientists are working flat out to find a solution, but our best hope is to sit tight, stay indoors and wait for the solar flare event to end in thirty-six hours."

"Does that mean I get to be an astronaut?" asked Elle. Charred, black stains marked where the burning welts had singed her pink onesie.

"Not if you don't finish your homework. For now, even the President says you've got to stay indoors."

"Spoilsport!"

A notebook landed on Sue's head.

"Finished. Can I go play now?"

"Have you listened to a word I've said? This isn't a joke."

Elle crossed her arms and sulked. Sue sighed, turning off the television to stare up at her daughter before reeling her in. Elle's upside-down face scowled back at her, nose to nose, as she kissed her on the forehead, avoiding the incandescent lump.

"Come on, let's turn that frown upside down."

She twisted her daughter around until Elle' floated, cross-legged and upright, grinning back at her.

"I get it. It's fun. But you have to be careful. There's so much we don't know."

"I'll be careful," said Elle, pushing away from her mother to float above the coffee table. "I wish you could float too, mommy."

Sue smiled. It did look like a lot of fun.

Sue spent the rest of the day playing with Elle, keeping her occupied, keeping her safe, and keeping one eye on the news for any update. At sunset, the northern lights returned, even more spectacular than ever, snaking across the sky. Her daughter had stopped bouncing off the walls.

"It's not fair," cried Elle, jumping up and down.

"Stop that! You'll damage the ceiling."

The news warned of the aliens increasing desperation to return to space, driven by the peak of the flare. Sue delivered supper from the top of a stepladder, although most of the spaghetti ended up on the kitchen floor. She'd never be able to forget the sight of her daughter squatting to perform a number two. Her hopeless aim would need far more practice if this became a permanent situation. The biggest challenge, however, had been the sleeping arrangements. Sue would have given anything for a nail gun. Instead, she stared up at her daughter laying above her on the cold plaster, teddy bear tucked under her arm.

"Night, night, my little star."

Elle yawned, tired after an eventful day. "Night, mom."

Sue adjusted the cord biting into her wrist before turning off the bedside light, the room bathed in the insipid, green light seeping through the blinds. Sue looked up into a constellation of red stars; the twinkling motes, brighter than ever.

She hummed 'Twinkle, Twinkle, Little Star' until she fell asleep.

Sue awoke in darkness, her daughter's teddy bear on her face. Her arm ached, dragged up in the air. Elle had moved during the night, but not far. A faint red glow still illuminated the ceiling.

Half-asleep, and wanting to avoid waking her daughter, Sue shuffled across the bed, twisting to ease the ache as she slipped back into a strange dream about astronauts fixing a space toilet.

With a groan, Sue turned off the alarm clock. Her other arm still floated above her, pins and needles running like electricity along its length. "Elle, time to get down."

She wiped the sleep from her eyes and looked at the coiled cord beside her. It took a long moment for her to spot the frayed strands lying on the pillow. She shot upright, arm still raised above her, stiff, impossible to lower.

"Elle!"

There was no sign of her daughter as she jumped from the bed. Her arm stubbornly refused to stop its bizarre salute, and she rapped her knuckles on the door frame as she ducked into her daughter's empty bedroom.

"Elle!"

She dashed from room to room—bathroom, living room, kitchen—all empty, not a sign of her daughter's passing on ceiling or floor. Then she saw it. The front door, wide open, the sun rising over the distant mountains.

"Oh, God. No! Elle!"

She sprinted to the porch, pain shooting down her outstretched arm as she scanned the garden, the sky. Down in the misty valley, a flock of startled birds took flight, and she watched them glide into the golden haze, heart sinking.

Far beyond, she could see people, arms and legs flailing as they rose, unwillingly, high into the sky. Victims of the alien motes.

Sue's legs gave way, but she did not fall, instead a pop followed by a wave of agony announced her shoulder dislocating. She hardly felt the pain as she looked to the horizon, eyes welling as the ground fell away below her.

"I'm coming, little star."

EVERYTHING YOU NEED

BY ANN WUEHLER

"Do you have everything you need?"

Tony put the small jar, containing a living Western Toad, down. He had been walking around, aimless, holding that jar against his chest, searching for anything that could not be left behind.

"I think so. Yes. Let me tuck this away."

He placed the jar inside the rounded case, with the other specimens he had collected. Bonnie had helped with a few of them. The garter snake. Had she not helped with that one when still only a little girl, with scabs on her knees from falling off her skateboard? A tap on the case, it closed up with a sucking sound that had always amused her. Until now.

"Are you driving, Bon? I fear I might shake too much."

"I can drive. Are you sure? We can stay here, have that picnic on the cheap carpet. It's lasted all these years, that cheap carpet." Bonnie put her foot on the red rectangle of carpeting she had found in the thrift store off Myrtle Road. Tony sat in his favorite rocking chair, hair snow white, face drawn and tired. He could not last another day here in this atmosphere, not another day. His hands shook with palsy; his skin had gone hot and loose and grayish.

And his eyes remained as kind and shy as that day she'd chanced across him trying to get a hissing, very small and incredibly angry garter snake into a collecting jar. A jar with a strange lid made from some bronze-like metal. The glass had a bluish tint, and a strange, deep sound when tapped with a fingernail.

"No. It needs to happen in that big open field. It's where the coordinates will place everything. I'd like to stay here, Bon. On this cheap, red carpet. Eat peanut butter sandwiches, drink lime juice. The powdered drink. That stuff…"

He accepted her kiss against his forehead, his smell one of faint rot and Old Spice. His disguise would slough away. If he remained on her planet, the real Tony beneath would die. Simple, brutal truth.

"Everything is packed? All of it? No pictures. Maybe I could pack you up as well."

"I got it all," she replied, taking up the pickup keys. "I'd go if I could. You know that."

Bonnie told him what he wished to hear, but the reality of all this meant a parting. She had said goodbye to those she loved; she had survived it.

"No pictures of you. It might lead to questions and checking stories."

But she had the one, in a small locket, tucked away at

the very bottom of her little girl's white jewelry box, that, when opened, displayed a twirling ballerina as pinging notes played. She refused to give that up, give up everything of her life with him.

"Shall we?"

"Maybe I'll tuck you away in a jar, Bonnie. Take you with me."

She laughed in his face, kissed his forehead, tasting death and rot on her tongue, smelling his Old Spice aftershave, which he wore to smell like so many other men. "I'd escape, be so mad at you."

She met his bleary gaze, saw a strange glitter far down, as if his real eyes hid behind the kind pair she knew so well.

Bonnie helped Tony out to their Chevy S-10 pickup, his cases covered by a blue tarp. But no one came out this way, to the very end of a dead-end road.

Small Creek Road had two houses on it. A five mile road, nearly, that ended at a small trailer house not many people even knew existed. Their only neighbor, Ross P. Lincoln, lived in a shack with his ten dogs and worked odd jobs, from helping out at harvests to collecting morels up in the mountains. Being a gentle, small man who kept to himself, he'd been near the perfect neighbor for Tony and his collecting—what Tony called his 'mission's aim'.

She drove halfway up the dirt lane that led to the highway, but turned left onto the rutted little road toward Small Creek itself. She drove carefully, and Tony put his hand on her leg. She noted his fingernails had started to fall off. The meat beneath them looked swollen and diseased.

"I can put the gloves on. I seem to be falling apart."

He tried to smile. She tried to smile.

"Only if you want to. I don't mind. I've lived with you for over twenty years. "

"Time is different here. Faster. I'm sorry. I'm not one of you. I thought I'd last longer." He turned his eyes toward her, the truck dipping and swaying as she navigated the road. "You look so pretty today. I like your hair up like that."

"Tony. You won't be dead? You said that when you go back, you'll recover. Be okay. Is that true?"

"Bonnie..."

He sighed, peered out the window at the long grasses, at the trees. A bit of his hair, attached yet to grayish skin, slid down the side of his head, landed on his shoulder. He picked this away, placed it in a small, metal box he kept for odds and ends. Had she not watched him pluck small mushrooms and tuck them inside such a box for later study and storage?

"Let's enjoy the picnic. I think I can get down one last sandwich. You make such good bread."

"I really do. This batch turned out. I tried that new yeast. I think I might try sourdough. I'm a bit scared of that. You have to feed it." Her lips moved; her heart spoke bloodied words. "Lie to me, Tony. Just lie to me. Don't tell me you're going to die, that you came here and you'll go back just to die with your stupid suitcases of samples. Please."

She stopped, the pickup stopping as well as she tried to breathe.

"I'm not going to die," Tony said, not looking into her

face. The pickup lurched forward and they both saw the rock-littered bank of Small Creek, the meadow on the far side, the trees that gave their shade yet. "I like how close this is. It's hell on the truck, but it's so close. Check that back tire. It leaks."

"Of course."

Bonnie parked. She tried to calm her thoughts, make them not scream that perhaps, in less than an hour, he would be gone from her life. She would have to tell everyone at work that he had run off. Make them believe it. She might have to find a new person, someone of her own species. Tony had been in her life since her childhood. Her hands took out the food, flopped the blanket down over the grass and dirt as Tony limped toward their spot, almost sacred now.

"Is that where you caught that poor, little snake?"

"I think so."

Tony allowed her to ease him down, the blanket an old, blue plaid number she had gotten for Christmas from her dad. The last present he had given her before his accident. He had swerved to avoid hitting a deer, smashed his little car beyond repair, along with his hearty, powerful body. He had died almost instantly, the police had assured her.

"What you brought me that first time. Peanut butter with raspberry jam. Bananas. Corn chips. A Ho-Ho. I was horrified. But I ate it. Every bit of it, just to make you happy with me. I think I loved you on first sight, Bonnie."

He smiled, tried to chew a mouthful of banana, but his teeth littered the blanket between his legs. Blood and drool and black liquids stained his chin, dripped onto his favorite striped shirt. White and gray stripes, so ordinary. His face, that disguise, so ordinary and forgettable.

"I'm sorry." He tried to pick up his own teeth, to take them with him. Bonnie caught his feeble hands, smiled, picked up his teeth, put them in the metal box with the bit of skin and hair. "Eat. I can sit here, enjoy you to the last moment."

"You flattering rascal." She winked at him, tossed her brown hair, gave a giggle, her heart so broken it had turned to powder and sand in her chest. "I suppose when you get back, you'll brag to all your fellow spacelings about how you charmed me into doing whatever you asked. You'll be a hit. That poor garter snake will be a star."

A strange little shiver went over him, a strange little smile lifted his drooping lips. "Spacelings. That's what I told you to call me—us, all of us. You stopped."

"Yes..." She could not continue this for a moment, this silly spate of words that hid nothing at all. "I fell in love and 'spaceling' didn't seem right. You were just Tony. It took me a while to love you, didn't it?"

"You were cautious, thought I was crazy. I trusted you. Showed you my collecting jars. Showed you the communicator, the little device with my language... You thought it was a trick. You were so mad at me for so long. 'Everyone laughs at me already,' you told me. You thought I was being mean."

"I did." Bonnie laughed, but her cheeks felt raw and wet. "I was an idiot."

Both turned their heads as a hum sounded, like a single

voice about to start a hymn, warming up by holding a single note. Tony tried to get to his feet; she helped him, the heat from his body like standing next to the stove as her bread baked. He wore a necklace, the pendant hidden down his shirt. For a moment, she saw a smooth cylinder about twenty feet across, with a walkway extending into the grass on the other side of Small Creek.

I am seeing a spaceship, she thought.

Tony turned to her, she could think of nothing at all but that she needed to check that back tire. The tarp peeled back, on its own. The cases and metal boxes and packages he had used to store his specimens floated toward the cylinder and disappeared inside it. Tony splashed through the creek, tripped and fell, but managed to crawl onto the walkway, his head turned to the side, his eyes trying to find her even as the walkway rolled back inside, taking him away from her. The entrance sealed itself. The air shimmered around that cylinder, standing at least thirty feet tall. Disguised. Gone.

Her spaceling was gone.

That hum again; she barely noticed it. She had not slept alone since their first time. The hum of machinery, the sliding of hatches, barely heard, as she went numb and cold just to survive long enough to get home to weep for days. A whoosh of air on all sides, as if something had surrounded her.

Bonnie forced herself to go back to a life without Tony and bumped against an unseen barrier, falling backwards onto leaves and soft earth, the sound of air being pumped into a room above her head. Like an air conditioner perhaps.

Her widespread hands encountered a smooth, cool surface. Behind her was the creek itself, a summer day captured in perpetuity. That special place she and Tony had shared, their oasis, their land of memories, chasing after small wildlife, laughing, kissing in trees. She could see their pickup, the food not yet eaten on the blanket, but it was maddeningly beyond the glass.

Something gripped the top of the giant collecting jar. Had she not helped Tony put so many little animals and plant samples in them over the years? From gophers to wildflowers.

A claw gripped the top of the jar—a jar sized for a human subject—and lifted it. She watched the ground recede at a steady pace, before the claw brought her into a tiny room, where her terrarium settled onto a purple-white floor. The sounds of the creek maddened her. Such a natural, known sound compared to the faint hisses and beeps of the spaceship hold or wherever this was.

"Bonnie..." Tony's recorded voice, breathing from above her, brought in with the air that kept her alive. The grass and bushes stopped at the blue, glass-like walls. "You're safe now."

"Don't trap me in this thing. Put me back."

"Don't you trust me, Bonnie? Don't you love me, Bonnie?"

His voice in her ears, soft and unnatural against the creek and meadow and summer sky. The mmm of the machine around her, the rustle of breezes in her new cage, the heat of sunlight on her upturned face as she looked, for the first time, into the face of her beloved.

"Shhh… It's all right now."

"You're not Tony," she whispered. "You're not Tony. He'd never do this to me. Is he dead? Just tell me. I'll behave. Just tell me."

The face drew back, except the angles and circles and ridges did not add up to faces as she knew them. The eyes seemed bulging, with no lids, too many pupils.

"Alalalpam arranged for your transport and safety years ago." The actual name escaped her ears; she heard Alalalpam from the cacophony. "You will grow used to your new life. He worked very hard at making this environment for you. If you walk down that body of water a bit, there's the home you two shared. Right down to the cheap, red carpet. We do not normally collect humans for study. You are rare and precious, a guest. You are the first for us. I will leave you alone. It's a long journey. I understand that Tony worked out weather patterns and…"

"Tony did this? For me?"

"Yes. Or we would have had to eradicate you. That is our law. He saved your life."

Bonnie could see nothing now but the place she had most loved. The glass had grown opaque. She stood in a giant collecting jar, a garter snake now. How long would this last? She beat her fists against that glass substance until they bled. Off she walked around Small Creek to find her trailer, exactly as she had left it. Her world had become glass walls. A replica.

Everything seemed too new, too shiny. The cheap, red

carpet seemed far too clean. No Tony to soften any of this. Bonnie sat on her own replicated bed, began to plan how to escape. They had left her rocks and trees and water. Death seemed better than the prettiest cage. Tony should have understood that. Maybe she had not known him at all. Doubts sliced through her very soul as she buried her face in the pillow that did not hold any of the known smells of her life. No Old Spice.

She would crack this damn glass, explode like gasoline if that was the case. Everything she needed was indeed in this bottle.

"Everything I need," she muttered.

Bonnie walked back to Small Creek, though the actual distance had been miles from her trailer. She found a rock that fit her hand. A deep strange boom sounded when she struck the glass. A tiny nick encouraged her. She struck that rock against the barrier over and over.

A hand on her shoulder, squeezing down, a voice she knew in her ear.

"Bonnie," and it was Tony, but it wasn't him at all. His hair held too much copper; his eyes had streaks of weird green; his shape seemed longer and thinner. The rock turned far too hot to hold and she dropped it.

"It's not you," she whispered, but he took her hands—her bloodied, broken hands—and kissed them, before leading her to the blanket beneath the cottonwood. He had no smell and his skin had the quality of plastic and shrink wrap.

The years passed. Seasons came and went with Germanic clockwork precision. Bonnie told herself she could smell Old Spice on this replica of the spaceling she had loved. When she tried to find rocks to bash her way free, they had been replaced with soft, spongy clumps designed to look like rocks. The new Tony would often go quiet, just watching her, with an expression so close to actual empathy.

Surely this cage, this prison, this giant collecting jar, had not been what her Tony had wanted for her. The glass remained opaque. She could not see out to whatever new world she now inhabited. She sat on the cheap, red bit of carpeting. It had become her most precious object here. The creek nearby murmured and flowed, like a fountain or an artificial pond in a garden. The new Tony handed her a peanut butter sandwich.

"Thank you."

She took a bite, chewed. It kept her alive but it had a faint taste of metal and salt.

"Perhaps…" The new Tony settled close to her. She winced, moved away before she could stop herself. "Perhaps you'd prefer to sleep." He looked upward, toward the giant lid that the sunny sky hid only a bit. "Your sadness hurts me."

"I'm fine," she said. She said this every time he asked her if she wished to sleep. Bonnie did not wish, just yet, to discover what he meant by that. "I have everything I need."

THE END.

MID MOURNING SNACK
BY RADAR DEBOARD

Mortimer noticed Andrea Stilton crossing the room, headed directly towards him. Her watery eyes were to be expected, given the circumstances, but Mortimer really didn't wish to empathize with anyone at the moment. Regardless, he did his best to hide his indifference with a solemn expression as the widow drew closer to him.

Andrea sniffled for a moment before saying in a quiet tone, "Thank you for doing the funeral on such short notice, Mr. Cunningham. It really means a lot to me."

"It was no trouble, madame," Mortimer slowly replied in his low voice. He quickly added, "My condolences for your loss."

"T-thank you," Andrea barely managed to stutter out before she started bawling.

Mortimer was about to leave the room, but before he could Andrea wrapped her arms around him in an embrace that was quite unfamiliar to him. He allowed the hug to go on for far longer than he wanted to, simply because force-fully pushing away a grieving widow was most certainly one

Hell of a social taboo. To Mortimer's surprise a sudden rumbling sounded in his stomach, causing a small pain to shoot up into his chest. A wave of confusion quickly followed as Mortimer tried to ascertain why the sudden hunger had taken hold. Surely it can't be because of the Widow Stilton being so close, he thought to himself. Another grumbling of his stomach finally forced Mortimer to gently push back the widow.

"My humblest apologies," Mortimer said with a slight bow, "but there are some business matters I must attend to. I hope you understand."

Andrea gave a small nod, "Of course...I understand." She quickly pivoted away from Mortimer, "I should attend to the other guests."

"Please do," Mortimer grumbled under his breath so Andrea would not be able to hear him as she walked away.

He scanned the lobby of his mortuary, disgusted to find it packed with people. Dozens of living, breathing human beings talked and snarfed down tiny finger-foods all around him. It repulsed Mortimer to see the living making a mockery of a place for the dead, even if they had no idea that they were doing so. Another rumbling from his stomach caused him to reflexively grab his abdomen. Mortimer couldn't fight it back any longer: he had to get some food, and fast. He frantically pushed his way through the pocketed gatherings of various persons while making headway towards the employees-only door located on the other end of the lobby.

Mortimer managed to exit the crowd without experiencing another unpleasant rumble, but he knew that another one was most likely on the way. He stumbled down the poorly-lit hallway that led towards the preparation room. A gurgling in his stomach caused Mortimer to stop dead in his tracks as he forcefully tried to prevent his body from ripping loose of the tight-fitting outfit he was currently wearing. It took several moments for the unpleasant sensation to pass, at which point Mortimer scrambled the last dozen or so feet into the pitch-black room before him. He immediately flipped the switch and patiently waited the few milliseconds it took for the lights to come on before progressing into the room.

He glanced over the options laid out before him, desperately trying to find a suitable candidate to meet his needs. Mortimer haphazardly pushed past the table containing the body of an elderly woman. She had died three days prior, so her flesh wasn't quite as fresh as what Mortimer normally preferred. Besides, she was well known in the town, so her funeral was more likely than not going to be an open casket. Someone would certainly raise concern if they discovered that the deceased body of such a beloved member of the community was randomly missing an appendage.

Mortimer didn't need to concern himself with the corpse of the elderly woman, or of the several remains laid out next to her. He pushed past them all until he reached the last body in the room. It was the corpse of a young man who had just been brought in less than a few hours prior. He had died in a horrific car accident which had ripped half his face off, among other gruesome injuries. The unfortunate soul's wife had managed to survive the crash, but she was in the hospital for the moment and would most likely not be out for the next week or two.

Mortimer knew that, based on the circumstances surrounding this particular cadaver, the body would be perfect for his needs. Thanks to the damage the individual had sustained before death Mortimer highly doubted that anyone would notice if something was missing. He eagerly picked up his bone saw from where he had last placed it and began hacking into the corpse's left hand, just above the wrist. Mortimer furiously worked, easily tearing through the tissue that was still relatively soft. It took but a few minutes to completely sever the appendage from the body.

There was a great deal of excitement that rushed through Mortimer as he picked up the limb and bit into it. The taste of dead flesh hitting his tongue activated his taste buds, causing him to let out a grunt of pleasure. It was only while eating such delicacies that Mortimer could really feel anything at all. Over the past few decades the amount of emotions and other sensations he had felt in his younger years had slowly faded; most of the things that had made him remotely human had vanished. Except for the physical pains of hunger, and being able to taste meat, Mortimer had grown into something truly unnatural.

His skin had long since lost its color, while Mortimer's body had twisted and grown to proportions that were not possible for any human. Thankfully he was able to force his shape to bend to that of a regular person through the consumption of deceased bodies. As for his skin the mortuary provided him with the proper equipment to hide his unnatural complexion under layers of makeup, meaning so far Mortimer had been able to live his grotesque life in secret for over two decades without anyone finding out.

Recently, however, Mortimer had noticed the hunger pains coming more often, causing him to feed at a higher frequency. This was a fairly large problem considering that there were not that many bodies that came through his door, and most had loved ones that would notice something amiss. Mortimer had resorted to waiting until after a cadaver was buried to exhume them and tear into their rotting flesh, embalming fluid and all, so to Mortimer the deceased motorist's flesh that he was feasting on was the equivalent of manna from Heaven.

Mortimer ripped off the last few chunks of flesh from the palm before ferociously gnawing at the bits of cartilage present between the phalanges. After a few moments of this Mortimer decided he needed more. He took the bone saw and began to rip into the right leg of the cadaver. Mortimer sawed with a vigorous speed, his body solely driven by the intense hunger that ate away at him. He was halfway through the bone when the sound of the door to the room opening caught him by surprise. Mortimer immediately spun around in a panic to find a small child waddling in.

"A child?" Mortimer muttered in confusion as he sat the bone saw down on the table.

He stared at the small human who was currently gazing around Mortimer's preparation room with a look of curiosity in its eyes. Mortimer cautiously approached the child, trying to ascertain more about it. He wasn't the best judge of human attributes, but as he stared at the child he approximated the kid's age to be no more than five, while also placing the being in the male category of the species. To Mortimer's surprise the hooligan wandered over towards him of its own free will. This made it all too easy for Mortimer to simply bend down and scoop up the child into his arms.

Mortimer examined the visage of the little pest while the child looked back at him in confusion. He noticed the kid's blue eyes, and how they seemed to sparkle from the dim light that shone off of them. The face of the youngling was a respectable one that had not yet been plagued by deformities or abnormalities of any kind. Though, most importantly for Mortimer, it was clear that the child did not have control over its auditory abilities yet, so there would be no way it could tell others of what it had witnessed him doing. Mortimer was just about to release the pest to wander off on its own when his stomach began to howl in pain.

"What the Hell?" Mortimer growled in agony as he tried to keep from dropping the small boy to the ground.

His gut roared with a ravenous hunger. He had just eaten a decently-sized snack, so that should have been enough to tide over his stomach for a bit, yet his gut called out for more sustenance. Mortimer closed his eyes for a moment. This managed to quiet his unruly innards for a brief respite, but the second he looked at the boy Mortimer's stomach once again roared. It took him a few more moments than it probably should have for him to finally piece together what was happening.

"Oh, my," he mumbled in a slightly amused tone, "It

seems my body's tastes are evolving. How interesting for me," Mortimer couldn't help but lick his lips as he stared at the boy he was still holding in his outstretched arms, "but how unfortunate for you."

GHOUL'S KITCHEN
BY NIKKI R. LEIGH

"We're going to go ahead and give that dish a solid score of four."

A dozen groans filled the audience, hands reaching toward the dishes displayed on the glass countertop under the spotlight. Mouths filled with sharp teeth salivated at the food, plated with a professional eye.

The protein was seared perfectly, sliced into thin portions the size of silver dollars. The meat swam in a puddle of au jus, rich, brown and thick. A dash of parsley, reserved so as not to upset one of the judges that detested the extra flourish, sat atop the gray-pink slices.

Pale hands lifted the plate and tucked it away for future consumption. The audience members pushed their restraints to the limits, trying to catch a taste of the food on their tongues swirling about their maws.

"Up next we have a dish from sous chef Aaron Shithe. He hails from Southern California, and is hoping to bring a little bit of Latin flare to his plate."

The host, a smiling woman with sparkling, white teeth,

held the microphone close to her mouth. Cameras circled Chef Aaron as he put the finishing touches on his dish. Bright-red ceramic holders, designed solely for the purpose of holding tacos, appeared on the screen, piled high with pickled cabbage, chunks of mango, and chopped beer-battered bits of meat.

Brain, to be exact.

Human brain to be even more precise.

Chef Aaron beamed, standing behind his plate with arms behind his back. He could feel his nails digging into the palm of his other hand, leaving half-moon marks in the flesh as he awaited his score.

It had to be perfect; he needed a score of five to be able to best his opponent and take his place in the competition. Impressing the three judges was no easy task. Their pedigree was intimidating at best, and completely demoralizing at its worst, so Aaron knew his technique and flavors needed to be spot-on. He hoped his culinary training would not let him down.

The blonde judge with piercing blue eyes shook her head. Aaron's heart sunk as she opened her mouth.

"Absolutely dreadful," she remarked.

The smaller, balding man with a paunchy belly spat the food to the side in a napkin, making a show of doing so.

"Indigestible. A travesty any day of the week."

The final judge, a restaurateur and Michelin-starred chef, wrinkled her nose in disgust.

"Take the 'h-e' out of this fellow's last name and you've got yourself exactly what this dish tastes like."

Aaron's heart may as well have been splashing about the floor by his toes, ripped out and discarded.

To put the nail in his coffin the head judge scooped up the plate and tossed it into the audience. Moaning bodies shuffled to the discarded meal, shoveling the bits of meat into their mouths as fast as they could, conveyor belts of palms whisking every last scrap into their faces.

Aaron stood in the spotlight, though instead of feeling the pride of success the circle of light only served to highlight his shame and disappointment.

Like hamburgers that had greasily adhered to a pan Aaron scraped his feet from the floor and shambled off stage. For the most alive person in the crowd he certainly felt the deadest inside.

"Stupid ghouls," Aaron muttered to himself once safely outside the building that held the syndicated TV success *Ghoul's Kitchen.* "They don't even know what they want. Hot brains? Cold brains? Whole thing's rigged anyways."

Aaron kicked rocks and empty soda cans down the street, vowing to himself that he didn't need the measly $100,000 or fancy job.

He continued to grumble as he made his way back to his tiny studio apartment. "Who wants to be a chef for the ghouls anyway?"

Aaron fumbled his keys, making his way inside. "I do," he conceded to himself, sighing.

He entered his apartment, the smell of the kitchen hitting him hard like a rotten fish slap in the face.

"Dammit! The brains are rotted again," he shouted into his apartment. He knew that smell, knew that meant he'd have to procure new meat before he practiced his dish some more.

"How'd it go?" a voice called from his couch, causing Aaron to jump and knock a metal spatula to the floor. A head peeked over the edge of the cloth sofa, bright-pink and spiky.

"Delia, hey," Aaron replied. "You scared the crap out of me."

"Sorry, man," Delia said, biting her lip. "Well, how'd it go? You going to be America's next Monster Chef?"

"You'll find out next Tuesday," he said, biting back a sob.

"That bad?"

"Worse."

"Did you have to run away, hands over your ears protecting your brains so the ghouls didn't steal what's left of them?"

"Okay, maybe not that bad," Aaron let out a sad groan, "but it still sucked. They ripped the dish to shreds and made fun of my name."

"Aw, that's low, even for a bunch of ghouls." Delia rose from her place on the couch and walked over to Aaron, wrapping her hands around his waist. "Well, the only place to go is up...and maybe to the dumpster with these rotted-out brains. Pretty rank, Aaron."

"You know you could have taken them instead of letting them fester."

"You forget: lazy."

"Ay, there's the rub."

The two walked hand-in-hand to the dumpster, a sack of spoiled brains gripped tightly in Aaron's free hand.

"Where am I going to get new brains?" He shook the sack, releasing a wave of fetid smells. "These were the last of my bribe to the funeral home."

"Maybe that's the problem," Delia said. "You bring your own food preparations to the contest, right? Including the brains?"

"We do," he said, stroking his hairless chin. "And I always try to bring the freshest, but maybe the brains are the problem. I'm stuck using days-old scraps. You should have seen the other plates, Delia. They were like the Kobe beef of brains, beautifully marbled. Not even a whiff of rot."

"We need to get you some better brains then."

"Smarter brains. Strong brains."

Aaron smiled an honest, real, excited smile. Maybe Monster Chef wasn't such a pipe dream title after all.

Aaron was relieved the first steps of his plan were so easy to put into action. He'd called the studio, begging for another chance. The assistant he spoke to relayed his message to the producers and they agreed to have him back, hoping that another complete demoralization of a contestant would boost their ratings. The audience was bloodthirsty, after all.

His episode would film in two days, another battle to get an apron and be in the running to conquer the culinary world. He had planned his recipe: a simple braised brains with shallots and a parsnip puree, beets pickled atop.

The acquisition of the brains was proving to be a bit more difficult. If Aaron and Delia's theory was correct they needed the freshest, most potent brains around to satisfy the judges. No more brains past their expiration date.

As Aaron looked at his target through his back window, a physicist at the local college, he felt a pang of guilt. He couldn't bring himself to entertain the morality of why this person's life meant less than his dreams of success; he just knew that he had goals, and TV fame and chef stardom mattered more to him than anything he could imagine.

Aaron crept towards the house, the spotlight in his mind blinding his ability to think like a human rather than a flesh-and-brain obsessed ghoul. They'd be his brains all the same.

He slid open the back door of the house, prepping the chemicals to knock his subject out. The professor entered the kitchen humming a jaunty tune while Aaron crouched out of sight, ducking behind the island. He heard her rummaging in a cupboard, then tiptoed behind her crouched form and pounced.

There was no time to scream, to fight back, only to slump into his arms unconsciously. He dragged her outside, and Delia pulled up with her car. Together they hoisted her body into the vehicle, stuffing her torso, then her legs, into the trunk as if filling a cordon bleu.

"The warehouse is ready," Delia said. She had prepared her art workspace for the professor, the solitude an artist requires coming in handy for criminal pursuits.

The two drove in silence, their anticipation to see if their plan would work frantically racing about their minds. Aaron was thankful that Delia was willing to put her neck on the line for him, but she knew as well as him that art and creative pursuits were the lifeblood they both thrived on. Besides, she had plans for an art installation using pieces of the body in ways that people would never guess it had once been human. Mad scientist creatives, the both of them.

They arrived at the desolate warehouse and set the professor up inside.

"What's the square root of forty-nine?"

"Seven."

"ABC's, backwards, quick."

"What is this, a DUI test or a brain teaser?"

"Fine, the ABCs backwards using the military phonetic alphabet."

"Foxtrot, uniform, Charlie, kilo to you."

Zap.

During the past two days Delia and Aaron had tenderized the professor's brain, pumping it full of logic problems, math, science, vocabulary, history...the list was endless, and so was the cattle prod shocking when the professor refused to answer a question. The pair believed the electricity would help get the energy flowing in the mind even if the brain teasers didn't.

On the third day Delia was lubing the professor's brain

with an abundance of knowledge while Aaron prepared his ingredients for his dish. His episode was set to film tonight, and he was buzzing with excitement.

He knew his dish would impress the judges. They had the culinary gift, something they retained once they transformed into ghouls, along with the entirety of a small town a few years earlier when a spell cast by an angry Dungeons & Dragons player went awry by becoming real.

The judges happened to be filming an episode of their hit cooking show in the town when the change happened. The yearning for brains was immediate, but rather than murdering the townspeople-turned-ghouls the media production companies got the bright idea to turn brain feeding into a pop culture phenomenon, and *Ghoul's Kitchen* was born. After studying the ghouls scientists discovered that the more brains one ate the more humane they became. Needless to say, the judges got the best and brightest of the recently deceased, and the cash began flowing; hordes of audience members craving gourmet snacks made for endless seat fillers.

As soon as Aaron saw the opportunity he knew he had to take it. No need to be chef to the stars when one could be a chef to the ghouls, always wanting more.

He reminded himself of this over and over again as he placed his ingredients in glassware to take to the show. Reminded himself of his desire, that he deserved the best and had worked so damn hard to get to this point.

So hard, he thought to himself, mallet in hand and bone saw in another. He wouldn't let a little soft murder get in the way.

He approached the professor, steeling himself for the gore he was about to create. She screamed, he struck, he sawed, and after fifteen minutes of effort he held her brain in his hands.

He resisted the urge to hold the brain high above him and scream in glorious victory. Not yet, not until that apron was wrapped around his body where it belonged.

Delia took her place in the human section of the crowd, ready to cheer her friend on to victory. Aaron proceeded through the pre-show set-up, going through hair and make-up while his ingredients were placed on the show table under the spotlight.

"Brains were legally obtained?" a show manager asked Aaron.

"You bet. Here's the paperwork," Aaron replied, handing the manager the paperwork for the brains he'd previously thrown away.

"Yeesh, date's a little old there. Can't wait to see them rip you one in front of the world."

"That's what I'm here for," Aaron said, shrugging.

"Don't forget to sign this. Gotta make sure we're all legal here, too."

"Got a pen?"

"Here you go." The manager handed Aaron a fancy pen. "Don't forget to read closely. Make sure you're okay with it all. No small thing, you know? I honestly can't believe you're signing up for this."

"Have to make it big somehow, right? Miss all the swings you never try or whatever."

"Yeah, but like this? Human to human, there has to be a better way."

"Only way I know how," Aaron said.

The manager shrugged, his hand running through his greasy hair. "Good luck getting torn to pieces, kid."

Aaron took a deep breath, readying himself for the heat of the stage lights. He heard the theme song playing, a quartet of ghouls singing live in glittering dresses, their wispy hair falling in tatters from their leathery scalps.

"I know what ghouls like,
I know what ghouls like,
Soft-eating licorice,
Cheerios and raw fish.
I know what ghouls like,
Ghouls like, ghouls like,
Me."

The ghouls in the crowd danced to the beat, enjoying the cheery introduction. They were already drooling, smelling the brains even before the aroma hit the air from the stove. They were loyal, never missing a taping, hoping for some of the best-cooked brains out there. Honestly though, they'd take anything thrown their way.

The lights centered on the host, who introduced the chefs for the day and urged the crowd to chant for their first guest.

"Aar-on! Aar-on!" they shouted, punctuated by gentle

groans and smacking of lips.

The host smiled, flashing white, pristine teeth, a contrast to the rotted mouths of the audience. "You may recognize Chef Aaron from a week ago. He presented brains so poorly cooked that even our audience members had trouble keeping it down,"

That's a lie, Aaron thought, stewing inside,

"but today he promises he's brought us a dish we can't say no to! He thinks this plate will set him on his journey to become the next Monster Chef. Let's see if he's all talk, or if he really does have the brains to get the job done."

Aaron waved to the crowd, then to the camera, trying to flush away his nerves. He imagined himself putting on the black apron, feeling its soft, firm cloth wrapping around his body. He got to work.

Aaron worked his way through his dish, braising and searing the brains and pureeing his vegetables and other ingredients to a fine consistency. He prepared the plate, spreading the mash across the ceramic surface before slicing and portioning out the cooked brains.

A *masterpiece*, Aaron thought, pride swelling in his chest.

The judges descended upon the dish, daintily forking the meal into their mouths, skin chapped and flaking as it hung off their chins and cheeks. Their faces lit up in excitement.

The first judge, the blonde chef, spoke. "This...this is incredible. Some of the best brains I've ever tasted."

The bald, male chef nodded eagerly, the thin wisps of

the hair he had left bobbing back and forth like dandelions in the wind. "A real turnaround from that crap he presented last week."

The final chef, notoriously the most difficult to impress, held her hands up, a smile creeping on her face, unable to speak. That said it all.

The host put her arms around Aaron's shoulders; Aaron felt tears of joy sprinkling his cheeks. He was almost embarrassed, but didn't deny himself the elation.

This is my dream, dammit. He laughed in disbelief that his plan had worked. He sent a silent thank you to the professor's spirit, sure that she was already haunting him for his misdeeds.

The host broke his excited frenzy by holding up a black apron to him, the *Ghoul's Kitchen* logo embroidered on the breast pocket. The brain with the knife cleaving it in two thumped under Aaron's buzzing fingertips, tracing the logo, making it feel as real as possible.

"Let's see you get that bad boy on," the host urged. "Wouldn't want to make too much of a mess on your nice clothes, now would we?"

Mess? Aaron stood suddenly still, confused. *Isn't the cooking over?*

"We've got a special treat for you all tonight. This dish was too good to share with our steadfast audience, but they still need to eat. We promised you a healthy serving of brain, and we don't ever disappoint."

Aaron felt his stomach drop. He frantically tried to remember back to his contract that he'd signed. What did he make legal? What did he sign away?

The host shot her hand out and grabbed Aaron by the throat.

My life, he thought. I signed away *my life.*

"We have a new segment of the show tonight. Not just a live taping, but a live feeding. What do you say, my ghoul-fiends? Are you in?"

The crowd moaned in a symphony of cheers.

Aaron looked to the rafters, to the human section of the audience. Their faces looked shocked and scared, Delia's among them. Aaron could see the tears sparkling in the light as they ran down her face.

The host grabbed a meat mallet from Aaron's table. It still glimmered with the professor's brain, as he had used it to tenderize his dish only minutes earlier.

She swung. The mallet connected with a muffled thump, and Aaron dropped like a sack of beans to the ground. He twitched, his body barely able to move under his commands. His fingers grazed the apron wrapped around his torso, trying to find some final sense of accomplishment amidst his twist of fate.

The host cackled, swung again, and cracked his head open.

His world went black, even as the spotlight stayed on his head, gray matter spilling to the floor only to be scooped up by the host and tossed into the audience.

"How about some brains tartare?" she yelled as the

crowd tripped over themselves to get to the mashed bits of Aaron being tossed into the sea of bodies.

As Aaron faded away he heard the theme song for *Ghoul's Kitchen* playing in his head.

I know what ghouls like,
Ghouls like, ghouls like.
Me.
And oh, how they did.

MALIK ALZALAM
BY HUNTER LACROSS

E ver since I was a young child I would hear the same sentence whispered in my ear whenever someone crossed me, the being's hot breath searing my cheek, "Aqtilah ya tifl, wahtadan alzalam badakhilik..."

I would later realize that it translated loosely to, "Kill him, my child, and embrace the darkness inside of you."

I will never forget the first time I heard this ominous sentence. My father Dougal, being an archeologist from Scotland by trade, had brought me with him to a newly discovered dig site just outside the heart of Cairo, Egypt in 1882. The site was an unearthed tomb that other archeologists, and even the local clergy, refused to go near due to its mysterious, ancient appearance. This tomb was thought to be far older, and more structurally unstable, than some of the other findings in the area.

My father was cautioned to avoid the crumbling pillars and sand-choked hallways by the site excavators, especially with a boy by his side, but he refused to heed them. Dougal was known for his bravery, with many people referring to him as the 'man with no fear', and this was not going to be the time he lost his reputation. He was always looking for ways to prove his fortitude, and the crypt was just another challenge for him to conquer.

We arrived at the dig site within mere hours of docking. My legs, still sea-wobbly, barely held me up as I trembled before the tomb. The moment I laid eyes on it a shiver wracked my body, as though warning me away from the gaping, maw-like opening that led under the scorching sands. Dougal refused to listen to my protests, and I was soon marched into the underground.

Come...

As much as I wanted to run, to turn and leave that death-house, the wind seemed to push me forward. My father, soon completely engrossed in his work, paid no attention to me. As he dusted away centuries of sand from a crumbling wall he failed to notice that I had left his side. Torch in hand I had turned down one of the branching paths of the tomb, and while walking down the halls I remember seeing images unlike most we had come across at other sites. I was guided with small gusts of air, until I came to a room with a large, black sarcophagus in the middle of it.

Without thinking I rested my torch on the sandstone floor, then I went over to it and slid open the lid; upon opening it, my strength seemingly bolstered, I felt a cold blast of too-fresh air, followed by a sentence whispered in a deep voice.

"Akhyrana, 'ana qadir ealaa nashr almawt wallaenat fi hadha alealam!" *(Finally, I am able to spread death and curses to this world!)*

My father must have heard the thud of the lid falling to the floor, because before I knew it he was rushing down the hallway towards me, a yell on his lips. I, however, was too engrossed with watching the human-sized swirl of smoke and sand spewing from the sarcophagus. A blast of putrid air burst around me, and I began coughing violently as I breathed in the sand and smoke.

"Boy, howfur kin you be so dunderheaded? Thae 'ere tombs haven't even bin explored, yit 'n' ye run off lik' a wee buffoon…"

He stopped mid-sentence, feet frozen momentarily until, with a scream, he leaped forward, bundling me in his arms and bolting from the chamber.

"Stupid boy! That be a sandstorm!"

I could smell the whiskey on his breath, feel his fingers digging into my side enough to leave bruises, but I didn't make a sound until we were at the hotel Father had paid for. That night my nightmares were filled with a man whose lower body was a whirlwind of dark smoke, his upper half a blur of crimson skin and black eyes. The being wore gold bands on his arms, the last light of an eclipsing moon glinting off of them. I told my father about my dreams the next morning, but he chalked it up to me being a scared boy.

He didn't have much time to deal with the petty fears of a child, and dismissed it as nothing.

That day I heard the same voice from the burial chamber speak again. My father was shopping for our breakfast in a bazaar, and I was petting a very sociable, mangy cat that looked as if he hadn't had a home in a long while.

"Aiqtalh, 'ayuha. Alfataa kasr ruqabatih alsaghira." (Kill him, child. Break his tiny neck.)

As the impulse to break the cat's neck swept over me the feline hissed, scratching my arms before running off in fear. The voice immediately resounded again, the whisper harsh enough to make blood trickle from my ear.

"laqad khadhaltani hadhih almarat. Walays maratan 'ukhraa." *(You let me down this time. Never again.)*

As I stood between the stalls, fingers clutched over my ear, a filthy, elderly man with tattered clothing approached me.

"You poor child...a shaitan has attached himself to your soul. You might as well be dead as you sit there, since even a homeless man such as myself is better off than you."

Before I could question him he walked off, melting into the crowd bustling through the lane. That night I tried to see if my father had heard of 'shaitans' after he came back to the hotel after meeting with the dig team, but he was drunk. Upon approaching him he stared behind me in horror, then he started to scream. I have never seen my father terrified, and I was unable to control myself as a burst of tears flooded my cheeks.

"Evil spirit!"

He was pointing to the swirls of red and black energy trailing across my flesh, and I felt a tug beneath my skin, as though something else was in there with me. Dougal hoisted his bottle, bringing the glass down upon my head. My vision blurred, another scream tearing from me as the voice crooned to me,

"La tubki, habibi. Sawf 'ushahidak min huna fsaedana. Sa'ajealuk 'aqwaa mimaa yastatie walidak 'an ykwn, hdha shukri litahririni." *(Do not cry, child. I will watch you from here on out. I will make you stronger than your father can be. This is my thanks for freeing me.)*

The next morning I awoke to my father and three other men strapping me down to a chair. He had told a local Priest of Toth about the being he saw behind me the night prior, and he swore on his life that it was not because he had been drinking. The clergyman believed him, as he could see the obvious fear in my father's bloodshot eyes.

This was the first time I heard the words that have followed me much of my life,

"Aqtilah, ya tifl, wahtadan alzalam badakhilik." (Kill them, my child, and embrace the darkness inside of you.)

My body began to glow with red and black swirls of energy, the djinn inside me laughing madly. I blacked out briefly, before coming back to consciousness with the three men and my father lying at my feet in a pool of blood. My father lay there with burn marks covering his body, his carotid artery burned away. The other three men were so disfigured from their burn marks that you could no longer recognize them.

"Ahsant, ya tflay. Hadhih mjrd bidayat alfawdaa alty sanantashiruha." *(Well done, my child. This is just the beginning of the chaos we will be spreading.)*

"No...!"

My desperate denial went unheeded.

After my father's death I was sent to the outskirts of England to live in an orphanage, as I had no next-of-kin. My new home was full of despair; the head mistress was cruel and abusive, and the other children bullied me as the rumors of my father's untimely demise spread. The longer I spent in that place the more I would hear the whispers of the entity that had murdered my family, and the more it became my only source of comfort.

One evening when I was walking back to the orphanage from the local market I was accosted by Edward, the lead bully at the orphanage. He cornered me by a farmer's fence, on a stretch of road with no one near enough to help me, his fists balled in rage as he shouted at me.

"Father-killer! I would have given anything to have a family, and you go and kill yours? You're mad!"

"No, I did not...!"

Before I could protest my innocence he thrust a pocket knife into my stomach, kicking me into the mud and leaving me there bleeding. As I crumpled to the dirt, a booming tempo pounding in my ears, I felt the air around me compress. I tried to crawl toward him, one hand pressed against my side, but he ran off. That was the first time I saw the entity without it being in a dream, and it was just as I had seen before. A tall, crimson-colored entity, humanoid body composed of half fire and half smoke, hovered before me. He held his palm out towards my wound, and with a shimmer of black and red energy my skin started to stitch itself back together.

"Anhad, 'ant taerif ma ealayk alqiam biha. Al'akhadh bialtha'ari! Aqtalahum!" *(Get up, you know what you need to do. Take revenge! Kill him!)*

The djinn leaned down, pressing its fingers to my forehead, and all thoughts except revenge left my mind. With a surge of energy my recently-healed body stood of its own volition, and I made my way to the orphanage. Immediately upon getting through the front door I snuck into the kitchen, unhesitatingly grabbing the largest butcher knife I could find. I hid it under my shirt, pretending my arm was hurt so I could cradle the knife close, and crept up to my bedroom.

Approximately two hours passed before the head mistress made her rounds to put us all to bed for the night. My room was always the last one she passed by, and my desire for justice still clouded my mind.

Or was it revenge?

Did it matter?

I had power, and I would use it.

"Goodnight Callum. It's time to shut your light out for the night, and do not let me catch you sneaking around again tonight, or else..." The headmistress said as she passed by my room.

Once all of the lights were shut off for the night I lay there, wide awake and ready to give my bully a taste of his own medicine. I knew Edward would be sleeping by then, and I planned on scaring him into leaving me alone. I would hold the knife to his throat for just a moment, making him beg sweetly for my forgiveness, and then I would sneak back to my room before he could call for the headmistress.

It was the perfect plan.

I slid into his room, creeping across the frigid floorboards until I reached his bedside. I gently tapped his shoulder, my fingers a bit rough.

"Wakey wakey…"

He stirred, eyes shooting open to meet mine as he sat up. Then they darted to the knife, which I quickly pressed up against his quivering throat.

"What in Hell? What are you doing in my room, you creepy bastard? Get out! Headmistress! Help…"

As he struggled to get the last word out the djinn materialized behind him, its hands snaking around Edward's neck. He nearly managed to scream, then the entity ripped his head off with ease, tearing the muscles and tendons to bloody ribbons.

"Hadhih hadiat litaeatuka. Qaribaan sawf takun li, ya abnay." *(This is a gift for your obedience. Soon you will be mine, my child.)*

I am not sure what happened next, the world around me going dark as my mind tried to come to grips with the hot, coppery-smelling chunks of Edward splattered across my cheeks. I awoke in bed the next morning, my once blood-stained pajamas clean, and by the time the constable arrived I had convinced myself that I must have just had a very, very vivid nightmare. It almost worked, and as the Constable equated Edward's death to some similar murders that happened about a year ago I let out a sigh of relief. He deamed them a sloppy copycat murder, someone playing at being Jack The Ripper, and Edward became merely another piece of paperwork for them.

After the murder the headmistress got more severe with

her punishments. Without us the government wouldn't pay her, and she saw her actions as a way to protect her income. Even back talking to her, or a simple disobedient moment, became something that would draw her ire enough to get us bloodied and locked in the corner closet for an hour. Her angry, severe tone worsened, and she would often throw objects within her reach at us if we were talking too much or playing too roughly.

Then my life changed. One day the Bishop family came to the orphanage looking to adopt a boy. They seemed like a genuinely happy couple, one who loved each other very much and were not afraid to display so even in front of us. We could tell by their obvious public displays of affection; they seemed to enjoy holding each other's hands, smiling and laughing at each other's jokes. One-by-one they had myself and two of my friends sit down with them to tell them a little about our past, as well as what we enjoyed doing for fun and some of our favorite foods.

The husband took an immediate liking to me when I told him my father and I used to explore archeological sites. He told me that, as a child, his uncle and he would explore the ruined castles in the Scottish Highlands. The wife, however, seemed like she was along moreso to keep her husband happy, and she seemed glad to be able to hold a conversation with a group of slightly older children than the toddler her husband was initially thinking of adopting.

After the couple left the headmistress pulled the three of us aside and prodded for information.

"What did the Bishops want with you lot? Do I have to

get rid of one of you piss-ants?"

Without thinking I spoke back against her.

"Aye, with hope she'll get all three of us out of this slaughterhouse! Who knows, maybe one of us will end up your next victim like Edward, ye bloody bawbag."

With that the headmistress sent the other two out of her office and beat me raw. I did not even see it coming - first came her fist at my face, then came the kicks to my ribs. I felt as if I was getting trampled by a rabid horse, and by the end of the beating I was spitting out large globs of blood. She dragged me to my room, slamming the door behind her. I wept, tears streaming down my face as my whole body throbbed. A whisper left my lips, the plea echoing around the emptiness of my room.

"I wish the head mistress was out of my life for good...I wish I could be with a family that treats me as if I am their own..."

This time he materialized above my face, a smirk plastered on his ruby lips.

"'Amnituk hi 'amri, ya tiflay." *(Your wish is my command, my child.)*

As the entity spoke he dissipated from view, my wounds once again healing. I was getting a bit too familiar with the sensation, and I cringed as the red and black energy prickled along my skin. Soon I felt an overbearing urge to go into the head mistress's private rooms, and as I made my way there, my limbs moving on their own like a puppet with strings, I heard her bath water running. I tried to fight the sensation, tried to turn around and cower back in my room, but the pull was too strong. I could feel my hands twitching, and I had an irresistible desire to drown her in her own filthy suds.

Her off-key singing covered what little sound my bare footfalls made, and I easily snuck into the bathroom where she was relaxing with her eyes closed in the nearly full bathtub. My arms reached out, my eyes watching as though I was looking at a stranger's hands. I shoved the headmistress under the water by her shoulders, calmly watching the air bubbles burst on the surface even as I vainly ordered my legs to turn and run. I felt the entity grasp onto my shoulders and speak, his energy and amplified strength continuing to course through my small body.

"Alamsat 'amnahak quti, ya tifli." *(I grant you my strength, my child.)*

As he finished the sentence my arms began to glow, as I was able to plunge the headmistress even further into the water. She should have been able to dislodge my weak grip easily, but there was nothing either of us could do against the power flowing through my arms.

She finally stopped struggling.

"'Aqtul akhar wasayakun jasdak li, ya tafli." *(Kill another and your body will be mine, my child.)*

I had no time to ponder his words. As soon as the puppet-like control over me dropped I ran, hiding in my room just as I wanted to. The next day one of the other children went into the headmistress' bathroom, since the only other latrine was occupied, and with a blood curdling shriek he came running towards the dormitory wing.

"She's dead! The headmistress is dead! The murderer

came back for his next victim!"

Within minutes the police arrived, and over the next few weeks most of us were parceled across the country to other orphanages. A few lucky ones like myself were adopted, and as I settled into a happy life I finally thought things were going to turn out alright.

Even though it has been a few years I can still feel the darkness inside me. I vividly recall the horror of the headmistress' struggling body finally laying still at the bottom of the bathtub, and of my father and Edward's blood. I try to shake my dark thoughts out, to keep them at bay, but this morning Mother Bishop accidentally knocked a cup of hot coffee into my lap while at the breakfast table. It hardly scorched me, but her apologies fell upon deaf ears as I heard that whisper once more,

"Aqtilah ya tifl, wahtadan alzalam badakhilik." *(Kill her, my child, and embrace the darkness inside of you.)*

THREE WISHES UPON A STAR

BY RONALD LINSON

WISH THE FIRST

Kenny pushed his coke-bottle glasses farther up his nose and examined the bong. At least the guy who sold it to him said it was a bong, or something. The conversation had only partly been in English, all of it Kenny's.

It was made of green glass and looked really exotic. Well, it was probably green, but it was hard to tell with all the crap on it. He spritzed it with blue glass cleaner and started rubbing with a paper towel.

A cloud of thick, purple smoke exploded from the opening right into his face, causing him to tip his chair back and crash to the floor.

"Kenny, are you all right!?" his mother shouted from downstairs.

"Yeah," he yelled back, "I was just cleaning!"

Righting his chair he staggered backward, nearly falling again when he saw what had appeared amid the clearing smoke.

Standing on his desk beside the bong was a grizzled little geezer, probably no taller than eight inches. And man, was he ugly!

"What the fu—" he started, before remembering he had his door open. More quietly, he said, "Are you what I think you are?"

"If you think I am a genie, then you are correct," he said in a three-pack-a-day voice. "It's the word I drew from your mind, though the proper word is 'Djinn.'"

"No fucking way," Kenny hissed under his breath. "You're serious?"

The genie sighed. He had a mop of frizzy hair, wispy whiskers, and wore a ratty, purple sequined vest with matching hot-pants and pointy slippers. "Yes."

"Awesome." Kenny quietly shut his bedroom door. "So, I get three wishes?"

The genie raised an eyebrow and smirked. "Sure, why not. Three wishes. Whatever you say."

Kenny opened his mouth but the genie held up a hand to stop him.

"Before you wish for something stupid, I am required to recite my terms of service."

Kenny groaned. "Do you have to?"

The genie nodded solemnly, then proceeded to talk nonstop for what seemed like twenty minutes straight. Kenny tuned out, not hearing a word of it. He stared, admiring once again the sexy poster of his favorite pop singer that hung on the wall above his desk, and knew exactly what he would wish for. He had originally wanted to wish for a new computer, but that was such a dork move. No, he wanted a girl just like her, and he couldn't get one even remotely decent the way he looked.

When the little man finished, he asked, "Do you accept these terms?"

"Yes," Kenny said.

"Splendid," the genie said. "I also know you weren't listening. That's fine; no one ever does."

"Okay, for my first wish," Kenny said, gesturing at his face, "I don't want to have to wear these stupid glasses anymore."

The genie smiled and snapped his fingers. "Done." He vanished in a puff of purple smoke.

Kenny waited, and waited, but nothing happened. "What a rip off, dude," he said. He reached out, intending to grab the bong and hide it in his closet to forget about it.

There came a knock at the door, which made Kenny jump. "Yeah, come in."

His mother had a big, happy smile. "Guess what honey, Dr. Hartman just called. You've been approved for contact lenses! Isn't that great?"

Wish the Second

After a jubilant "Woo!" and a hug from his mother, Kenny waited until she left before again closing the door and returning to sit at his desk, ready to make his next wish. He knew exactly what he wanted. He felt a twinge of disappointment that the genie hadn't just fixed his eyes magically, but whatever.

He gave the bong a good rub. Instead of a blast of purple smoke the tinny voice of the genie echoed from within:

"As per my terms of service, only one wish may be made per week. Please try again in six days, twenty-three hours, and 49 minutes."

Well Hell, that sucked, but he could wait a week. He set an alarm on his phone to alert him the instant time was up.

The next day after school he received his contacts. He had to admit he did look a whole lot less like a Revenge of the Nerds reject. It would take some time for the little grooves on his nose to disappear, but that couldn't be helped.

His social life at school instantly went from abysmal to merely pathetic, a definite improvement. Less bullying was good, and even the dipshit jocks passed him by more often than not for more obvious targets now.

Kenny wasn't the only one whose life improved suddenly. His older brother Reggie got a new job as some kind of assistant at the hospital. Mom and Dad were ecstatic about this turn of events because it meant they didn't have to dole out so much for Reggie's pre-med program, and the good luck train kept steaming along. Kenny got a brand-spanking-new laptop, faster, more powerful, and, best of all, it sported a humongous three terabyte hard drive, all the better to store and view all the pictures and videos he could find of his favorite star.

When time was almost up—one minute, to be exact—he set the bong on his desk and waited. The alarm went off, and he gave it an extra ten-count. He wasn't that desperate, after all.

He gave it a good rub, and it squirted purple smoke in his face. As soon as he saw the genie standing beside the bong he made his wish.

"I wish to be popular!"

The genie regarded him with a gimlet eye.

"Well?" Kenny asked. "I made my wish. Do your thing."

The genie sighed. "As per my terms of service, wishes must be grounded in reality."

"What does that mean?"

Looking Kenny straight in the eye, the genie said, "It means any wish you make must be actually possible."

"Ow."

The genie nodded. "Sorry."

"You know, why didn't you get me laser eye surgery instead of contacts? That would have been awesome."

The genie shook his head. "Your doctor did tell you that you were not a candidate. You seem to have a bad habit of not listening to important information."

"Yeah, I guess." Kenny sighed. "So, anyway, I guess that rules out immortality or unlimited wealth, huh?"

"Yes, but wealth is possible in reasonable amounts."

Kenny brightened. "Is that so?"

The genie held up a hand. "As per my terms of service, monetary wishes are limited to accessibility."

Kenny growled. "Does that mean I can wish for money, but only as much as can get to me, right?"

Another nod.

"Fine, I'll play the lottery. Make me win."

The genie cleared his throat. "As per my terms of service, wishes are bound by the laws of the jurisdiction in which the wish was made, and since you are a minor—"

"God damn it," Kenny said, swiping his hands over his face. He leaned back in his chair and stared up at his beloved poster.

He'd had it blown up and printed from a picture he'd found on a paparazzi website on the Gray Web. It showed his all-time favorite babe, April-Mae June, the most popular singer out there at the moment. It was a shot from her concert last summer at Ipanema Beach. It showed her on stage holding a pink microphone to her mouth and pointing at someone in the audience, probably her BFF Madison, with a sassy look on her face.

What made it his favorite, though, was what she was wearing: an itsy-bitsy, teenie-weenie, yellow polka-dot bikini. In fact, she had been singing her cover of the song with that title at the time. Mom had been less than enthused when he'd plastered it onto his wall, but Dad had said it was 'healthy'.

The genie turned to see what Kenny was looking at, and asked, "Who is that?"

Kenny told him in great detail. In excessive detail, actually. He knew every public fact about her, and some that weren't: her preferred nail polish color, the name of her dog's veterinarian, her measurements, and, most important, her concert schedule for the next two years.

"And she's hot!" Kenny finished.

"She is but a child," the genie said disapprovingly.

Kenny snorted. "She's not a child, she's my age."

"And you are a mere boy."

"I'm a young man! I'm fourteen!" Kenny cried, his voice cracking.

The genie shook his head, but said nothing.

Kenny tapped his fingers on the desk. "Money...aha, I know what I want. I wish for enough money to buy all her stuff. Her tickets, her merch, all that shit." Her next concert would be right here in town next week, in fact, so it was perfect timing.

The genie nodded, raising his hand to execute the command, but then he hesitated. "Merch?"

"Yeah, merchandise. Here, look." He dragged his new laptop over, brought up April-Mae's official site and showed the genie, scrolling down the page slowly.

"I see. Interesting."

"Isn't it, though?"

"You would like to purchase all of this?"

"Yep."

The genie pointed at the screen. "Does that include girls' underwear?"

Kenny slapped the laptop closed. "That's none of your business. Now make with the wishy-wishy."

"Done." With a snap of his fingers and a puff of purple smoke the genie vanished.

Given what happened last time he figured it would take a little while for the wish to kick in, so he opened up his laptop again and started surfing for new paparazzi shots of his girl.

About half an hour later an email arrived. It was from his Aunt Rita, his very rich Aunt Rita.

It read:

"Hi, dear! Sorry I missed your birthday. Busy busy! You know how it is. Anyway, here's a prepaid credit card! Happy belated birthday!

Auntie Ri."

The amount on the card was a whopping three thousand dollars. Kenny's mouth fell open, and he fell out of his chair.

Wish the Third

A little over a week later, on sunny morning, Kenny sat admiring the first load of merch he'd ordered. Some of it he'd had to hide for more private, late-night admiration, but the posters, keychains, stuffed animals and other assorted products in girly colors held prominent positions around his room.

His mother, again, was openly disapproving, but this time his father hadn't said a thing. He'd looked around at everything, stared at Kenny for a moment with a strange expression, and then left.

But the one thing he was most psyched about was the concert ticket. Buying all that crap had netted him a sweet discount on tickets for her "Petals Down Under" tour. He'd used the seventy-five percent discount on a front-row ticket for her show tomorrow evening right here at the local Amphitheatre.

He wasn't too clear on why the tour was called "Petals Down Under" since none of the shows were to be held in Australia, or even anywhere in the southern hemisphere, for that matter. Nor did he get why the ticket was labelled "flower-sniffer seat."

Whatever. It was now time to make his final wish, and he had it all set up with that ticket.

"I wish for April-Mae June to become my girlfriend," he told the genie once it appeared.

"As per my terms of service—"

"What the fuck, dude," Kenny said, not caring that his door was ajar. "Are you telling me she has a boyfriend already? I checked. As far as all the gossip sites say she doesn't."

"That is correct," the genie said. "She does not have a boyfriend."

Kenny noted the emphasis on the word 'boy' and sat down on the floor, stunned. "Are you serious?"

The genie nodded.

"But...but that's something everybody would know. Hold up, are you saying Madison, her BFF, is actually her..."

The genie nodded again.

"Oh, wow," Kenny said, digging the heels of his hands into his eye sockets. "But she doesn't—I mean, they don't..."

"She is your age, remember?"

Kenny laughed. "Well, I still think she's hot. And I still love her music." He thought hard for a moment. "Okay, I have a wish in mind. I'm going to hate myself for it, and it's totally pervy."

The genie waited, expression impassive.

"I wish for nude pictures of April-Mae June."

With only the slightest hesitation the genie raised his hand to snap.

"Wait," Kenny said. "Aren't you going to give me that 'terms of service' bullshit? You know it isn't legal."

"It depends on context," the genie said. "There are certain exceptions."

"Huh, I didn't know that," Kenny said. "What kind—no, never mind. Go ahead and do it."

The genie snapped his fingers. "Done." He vanished in a puff of purple smoke, and so did the bong.

As he was wondering how this wish would manifest his father yelled up from downstairs, "Kenny, get your ass down here!"

Groaning, Kenny got up and went to see what his father wanted.

Be Careful What You Wish For

His father was royally pissed because Kenny had blown off his chores for weeks, and he made him do all of them: wash and wax the car, paint the fence and sand the floor. He complied only because he needed a ride to the concert the next day.

The chores took all day. It was evening when he was done, leaving him exhausted and sore. All he wanted to do was eat and go to bed. On his way to the kitchen where his mom was reheating his dinner he caught snippets of the news drifting in from the den.

"Early this morning...tour bus...catastrophic traffic accident...were killed instantly."

Reggie came in while Kenny was eating his tacos. It looked like his brother had had a rough day too. He was still wearing his scrubs, and there were dark circles under his eyes.

He came into the kitchen and set his valise down on the table across from Kenny. "Hey," was all Reggie said to him.

"Are you all right, honey?" their mother asked, coming into the room.

"Yeah, just one of those days." Reggie sighed. "Don't really wanna talk about it now." He picked up his valise. "I'm going to bed early. Goodnight."

As he lifted the case something small skittered out of it, ending up underneath the edge of Kenny's plate. He fished it out. It was a USB drive. He opened his mouth to tell Reggie, but he had already left.

He stowed it in his shirt pocket, finished his dinner and headed to his room. His father seemed much happier now, even praising his work with a pat on the shoulder as they passed in the hall.

Extremely curious about the USB drive, he decided to take a quick look before crashing. Plugging it into his laptop he saw that it contained several folders, each with a person's name.

One name popped out at him right away: "Hawkins, April-Mae June."

"What the hell?" he muttered. What would Reggie be doing with a folder on his USB drive with the full, real name of April-Mae June?

He opened it and was presented with a list of twenty image files. All had filenames that were just jumbles of numbers and letters, all but the first, which said it was an ID card.

It was indeed a copy of April-Mae's California state ID card. Neat. He copied it over to his super-secret April-Mae June stash.

The second picture…was of her face and bare shoulders. Her eyes were closed and dark bruises marred her exquisite features, and her neck looked…wrong.

Swallowing, Kenny closed the picture and opened the next.

This one was a wider shot, including her chest. Her breasts were clearly visible, along with more bruising and deep punctures and lacerations.

Feeling like his dinner was about to reappear, Kenny closed the picture. Then he saw the name of the USB drive at the top of the window:

Eastside Hospital Morgue – Postmortem Images.

WAILS OF ANGUISH
BY JESSICA CASEY

It was another dark and dreary day in Ardara, a quaint town in Ireland. School was out for the weekend, and kids were beginning their treks home. Most of her elementary school peers ran off like bolts of lightning, but Kira was in no rush. She loved days like today. Drizzly rain tickling her face and jumping in puddles to get her shoes mucky were some of her favorite things to do. Her small, red head bobbed and weaved as she slalomed up the road, hitting every puddle in her path.

She heard laughter from the other children ring out. They were probably on their way to sleepovers or playdates, or some other weekend adventure they had planned. Kira was what they liked to call 'weird'. She seldom got invited to things, and if she did it was usually a pity-invite to a birthday party. She sat at a corner desk in the back next to a window, and spent most of her time with her chin in her hands thinking about being anywhere else. Most of the other kids didn't outright bully her, but Kira could hear their whispers.

She was more than halfway home when the joyous

chatter in the air turned into soft sobbing. There were no longer children running up and down streets, and the rain began pouring down. Kira's wet hair was plastered to her face, and her body involuntarily shuddered. She stopped dead in her tracks as the crying grew louder.

"He-hello?" she stammered, waiting for a response. The cries continued. "Hello? Are you alright?" she called out, this time with more confidence in her voice. The sobbing grew even louder.

Kira hesitantly continued her walk home, the crying intensifying with each step. By the time she reached the fence gate deafening wails rang in her ears. She placed her hands over them to muffle the sound, but it resonated deep inside her head. She couldn't escape this noise!

She ran up the stone path and threw open her front door, falling on the floor in the entryway. Tears leaked down her cheeks. "Stop! Why are you crying? Please! I don't know what you want!" Kira screamed out. Through the wide open doorway she saw a woman dressed in a white nightgown, hair so red it could have been on fire. Her skin was pale, and her eyes were puffy and red. Her frame was small and frail, her mouth hanging open as tears of blood streaked her gaunt cheeks. Across her stomach was a large gash that seeped blood, one hand holding in her entrails. The woman locked eyes with Kira as she let out a bloodcurdling scream. She charged toward the house, her feet hovering above the pathway.

Kira let out a frightened cry and scampered to her feet, slamming the door shut. She pulled the curtains aside with trembling hands and peeked out the window beside the entrance. There was no sign of the dreaded woman. She opened the door a crack to be sure, but all she saw was rain pouring down. Shaking her head she closed the door once more. What was that thing she had seen?

"Kira, is that you? I've got some sad news, a leanbh," her mother said, wiping her eyes with the back of her hand. She looked at her daughter's face and saw fresh tears. "Have you already heard?" she asked, perplexed.

"Heard what?" Kira replied with a confused look.

"Your gram passed away this afternoon." Her mother's eyes welled with tears and she blew her nose with her hankey. "It looks like you've been crying. I thought someone may have told you on your walk home."

"Ma, I saw a lady! She was floating—" Kira explained before being interrupted by her mother.

"That's enough of that, Kira! I don't have time for your stories right now. There's too much I have to get done," she said with a sniffle before returning to the kitchen to make phone calls.

"But it's not a story..." Kira said to no one. She walked to her room and sat on her bed. Every time she closed her eyes all she could see was that horrible woman. Her stare penetrated her soul, filling her with fear and dread.

For several months her sleep was plagued by nightmares of the lady covered in blood. One night she awoke with a bloodcurdling scream, sweat dripping down her back despite a deep chill in her bones. She grabbed a flashlight from underneath her pillow and shouted into the darkness.

"Leave me alone! Get out of my dreams!" She pulled her blanket over her head and clutched the flashlight tightly, crying softly.

Outside her bedroom her mother gripped the doorknob. "It's happening again, Sean. I hate seeing her like this. It's almost every night now," she said with a sigh.

"You remember what the doctors said: she needs to learn that these nightmares are just in her head. They're not real."

Her mother's hand dropped to her side, dejected. "I know," she whispered. "Let's head to bed. I think she's calmed down."

Months turned into years, and Kira's nightmares became less frequent. Just after her 16th birthday, while working on homework at her desk, the temperature in her room dropped rapidly. She could see her breath escape from her lips. She looked toward the window for a source of the sudden chill, but it was shut tight. She shivered uncontrollably. That ghastly woman from years ago appeared from thin air in front of her bedroom door, only this time she wasn't dreaming. Kira tipped over her chair as she scurried to the corner of her room, trying to put as much distance between herself and the frightful woman. She opened her mouth to scream, but there was nothing but silence.

She was paralyzed with fear.

The woman wailed inconsolably, high-pitched screams filling the room. Blood dripped from her eyes and the ragged gash on her stomach, but the floor remained unsoiled. Her hands and neck cracked and contorted as if all her bones were breaking, reaching out as she glided toward the girl. Her mouth hung open inches from Kira's face, emitting the loudest, ear-piercing scream imaginable. Kira whimpered and flinched in fear, squeezing her eyes shut tightly, hoping she would disappear. She felt like her ears were bleeding from the sound.

An intense cold ripped through Kira's body as the screaming woman passed through her. She breathed out a white cloud of air and shuddered uncontrollably. As soon as she opened her eyes the room was empty; besides a lingering coldness in her bones there was no sign that anything had happened. Tears rolled down her cheek as the memories of the woman came flooding back. The terror and anguish she had felt as a child had amplified tenfold the second she was touched by the frightening apparition.

Her breaths came quickly, shallow and raspy. Her chest heaved faster and faster, and with her head in her hands she slid down the wall to collapse onto the floor. As she sobbed into her arms her bedroom door creaked open. Kira's father stood in the doorway with his phone in hand, his eyes misted over. The phone clattered to the floor as he rushed to console his daughter.

He held her in his arms, gingerly stroking her hair as he sobbed along with her. She had no idea if he had seen the bloody woman, but she was too afraid to ask. He managed to choke out a few words before completely shutting down. "Your ma...she's...there was an accident..." Kira's eyes went wide, and her entire body fell limp. *This can't be real. It has to be a nightmare. She had spoken to her mother only an hour ago. She was just getting groceries. How could she be dead? It isn't right. Someone must have been mistaken.* But she knew that wasn't true.

It wasn't just in her head.

Kira let thoughts of the bloody woman creep back into her mind. She felt like she was slowly going crazy. The screaming was so loud it seemed impossible that no one else could hear her, yet her father didn't run in here when the shrieking started. *Why does she bring death outside my nightmares? First Gram, now Ma. Is she some kind of twisted Grim Reaper?* It was all too much for Kira to process. All she knew was that her mother was dead, and now she was left to gather up the broken pieces of her family.

After her mother's funeral the nightmares came back, now with visions of her own gruesome death. The woman covered in blood was there, screaming over Kira's lifeless body as it lay in a pool of blood. She didn't see what had happened, just the images of her broken corpse. Usually in nightmares you see everything leading up to death, but would wake up before anything happened. These were the exact opposite. Everything leading up to the death was a mystery, but she always woke to the image of her mouth open with thick, dark blood pooling out around her. She shot up in bed, drenched in sweat, her heart practically pounding out of her chest. Kira hoped the nightmares would start to fade away, just like they did when she was younger, but the older she got the more frequent they became.

Now, any time her eyes shut, all she sees is the bloody woman. Kira's puffy, bloodshot eyes skimmed over her textbook, unable to focus. She continued to ignore her father's knocks on her bedroom door, and with each passing day in Ardara it became harder to pretend that everything was fine. Everywhere she looked she would see that hideous woman. Always wailing. It was exhausting; Kira felt like she was being stalked by death.

She felt like her only escape was to move, so as soon as she finished her schooling she packed up her things and moved to Dublin. She hoped that the cacophony of the city would be enough to drown out the constant screaming she heard in her head. She found a shitty apartment in the sketchy part of town, perfect for someone trying to hide from something impossible to avoid because everyone else there was doing the same thing.

And that's where she met Conor.

Like Kira, Conor had moved to Dublin to escape something. He had racked up a fairly hefty gambling tab that he couldn't pay for, so he ran. He was verbally and physically abusive, but Kira felt like she deserved it. He helped her numb everything around her with drugs and alcohol. Conor's drug of choice was heroin, and the first time Kira tried it the screaming that plagued her for years suddenly stopped. She couldn't remember the last time she experienced silence. A small smile pulled at the corners of her mouth as she drifted into peaceful slumber. No red eyes or wild hair of that bloody woman, just nothingness.

And it was absolutely perfect.

Kira and Conor spent the next few years working just enough to cover their drug habit. The more she did it the less effective it became at stopping the woman from showing up, so Kira would do more until she got the silence she craved. It was a completely miserable life, but it beat sleepless, tormented nights seeing herself die. She didn't think she would be able to survive it again.

One day everything changed. Kira noticed her period had stopped. She clutched a pregnancy test in her hand, selfishly hoping it would be negative. She wasn't ready to give up numbness, but there was no way she could continue using if the test was positive. Even if it killed her. She was tired, though, tired of always having to be high just so she could function.

As she anxiously awaited the result all she could think of was the bloody woman. It had been years since she heard that horrible crying. Her heart beat faster the more she pictured her, and fear consumed her again. With a deep breath she took one more hit off her pipe before placing it back on the bathroom counter. She didn't know why, but Kira felt like it would be her last time doing that. Her heartbeat began to slow as the image of the woman faded into nothingness; just then the timer on her phone went off. With a deep breath she picked up the test: two lines. It was positive.

The first few months were absolutely brutal. Her nightmares came back almost immediately. It was agonizing watching Conor in his drug-induced haze, but it was even harder hiding her pregnancy from him. She wasn't sure how he would react, so she just tried to avoid it. She had to keep him distracted when they smoked so he wouldn't notice her pass the pipe back without her taking a hit. Her wardrobe became oversized sweatshirts, and luckily most of her clothes were big on her now.

She was able to carry this on for almost eight months without him catching on, but she knew she couldn't keep it from him forever. Pretty soon there would be a baby, and she had no idea what she was going to do then.

She just had to tell him.

"Conor, I have something to tell you," she said quietly.

"Hmmm? What'd you say?" he replied, half asleep. The TV played quietly in the background.

"I'm pregnant."

"What!?" he shouted, sitting up. "When?" She could see him trying to do the math and figure out when this could have happened, but he could barely remember what they had to eat last.

"Almost eight months now." Kira turned her head and looked at the floor, her fingers fiddling with her white nightgown. She could feel his eyes staring at her.

"Eight months? Are you kidding me?! Why did you wait? Now it's too late," he said, quickly getting to his feet. He began pacing back and forth, muttering to himself. She knew he was going to be mad, but it was still upsetting.

"I was scared. I didn't really know what to do, so I didn't do anything—"

"SHUT UP! Stop talking! I don't want to hear your fucking lies anymore!" he screamed as he punched Kira.

She saw a bright flash of stars before everything went black. A few minutes later her eyes fluttered open. Her head was pounding, and she could hear Conor rummaging through the drawers in the kitchen.

"Conor, what are you doing?" she asked groggily. One hand was on her stomach, while the other was rubbing her head.

"I told you to shut up," he answered. She could see metal glistening in his hands as he walked back towards her. Kira tried getting to her feet quickly, but Conor shoved her back onto the futon. "You're not going anywhere," he cried as he plunged a knife into her stomach.

Kira screamed in agony as he stabbed her again. She dropped to the ground and dragged herself across the floor. She could see her reflection in the mirror on the back of the door: her nightgown was soaked in blood, and her hair was matted. As she looked at the life fading from her eyes she noticed the bloody woman appeared behind Conor. Her screams and cries were indistinguishable from her own. With each blink the woman came closer and closer in the reflection, until she was standing directly behind Kira.

That was when she noticed the resemblance.

Their bloody nightgowns were a perfect match, along with the gash across their abdomens. The whole time she had been seeing herself, at this very moment, and those cries of anguish she had been tormented by for decades had been her own. They were the very same ones escaping her mouth now as she bled out.

Conor walked over and kneeled in the blood on the floor. "You made me do this, you know. It's all your fault," he said through tears before raising his hands and stabbing her one more time through her back. Kira looked at the mirror, and with her final breath she watched as the apparition of herself disappeared.

I'm sorry, baby. I'm sorry I carried you with me this long just for your life to be snatched away. You didn't even get a chance.

There was nothing but darkness for a very long time, but she was compelled to return home. She passed through the door of her childhood home, then up the stairs to her parent's room. She entered and saw her father lying in bed. He was so small and frail. In a chair beside the bed a young woman was sitting and holding his hand. Her hair was the same vibrant red as Kira's, and there was something strangely familiar about her. There was a connection to this woman she had never met, and then it clicked.

"I'm here, Grandpa. I love you," the woman said sweetly as she brought his hand up to her lips and kissed it.

Kira's shrieking stopped as she moved to the woman. All of that sorrow and guilt she felt about her baby's death suddenly lifted as she placed her hand on the woman's shoulder. She noticed her shiver a bit, but her eyes never left her grandpa. Kira couldn't believe that her baby had survived. She walked to her dad and kissed him on the forehead.

She could finally be free.

THE BANSHEE AND THE BOSUN

BY JOSH SIPPIE

I preferred my old shipmates to my new one. I missed the captain and his gurgling growl every time he saw something mildly displeasing, missed the seacook and the way he made molded bread taste digestible. Missed the call of the lookout, "Starboard, Ho!" It's just me now, holed up on deck, knowing what awaited me at night. Knowing I was the last one, the last one with a harvestable brain to be slurped out of my skull until consciousness abandoned me. I heard it happen to the lookout, a sickening, sloppy sound, like twisting a fish. I saw it happen to the second mate. His eyes rolled up into the top of his head as his breath forfeited.

And she—it—was there, with her starlight eyes in a sea of black and grey framed by the opaque night. Her eyes saw mine, but she had eaten already so she just smiled, her teeth blacker than the night that bore her. Her blood-soaked, violet tongue lolled out the side of her mouth like a flaccid, lifeless eel.

In that moment I knew what awaited me. I knew that death had found this ship before this ship had found the land it sailed for. There was nowhere for me to go that she couldn't, no weapon I could use that would fell her. We'd tried guns, swords, hand cannons and fire. She withstood it all, smiled, then shrieked with pleasure as bullets passed through her skin as if she were made of mesh that healed itself.

Tonight was my night. As I watched the sun set on my final day I reveled in the glowing, orange embrace of the horizon like never before. The sky was red this morning, and every morning for the past month. It would be red tomorrow morning as well.

I did wonder how I'd made it to last. Perhaps I had just the right mix of bravery and cowardice. I wasn't so brave that I'd go after her with dual sabers, and I wasn't so cowardly that I shivered in my boots with locked knees. I was brave enough to move, cowardly enough to hide. Brave enough to watch, cowardly enough to know when to flee.

It surprised me how modest of an eater she was, if I dare use the word. Only one brain per night, nothing more. She never had seconds, never had an appetizer.

A shriek sounded from below decks and my skin prickled. She woke from whatever Hellhole she sprung from, though I doubted she ever slept. The wailing, even so far away, rang in my head like a resounding hiss, penetrating deeper than any sound had ever gone before. It consumed my thoughts, which left my body rooted. She had shrieked and wailed plenty of times before, but never like this. It sounded almost distressed.

It neared. She never breathed, or perhaps she had two air ways: one for breathing, one for screaming. What creator would provide such a supplement, I cared not to know. Not my creator, surely, not the one I would see sooner than I might like.

As soon as the sun ducked below the horizon she arrived on deck, taking the stairs as if she were any ordinary creature of flesh and bone. She toyed with me, I had no doubt. I would not give her a hunt, which I assume she wanted, for she seemed to revel in bounding after my crewmates; trapping them, torturing them, letting them flee again before she pounced, slayed and feasted. She saw us as sport first, supper second.

"Where are the rest?" I had never heard her speak before and, on hearing it for the first time, I wished she'd never spoken at all. Her voice was harsh and grating, grinding out of her vocal cords like all that screaming actually did some damage to her. Like a door hinge swaying back and forth. Maybe speech was not a primary function of her larynx, assuming she had one of those.

I turned to face her and my joints tensed. She stood passively, not ready to bound, but merely looking.

"It is only me," I managed to say. I hoped it sounded more confident than it felt. I'd been preparing myself for this moment for a while. I wanted to go bravely, to go to the gates of God knowing I had been my best until the end.

She craned her neck and looked side to side.

"This will not do," she said.

"Go find another ship if you need more, heathen." My skin crawled as I said it. Being brave felt satisfying, but a part of me still didn't want to provoke her, as if my life might still be spared.

She smiled at me, her glowing eyes narrowing, her blocky, black teeth leering like bloodthirsty, boxy beetles.

"You know nothing."

I shook my head. "About you? No, I don't. Nor do I care to."

She continued to scan the deck and the waters beyond her. It was a clear night, and had been since she arrived. This was added cruelty to the situation. As a crew we relished kind weather, but we could not properly enjoy it knowing what waited for us every night.

"Lower the sails," she said. I must have misheard her, so I asked her to repeat herself. "Lower the sails!" Her voice shook the boards this time, rattling my very spine.

"Why—" my voice caught in my throat. "Why would I do this? Why do you want this?"

Her smile widened. I grew tired of her company all over again. I felt the threat diminishing by the moment, even as I refused to allow myself to relax. Perhaps it was her final charade, a game to liven the sport.

"Do as I say," she said, her abnormally long finger pointed at me, the sharpened tips of her nails as black as her teeth.

"If you intend to kill me, I'd have you do it now. I will not be your plaything."

She walked silently, her feet making no sound as she approached. Every step closer I saw how reviling she truly was.

Her skin, where it was exposed around her neck and arms, was cracked like an arid desert. Her face was too, though it was harder to see from the blinding glow of her eyes. Her eyebrows—shadowy and angular, like the rest of her—sat just above her eyes. Her thin, purple lips might as well not have been there.

"I do intend to kill you, but not yet. You will live until I find fresh sport."

I swallowed, failed, swallowed again. My throat had gone dry as she circled me as sharks circled the boat, waiting for the next victim to be buried at sea.

"Lower them," her voice, now an unseen growl from my right shoulder, was losing its menace.

"Tell me why," I said. "We can be civil here."

Her silent steps gave no indication of where she was behind me, but I flinched as she appeared by my left shoulder and stood there, breathing her foul breath of rust, worms and rot. I had some power here, I felt, something she needed that I did not understand, but as long as I held it I wished to know what it was.

"I will do it," I said, seeing the benefit to my own situation if the ship moved towards anything other than the great, blue void. "If you tell me why."

She seemed to consider this for a moment, and for the first time I felt that I was having a conversation with a civilized entity and not an amalgamation of evil; though she still contained the qualities of the latter more than the former. Still, I had never seen her think as she was now.

"I hunger," she said. "You are meat, but you are all I have left."

I nearly laughed, but for the fear of making any sudden sound and prompting a spontaneous decision from her.

"I travel on the fog. There is none. I cannot consume you until I know what I may consume next."

I couldn't stop from smirking. She wasn't a blinded predator after all. She thought ahead, forecasting her survival like the rest of us. Like me, if she expected me to sail this ship solo when I had no benefit of a navigator, captain, lookout, or anything else for that matter. I considered her viability as a crewman. I considered what deals I could make with her, but only one lingered—

"If I find you more food," I said. "Will you let me live?"

Her smile sickened me and my smirk turned to a grimace. Her teeth, up close, proved stained with caked blood—that of my crewmates. My stomach tumbled across my diaphragm, unhappy with the thoughts I gave it.

"I will consider it, but if I refuse?"

"Then I slice open your brain while you still live, and devour your brain piece by piece. A foolish question. Do not waste my time."

"Very well," I said, my brain itching either from the weight of threat, or because the dilemma that now presented itself lodged into my cerebral cortex like a wayward fish hook.

I walked to the gunwale. She shadowed me with every step; silent. No breath, no footfalls. Just lurking out of the corner of my eye, her eyeballs like hollowed-out moons looming over my shoulder. But she needed me, I knew that much, and as long as she needed me I was safe.

I let down the sails as I'd seen it done before, doing so remarkably easily, giving my confidence a boost despite my unwanted shadow. What little wind there was caught in the canvas; the ship lurched, groaning, as if it knew what horrors had transgressed in its very own bowels. I walked to the helm. I never had the chance to dream of being captain. My duties on the ship were much different, they kept me busy, kept my pockets and stomach full, so I had no reason to aspire.

As I gripped the wheel in my hands, forgetting myself for a moment, I felt a swelling of pride and dread. My pride was checked by the lurker with the grey and black cracked skin. I saw now, my eyes having acclimated to her sheer darkness, that she had other entities dawdling about on her skin. Maggots, I expected, picking at the dead flesh she had become, though I knew not what she had been before her current form.

I turned the ship north, the direction we had come from, back towards the Canary Islands. Back towards home, family, civilization.

Meat, as my shipmate would see it.

Then I spun the wheel back around. West, to nowhere. My service ended long ago, when she first boarded this ship, or so I had thought. My last service wasn't to my crew.

It was to everyone else, that they be spared an end by this banshee..

WHERE THERE'S SMOKE

BY WILLIAM STERLING

The girl sat with her back straight and her arms pulled tight behind her. She had fiery red hair, half of which was still glamorous, in a full-bodied, curly updo, but the other half was down, glued against her head with a combination of blood and sweat. Her bangs dangled freely in front of her eyes, making it hard for John to read the expression on her face.

John's pledge-mate, Chad, stood on the last of the basement steps, blocking the exit as he tried to explain his actions to one of the senior members of their fraternity: Alex. But for all of Chad's hurried, breathless attempts at explanation, his story made no sense.

"She's a witch!" he insisted, for the hundredth time.

"What do you mean she's a witch?" Alex asked, rubbing the bridge of his nose in frustration.

"I mean...she cast a spell on me or some shit. I don't know!"

Alex rolled his eyes.

"So you tied her to a pipe in the basement?" John snapped, still looking at the girl and wondering what he could do for her.

"Yeah! I didn't know what else to do. I couldn't just let a blood-drenched witch go running out into the front yard, you know? I had to think about the rest of the brothers!"

"Blood-drenched?"

"Yeah!"

"Why is she bloody, Chad?"

Chad paused, looking down at his crimson knuckles in confusion, as if he needed to confirm his story before speaking it out loud.

"Because I slugged her!"

John glanced away from the girl, back towards the other two guys.

"You punched the girl?" Alex grumbled.

"Well, what else was I supposed to do?"

"Why did you punch a girl?"

"She's not a girl! She's a witch!"

John took a couple of steps away from the stairs and away from his friends.

No.

'Friends' wasn't really the right word.

They hadn't developed that much of a relationship yet. 'Acquaintances' was more accurate. 'Mutuals who hit each other with paddles for the promise of an eventual friendship' was probably even more accurate. But not friends.

Especially not after this.

God, John had known that Alpha Sigma Sigma wasn't made up of the best people, but this was unfathomable. How had he let himself get drawn in with this crowd?

John moved towards the row of refrigerators lining the basement's leftmost wall. He opened the first refrigerator and frowned at the never-ending collection of beer bottles and cans.

"She lit my pants on fire, dude." Chad was still trying to explain himself near the steps.

"What, like with a lighter? Did you back into a candle that you lit or something?"

"Candle? What? Nah, Alex. You know I'm not into any gay shit like that. No, she lit my pants on fire. With, like, magic or some shit."

John closed the first refrigerator and opened the door to the next one, finding nothing but another stockpile of alcohol, alcohol, and more alcohol.

John heard Alex sigh as he opened refrigerator number three.

Tah-dah.

There was a lone water bottle discarded in the back corner of the appliance. John didn't want to guess how long it had been back there, but it stuck to the bottom of the fridge when he tried to lift it up. If there was ever a reason for water bottles to have expiration dates, then this bottle would have been patient zero.

But water was water.

Probably.

Right?

John snapped the top off and sniffed its contents.

It smelled like water.

Or, at least, it didn't smell like vodka.

That would have to be good enough.

John walked over to the redhead who was tied to the pipe and knelt beside her.

"Pledge! Don't speak to the witch in question!" Alex demanded, but he wasn't really paying attention to John.

"What do we do now?" Chad was asking the older fraternity brother.

"I don't know. None of our pledges have been stupid enough to get in a situation like this before. Jesus, Chad. You tied her up in the basement! The council is probably going to kick you out of the frat for this."

"No! Please, no! I'll do anything!"

John tried to tune the other two out as he held the water bottle out towards the girl.

If this was what frat life led to, then John was out.

He was quitting.

Blood oaths and sacred pacts be damned, this shit wasn't right.

John was ready to yell all of this at Alex, but Alex wouldn't have paid any attention to him. He was too busy drilling Chad with insults to pay attention to John. Same as always. If John had a superpower it would have been invisibility. Same as it had been in high school. Same as it had been in middle school.

This fraternity was supposed to help him become somebody. The promise of camaraderie in a terrifying new environment had lured him in. The beer had sealed the deal. But at this price? It wasn't even close to worth it.

"Drink some water," John whispered to the girl.

For the first time that evening, the girl raised her eyes and met John's. Her right eye was bruised purple, split and bleeding from where Chad had hit her. But despite the wound, the girl's eyes were sparkling with a sense of clarity and anger instead of fear and pain.

The look caught John off guard and he had to fight the urge to back away from her.

He lifted the bottle to her lips instead and she drank enthusiastically, as if she had been deprived of hydration for days, not minutes (or had it been hours? When had Chad done this?)

John pulled the water bottle away from her lips and let her breathe.

He stood straight and glanced behind the girl, to see how she was bound to the basement's pipework.

Thoughts about freeing the girl flitted through John's mind. Could he get her past Chad and Alex at the base of the steps? John was much smaller than either of the other two. He had never been much of a fighter. He—

The girl's hands were unbound. The rope which Chad had originally used to confine her lay limp like a dead serpent against the concrete and the girl's hands were rotating freely behind her as her fingers contorted and wrapped over themselves and under themselves in a curious, rhythmic fashion. They looked like ten snakes dancing across her palms.

John looked back towards the girl's face and caught her smiling.

She winked at him.

John dropped the water bottle and took a step back, unsure what was happening.

On the other side of the room, Chad and Alex finally stopped talking.

Chad's eyes grew wide as he stared, slack-jawed, his hands rising slowly up in front of his face. He gritted his teeth together and a vein popped out on his forehead as Chad strained to do...something...but there was no telling what.

The other pledge looked odd, as if he was trying to deadlift his max and needed a spotter to intervene. More veins bulged against his neck and his jaw clenched shut.

"What's happening?" he scream-mumbled through clenched teeth. His fingers uncurled themselves and wriggled as they rose, creeping from beside his waist straight towards his eyes. His neatly trimmed fingernails scratched the air beside his nose.

Alex jumped forward, recognizing that something was wrong, and he tried to grab Chad's hands to pull them away from his face.

Alex was too late.

Or too weak.

Or both.

Chad screamed and John watched in terror as his fingers pressed against the whites of his eyes, compressing them back into his skull until his fingernails split the delicate orbs, spilling clear, aqueous humor down his cheeks.

John wanted to look away, but couldn't. His head felt frozen in place, his eyes held open by forces he did not understand. Chad's self-mutilation was a spectacle to which John was a captive audience. And it wasn't over yet.

Chad's knuckles turned white as his hands rotated, drawing his fingers to the outer rims of his mutilated eye sockets. His arms flexed and strained and John learned what sound a skull makes when it splits in two.

Chad finally stopped screaming as he fell to the concrete floor of the basement, the skin on his forehead stretched thin, fragments of bone jutting out around the chasm which had opened across his forehead. Blood poured forth, fast and furious.

"Y-y-you killed him! How?" Alex screamed, turning towards the redhead who was still seated on the floor.

She rose, silently, to her feet and with a casual, final flick of her wrist and a snap of her fingers, she disposed of the fraternity brother.

Flames erupted inside Alex's pants, surging up his torso as if being blown from a flamethrower. The resulting rush of heat slapped John in the face and knocked him backwards to the floor. The hairs on his arms and face were singed away in an instant, and his eyes flooded with tears.

Alex was gone before John could get his bearings enough to look up. In his place, a garden of red and orange flames had bloomed across the basement, dancing on each and every wooden surface. The row of refrigerators had been knocked over by the explosion like dominoes, and the only evidence that Alex had ever existed was an imprint of his shadow seared into the cement of the unfinished basement's back wall.

John screamed and contorted his body, trying to scramble away from the witch at his side. The path to the basement's steps was clear now, save for Chad's corpse and the pool of blood expanding around his head.

The witch turned towards John and picked up the water bottle which he had offered. She tipped it upside down, drenching John with the liquid, smiling at him, then gliding towards the burning steps. She was leaving John, alone and confused, in the furnace-like underbelly of Alpha Sigma Sigma.

The flames dared not bother their summoner, and John stared incredulously as the fires parted before the witch like the Red Sea before Moses, the charred, wooden steps supporting her ascent like palm fronds in Jerusalem.

The witch opened the door to the frat house's main floor and turned back to John.

"You should really choose your friends better," she said.

And then she was gone, disappearing into the mad rush of pledges and college bros who could be seen through the doorway, escaping the burning house en masse.

The door slammed shut, either from the witch's powers or from the fraternity members' desperate effort to push past the obstruction. Really, it didn't matter much.

John was trapped.

He watched in terror as the steps to the basement imploded, caving inwards as the flames consumed their support structures.

The flames rose higher and higher, and John choked to death on the smoke once, twice, a thousand different times.

The heat increased until it became insufferable, and then it continued to increase more and more. John felt the blood in his veins boil, felt the crackle and pop of his own fat separating from his muscles as they cooked. John screamed through it all, somehow never succumbing to the endless dark which he kept hoping for. Although he begged for death to take him away, the Reaper eluded him.

The water on his skin stayed in place, John's wet clothes hugging him, acting both like a blanket of protection and a sous vide bag at the same time.

A blessing and a curse.

The firefighters didn't reach John until it was nearly morning.

His survival was deemed a miracle.

John wasn't so sure.

The fraternity offered him a spot in their brotherhood the very next day: a token extension of pity for what he had been through. Hush money to never speak of what Chad or Alex had tried to do.

John turned down their invitation.

He needed to choose his friends better.

FOUNDATIONS

BY GEORGIA COOK

She had a customised door chime. He hadn't expected that.

Jonathan listened numbly as a muffled rendition of 'Twinkle, Twinkle, Little Star' echoed through from the other side of the tiny apartment door; a spark of the normal world, flickering past him in the darkness.

There was a pause, then a cheery voice called out from inside, "Come in! Door's unlocked, kettle's on!"

Jonathan steeled himself and gave the door a push. It creaked open, dispersing a wave of artificial lavender scent into the hallway. He coughed, pressing a hand to his mouth until he felt better, and stepped inside.

The apartment was a cramped three-roomed affair—same as Jonathan and Lydia's apartment downstairs—made even smaller by the volume of possessions. Furniture hulked at strange angles; armchairs and bright kitchen stools arranged around a multitude of coffee tables and cabinets, each one overflowing with knick-knacks and curiosities. Glass eyes peered down from every corner of the crowded sitting room, a tribe of antique china dolls. And within it all, perched on an overstuffed blue sofa, was Madison Nicnevin.

She was younger than Jonathan remembered; red-cheeked and smiling, bordering on middle-aged, with a mess of gingerish hair and an orange jumper.

"Jonathan!" she trilled, rising to her feet. "Do come in, come in! What a lovely surprise!"

Jonathan swallowed. What had he expected to find up here? An empty apartment, dark and cold? Dried bats hanging from the ceiling? A cauldron bubbling over an open fire?

God, he needed sleep.

"Uh...thanks..." he mumbled, closing the door behind him. He immediately wished he hadn't; the curtains in the apartment were drawn, lending the light a thick, reddish quality. The air was soupy with summer heat, punctuated by that same stifling lavender. Already Jonathan could feel himself starting to sweat.

Madison shuffled past him to the tiny kitchenette on the other side of the room, motioning for him to sit. "And how is dear Lydia?" she called over her shoulder.

Was there a twinkle in her eye as she asked? A sudden sharpness to her smile? Jonathan stiffened. No matter how often he heard it, the question still hurt.

"Same as always," he said. "Thank you."

"What a shame. Such a lovely girl."

There was a click and the soft roar of boiling water. Jonathan stood awkwardly in the middle of the living room, trying not to catch the eyes of the dolls. A door on the opposite side of the room sat ajar—probably leading to a bedroom, Jonathan thought, but something about the darkness behind it unsettled him.

Madison reappeared, holding two steaming mugs of tea; one pink, with dancing cartoon rabbits printed across the surface, the other narrow and white, bearing a picture of a beaming, anthropomorphic flower.

Madison forced the pink rabbit mug into Jonathan's hand and ushered him into a chair. "And to what do I owe the pleasure?" she asked, settling down on the sofa.

Jonathan took a deep breath. Here it went; admitting to the madness. Finally bloody giving in.

"I've heard..." What had he heard? Stories. Stories from all over the apartment block. "I've heard you...know... things..."

Madison smiled at this. "I know many things, my love."

"Things." Jonathan could feel his face growing hot with embarrassment and anger. "You cured Mr Evalet's wife down in number 5. You found the Linderhurst's missing cat..."

Alive and well. Days after it had been spotted dead on the side of the road.

Madison settled back, her smile replaced with a strange, piteous expression. Jonathan hated it; he'd seen it too often over the past few months, arranged across the faces of friends and neighbours, sat behind murmured platitudes and hushed whispers.

"And now you want the same..." said Madison.

Jonathan made to stand, fumbling in his pocket for his wallet "Look, I have money! I can pay!"

Madison waved him down. "There is...one spell. A ritual I know. For your poor wife."

God, she'd said the words. Spell. Ritual. Descending the final steps to madness. What would Lydia say to all this? To Jonathan visiting a—

"What do I have to do?" he whispered.

Madison was quiet again for a long moment. Jonathan's heart pounded. The heat swirled about his temples. Was she smiling again? Was that an arch of amusement to her brow? Finally, she set down her mug.

"Something of this kind," she said. "It requires...sacrifice."

Jonathan's blood ran cold. He tried to laugh, but the sound caught in his throat, high and hysterical. He felt as if he were standing on the edge of a deep precipice. "What do I do?"

"You must take something precious and bury it. Bury it in the foundations of this place. Make it protector and sentinel; ward off all things against your love."

The heat was rising now. Jonathan could feel the sweat dripping down his forehead. Madison's face seemed to glow in the sunlight, tinged crimson and gold.

"Bury what?" he asked.

Madison Nicnevin took a long sip of tea. "A heart, pet. A living heart."

Out in the corridor, Jonathan slumped against the cold brick wall, his breaths hollow and flat, his eyes sharp with tears.

A cold breeze whistled through the hollow walls, twisting down the empty staircase, bringing with it the scent of old urine and the dampened roar of distant traffic. Jonathan closed his eyes, savouring the tepid air. He felt as if he'd returned from another world; back into the grey oppression of the apartment block.

When he opened his eyes again, he felt almost normal. He wiped his mouth viciously on a sleeve, hating the cold sting of sweat across his forehead, the lingering scent of lavender on his clothes.

A heart. Christ.

Lunatic old bat.

What had he expected? Reassurances? Medicine? A spell to fix everything wrong in his fucking life? He was desperate—everyone in the damned block knew he was desperate—and here was a stupid, old woman, either mad or deranged or evil, willing to prey on that desperation. Like fortune tellers promising the world, or psychics pretending to contact the dead...

He wouldn't tell Lydia. He'd been right not to mention this to her in the first place; better not to upset her. Better to forget the whole fucking thing.

Mind made up, Jonathan straightened, clawed his hair out of his eyes, turned back to the stairs, and began the slow, echoing descent back to his apartment.

Miss Nicnevin had lived in the flat directly above Jonathan and Lydia's for longer than anyone could remember. She was a staple of the apartment block, a permanent fixture. Despite her relative youth, and the existence of far older and more reclusive old women, rumours seemed to enwrap her like a shroud. Children whispered behind their hands as they passed her door, eyes gleaming with interest and horror. The more superstitious avoided the fifth floor altogether.

Children knew these things. Children always knew. They were the carriers of folk and fairytale, and every community needed a witch.

As he rounded the corner onto his own floor, a large, ginger shape darted from the shadows and streaked past Jonathan's feet. He swore and lurched back. It was a cat, hulking and grizzled. It hissed and swiped at Jonathan's ankles, its collar glinting in the sunlight, before disappearing into the cat flap at number 15.

The heat of humiliation and hatred flared in Jonathan's chest, filled with the unease of the last hour. He resisted the urge to give the cat flap a kick, instead making his way past the row of identical white doors to his own at the end of the corridor. It was still locked; Lydia hadn't left this morning.

Jonathan listened at the door. No sounds from inside; no shuffling footsteps, no rustle of clothes. Once—years ago, it felt now—he might have heard Lydia singing to herself in the shower, pottering about the kitchen as she cheerfully burnt breakfast, any of the normal, beautiful little things that were now almost impossible. Slowly, gently, he eased open the door.

"Good morning."

Jonathan's stomach gave a lurch.

Lydia was waiting for him in their tiny living room, propped up on a mound of pillows. Usually, her chair was angled towards the windows, so she could watch the view outside, but this morning she'd turned it towards the door to wait for him.

She looked so much smaller this morning, grey and thin, hair spread out around her like a brittle cloud.

Jonathan leaned down to kiss her forehead. "You should be in bed," he said.

Lydia waved him off with a weak little smile. "How'd it go?" she asked. "Visiting the neighbours."

"Fine, fine."

"You sure?" she drew back, studying him critically. "You don't look fine."

"Just spooked by Mrs Roud's stupid, old cat."

"She dotes on that cat," Lydia spread her hands across the blanket over her knees. "What's its name? Callous? Carrow?"

"Cassius." Jonathan couldn't keep the flatness from his voice.

"That's it!" Lydia laughed lightly. "Cassius. Do you think—"

She was interrupted by a sudden round of coughing, shaking her frame and dislodging the cushions around her head.

Jonathan reached for her in alarm. Lydia waved him away. "Sorry, sorry. I'll be fine. Just a second."

She continued to cough as Jonathan rose unsteadily to

his feet, heart pounding. It hadn't lessened; that horrible, sick feeling of helplessness, deep in the pit of his stomach. Not after months of this, as the world slowly disintegrated around him.

"I'll just... Just give me a minute."

Jonathan hurried to their bedroom, stumbling on the carpet as he went, and shut the door behind him with a click. The room was still and cramped. Heat swirled in the air, filled with the rhythmic click and beep of Lydia's machinery. Jonathan slumped against the door, head in hands, and swallowed back a sob.

What had he done? What had he thought he was doing? Visiting a mad, old woman in her grotty apartment. Listening to the advice of some whack-up hedge witch.

What had she said?

A heart.

Bury a heart in the Foundations. Protect Lydia. Make her well.

They'd tried everything, and nothing seemed to work. Lydia was still sick, still fading; becoming smaller and thinner, like a paper girl, ready to crumple at the slightest breeze.

A thought arose in Jonathan's mind, terrible and sharp, twisted with desperation.

A heart didn't have to be human. A heart could belong to anything! The important part was the living aspect. He just had to choose something small. Something that wouldn't be missed.

A second thought arose, softer and quieter than the first, as if it had simply been waiting all this time for Jonathan to agree. It came accompanied by a flash of ginger fur and a malevolent, green-eyed gaze.

He knew exactly which heart to use.

Out in the living room, Lydia's coughs had subsided to low, rattling breaths. Jonathan's stomach clenched. Slowly, slowly, he eased himself back into the room.

Their apartment was identical in layout to Ms Nicnevin's, with a small kitchenette attached to the wider living area. Jonathan crept into the kitchen, careful not to draw Lydia's attention. He selected a knife from the kitchen block, watching it glint under the lights, then slipped it into his pocket.

It couldn't be that difficult, surely? He'd carved chickens before. Cuts of roast beef, Christmas ham. They were all the same, weren't they? When you got right down to it.

All meat.

He moved back into the living room and kissed Lydia gently on the forehead. "I'm going out."

She stared up at him with pale, exhausted eyes. "Where?"

"Just out. I'll be right back."

Jonathan left the apartment without looking back, locking the door carefully behind him.

The hallway was empty. Soft footsteps and muffled voices echoed down from the higher floors. On the street outside, the high, bright laughter of children and the thud of a football filtered up through the windows. The world was tinged with golden sunlight, casting a sheen across the concrete walls and dank stairwells.

Something moved in the shadows by number 15. A ginger shape padded out into the sunlight. Jonathan held his breath.

The basement. There was an old maintenance room in the basement— he'd seen the door ajar once on his way past reception-- filled with tools and cleaning products. He could steal a key from the security room, find his way inside. Nobody would find him; nobody visited apart from the night shift, and even then only rarely.

It would be so easy. So easy...

The cat brushed against his leg, mewing softly.

Gently, gently, Jonathan reached down and picked it up.

It was dark by the time Jonathan climbed the stairs back to the apartment. A crimson sunset blushed the walls, turning the world red and gold. Shadows lurked in distant corners, spreading out across the concrete.

Lydia was asleep on the sofa as he unlatched the door, chest rising and falling almost infinitesimally. Jonathan stood in the doorway a moment, watching her, before he walked to the bathroom and flicked on the light.

His reflection stared back at him in the bathroom mirror, pale and dark-eyed, hair a mess, a long, ragged scratch peeling down his left cheek. His hands itched. He'd scrubbed them in the basement's tiny porcelain sink, scrubbed and scrubbed until the skin was red-raw, but it hadn't been enough.

Jonathan reached out and turned on the tap. Water gushed into the bowl, filling the bathroom with rising steam.

He heard the soft chime of the doorbell outside, followed by Lydia's unsteady footsteps, then the click of the latch.

"Sorry to bother you, dear."

"Not at all. Can I help you?"

Jonathan peered numbly out into the hallway.

Mrs Roud stood on the doorstep, small and frail in her oversized house coat, holding a little, purple cat toy. It jingled sadly in the corridor gloom.

"You haven't seen my Cassius, have you?" she asked. "He's gotten out again, silly thing."

Lydia shook her head. "Sorry, Mrs Roud, we haven't seen anything." She looked over her shoulder. "Have we, Jonathan?"

Jonathan shook his head. He'd vomited earlier, and he could still taste it in the back of his throat.

Mrs Roud nodded, wringing her hands together fretfully.

Jonathan went back to washing his hands. The light in the bathroom flickered fluorescent white, deepening his eye sockets, tinging the world in unnatural brightness.

That night, Jonathan dreamed of an impossibly tall apartment block; empty and cold, wind whistling through its hollow bones. He pictured it growing out of the earth like a sapling, rising up and up and up, sinking deep roots under the soil. He pictured a staircase winding straight down through the centre, ending at a tiny, cramped room, raw with stifling heat and lavender stench, filled with the clutter of millennia. A thing unchanged, undaunted by the centuries, home to something older than the ancients.

And beneath it all, endless and eternal, the low, thudding boom of a thousand human hearts...

Jonathan opened his eyes. The bedroom was dark and stiflingly hot. Lydia's monitor beeped on the floor beside the bed. Her form beside him was small and pale, thin beneath the layers of blankets. No change, no difference, nothing at all. Jonathan lay for a long time, staring at the ceiling, his chest burning with shame and self-loathing.

Stupid, stupid! He'd been so stupid. It wasn't an animal heart he needed. Lydia was worth more than a damned cat.

...but God. He knew what to do. The dream had told him. The cloying heat of Madison Nicnevin's apartment.

Jonathan knew exactly what to do.

It was still early in the morning. Thin, grey sunlight seeped across the apartment complex, highlighting faded brickwork and ancient graffiti, leaking through doorways and turning the shadows a subtle yellow.

Jonathan knocked softly on the door of number 15. "Mrs Roud?"

Lydia was still asleep. She hadn't woken as Jonathan left; she wouldn't even know he'd gone.

Nothing stirred beyond the door. Jonathan was about

to knock again when a thin voice floated through from the other side. "...Hello?"

Jonathan took a deep breath. "Mrs Roud? It's Jonathan, from across the hall?"

"Oh!" the voice brightened. "Jonathan dear! Just give it a shove. It's not locked."

The door creaked open with a gentle push. Jonathan glanced over his shoulder; no cameras in this corner of the building, nobody awake this early. The night workers were still travelling home; the early risers had already left. Nobody was around to spot him. Nobody around at all.

He eased open the door.

Mrs Roud's apartment was small and neat, sparse in a well-cared-for way. The air smelt faintly of disinfectant, strung through with the sharp, unmistakable scent of cat piss. Cassius's bowl sat forlornly in the corner, filled to the brim in a sad but hopeful way.

"Come inside, dear!" Mrs Roud warbled from the kitchen. "I'll be right with you."

"It's no rush."

Jonathan stepped inside and closed the door gently behind him, locking it with a small click. The knife behind his back glimmered in the almost-dawn.

It was a mercy, he told himself. A small mercy, really.

She wouldn't feel a thing.

This time, the process was quicker. Mrs Roud was lighter than he'd expected, the basement lending a comforting, subterranean chill to the air.

Afterwards, Jonathan scrubbed his hands in the basement sink for almost fifteen minutes, but even in the gloom he could see it had done nothing. He was getting used to that.

He climbed the basement stairs in silence, a terrible relief filling his lungs.

It was done.

The sun had finally risen. The apartment block echoed with distant noise; footsteps and muffled voices. Jonathan paused in the lobby and closed his eyes, willing the world to be different, willing something to have changed. Was there a tinge of summer softness to the air? A new layer of red? Could he hear the refreshed heartbeat of the apartment building, pounding through the walls, keeping Lydia safe?

Nothing. He heard nothing. Nothing felt different.

Jonathan's stomach clenched.

Hadn't it worked? Hadn't he done exactly as asked? His hands ached from the frenzied scrubbing. The smell of copper and meat hung thick in his nostrils, saturating his clothes. Why did nothing feel different?

Jonathan's eyes flew open. All around him, the sunlight cast dappled patterns across the apartment walls. Outside, the usual gaggle of children had gathered in the morning heat to play football, their shouts and cries echoing up from down below. The sounds of a living space shared by hundreds of people.

A place needing sacrifice.

Jonathan's heart sank. The knife felt heavy in his pocket.

God... God it made sense, didn't it? Something precious, something loved. A heart untouched by the cares of the adult world.

The perfect protector for his Lydia.

Feeling nothing, nothing at all, Jonathan turned and descended the stairs. Down, towards the sunlight and the joyous laughter of children.

It was dark by the time Jonathan returned upstairs. His brow was caked in sweat. His hands shook. He'd removed several layers of skin with his scrubbing.

All was quiet and still in the apartment. The curtains rippled in a soft summer breeze. Jonathan stepped forward. A floorboard creaked beneath his weight.

Lydia's voice filtered softly through from the bedroom, accompanied by the rustle of the duvet. "Johnny? Johnny, is that you?"

Jonathan flinched.

He could go to her now, forget this whole wretched business. He could hand himself in, save Lydia the heartbreak of finding out...

But what good would that do?

Nothing would change. The ritual still wouldn't have worked. Lydia would still be...

"Jonathan?" Lydia's voice was weak, sandpaper rough.

Jonathan ignored it. He selected a fresh knife from the block in the kitchen. This one was long and serrated— a bread knife, still beaded with tiny crumbs.

When he left the apartment this time, he locked it from the outside. Just in case.

The room was darker than he remembered. Moonlight filtered through the drapes, barely stirring the fetid air. Dust swirled in the sweltering heat, adding texture to the shadows. The mismatched furniture loomed on all sides, threatening to topple any moment, converging to swallow Jonathan whole.

And there sat Madison Nicnevin, red-cheeked and smiling. Waiting for him.

Jonathan lingered in the hallway, hands itching, vision swimming. Sweat dripped down his forehead. How long since he'd eaten? How long since he'd slept? God, a day? Two days? It felt like a century.

"Why isn't it working?" he whispered. The smell of lavender was choking. He could barely breathe.

"Why isn't what working, pet?"

She was smiling at him. He knew she was smiling at him.

"Your fucking spell. Why isn't it working?"

She was mad. He was mad. They were both fucking mad. He'd done this because she'd told him to.

At the back of the room, Madison Nicnevin's bedroom door hung open into total emptiness; a pitch black void. No shapes, no furniture, nothing at all seemed to penetrate the shadows...

"I did exactly what you asked!" Jonathan snapped,

struggling to focus his attention. "The cat, the old lady, the damned—" He couldn't say it. "And Lydia's still…"

Madison's smile widened.

A thought arose through the tangle of Jonathan's mind: how old was Madison Nicnevin?

She'd lived here as long as anyone could remember. Jonathan remembered his dream. He pictured a vast stone tower, rising out of the landscape in the mists of pre-Londinium Britain. He pictured stone and moss, giving way slowly to plaster and wood, then concrete and twisting iron, strong and eternal, constant even in war and plague and fire.

Blood in the walls. Blood in the Foundations. Blood in the bones of this place. And how long had Madison Nicnevin lived here, gently stoking the flames? Keeping the land fed? How many others had she coaxed to do her bidding, promising them life and love and protection? If they only did as she asked…

And who among them, once they'd started, had found themselves able to stop?

"—did you?" Madison's voice cut through his thoughts.

Jonathan's blood ran cold. "What do you mean?"

Madison smiled, face shadowed in the stifling, red light of her apartment. The glint of bared teeth, locked under the gaze of a hundred, glassy-eyed dolls.

"What heart do you have left, my sweet?"

Jonathan descended to the basement in total darkness. The world was silent and still, filled with a sickly, summer warmth. The wail of police sirens rose in the distance. Somewhere, a frenzied mother called desperately for her child, but it was all background noise. The soft chatter of the building.

Jonathan understood now. He knew exactly which heart had to live in the apartment walls. A willing heart; a willing sacrifice. To keep the walls standing. To keep Lydia safe.

He knew exactly why Madison Nicnevin had chosen him.

Jonathan drew the knife from his pocket. It glinted in the darkness, crusted with brackish-red.

Would it hurt? He'd gotten very good at it, knew exactly where to cut, exactly where to place the blade. Lydia would be so proud of him.

Jonathan's grip tightened on the handle. He would keep her safe. He'd promised. He'd promised her.

The thought followed him the rest of the way down the stairs, hammering with every footstep, with each beat of his own pounding heart:

Keep her safe...
Keep her safe...
Keep her safe...

ON THE RUN
BY ROWAN HILL

The knife handle rested sticky in Teresa's palm, tacky with congealed blood. Whether it was Mike's, her own, or from Stacey's gut wound, she didn't know.

It probably didn't matter now, or rather it was too late to worry. Stacey had keeled over and Teresa hadn't even thought about hygiene or blood-borne diseases. Her friend and partner had been gutted—the knife was a surprise from the man's belt—and she had rushed in before Stacey even hit the ground. Sweaty hands with broken knuckles covered the gash above her crotch, pushing down and praying the bulge pressing back wasn't Stacey's intestines trying to escape.

Now Teresa was running. Frantic. Harried. But alive.

The bayou thrummed in the late hour. It whipped past in her frenzied state. A barn owl soared through the air. Moonlight streamed between behemoth cypress trees, arms languidly melting with grey Spanish moss down to gently rippling water. Teresa leaped over a fallen log, necklace bouncing against her chest, sweat running down her back, every muscle screaming, howling, with effort.

Oh god, she was so scared.

The owl screeched as it found dinner and, in Teresa's imagination, she thought a man shouted alongside it, wondering where she was. But that wasn't right.

She was so scared but so alive. So fucking alive she wanted to scream and vomit and run all at once.

It was too much. She would miss something. Make a mistake if she went too fast.

So she knelt by the bank, closing her eyes against the dark, humid swampland, ignoring critters and crawlies on their nightly routines. Adrenaline roared in her ears, her heart a drum, wild and harsh. She exhaled, willing quiet. Willing blood to slow, the fear of being caught to dampen, to control how this would end.

Crows cawed in a distant nest, a possum snuffled in the brush, a gator lazily pedaled water.

Slow, Teresa, she thought.

How long had she been running? Thirty minutes? An hour? The trio had driven the Bronco down the dirt track for at least four country songs. Deeper into the National Park hugging the Mississippi, right up to a little cloistered spot Mike knew. They had to be at least fifteen miles from Grady's Corner, the nearest podunk town. She cursed herself. All her instincts were shot to hell after three years of taking it easy in her momma's basement, living off VA cheques, playing Sudoku to keep her mind 'sharp', and walking to the Piggly Wiggly for exercise.

She didn't even notice when Mike casually dropped a pill into Stacey's drink.

And now Stacey was dead.

Branches crunched under feet, their rhythm broken, hobbling but fast. Her eyes shot open to nothing but the wall of trees lining the water. Something heavy and careless was stomping like it was at a hoedown. Letting the whole bayou know it was there and in a hurry.

Teresa ran.

The full moon's blaring light pierced the canopy of the woodlands, speckling the ground full of detritus. Thin, blue beams caught dust and grit, white flecks against black night, and Teresa was in Afghanistan again. She blinked away the memory, the tall, slender trees returning. She ran hard, light on her feet, moonbeams flashing faster and faster against her eyes, blinding her from one second to the next.

After a thirty-second sprint, thin branches lashing bare legs and sandals nearly falling off, Teresa stopped and knelt by another tree. Fire seared her lungs and she smothered it with deep, silent breaths.

Her head tilted. They were also running. Branches swishing against footsteps in that same broken rhythm.

Where did they expect her to go? Were they heading for the main road? The town?

Opening her eyes, she was back in the ruins of Malsapa village, mudbrick walls of dilapidated huts transformed grey in the full moon. Holes in the ceiling admitted moonbeams appearing as translucent sylphs. Lunar ghosts. The village was a warren of confusing tunnels and shafts illuminated by the blazing moon.

It was on its way down when Teresa spotted it.

A wolf. But not a wolf. Not like any wolf she had ever seen. Not like the coyotes while deer hunting in Arkansas. Not like the wolves of Alaska, where she went through boot.

It wasn't just bigger. It was nastier. Feral. A savage beast in a savage land.

Serving Recon in the Balls to 0200 shift in her observation post by the light of the moon, Teresa watched it stalk from the desert foothills into the empty town, a shadow against shadows. From her elevated position, without binoculars, she thought it was Taliban. But it was too fast, too low. There was discernible intent in it, and it wasn't trying to stay hidden. She told her buddy she was walking the perimeter and he sleepily agreed.

A howl cut through the bayou chatter and Teresa couldn't tell whether it was from her memory or in this time and place. Her neck ached and her free hand massaged it, the knife wound in her upper arm slowly giving her grief. A creeping soreness stiffened her bones, as she seeped life into the foul swamp air. Her right hand was caked with blood and she knew for sure it was Mike's. It cracked and flaked away as her dirty fingers kneaded the knot beneath her skin and she smiled, remembering the surprise on her date's face after the slippery knife had fallen from his grasp and right into hers.

Straining in her crouch, her sandal strap finally broke and she slipped both Walmart cheapies off, throwing them away in frustration. How had she become this? She had returned from war, an honorable discharge wrangled after a few misdemeanors, and life became pointless. Boring.

Boring until she met Stacey.

Another howl pierced the muggy night. But instead of a hunting cry, it was warbling, weak, in pain. It made her think of Mike and she wondered how he was liking his new look. It wouldn't suit him at all. He was too beautiful with his blonde hair and piercing, electric blue eyes. The symmetry of his face was eradicated.

Teresa stood, honing her ears for the direction of the howl, but it was everywhere and nowhere. Ricocheting between trees like a goddamn bouncy ball.

The main road was her best bet. The moon was useless for guidance while beneath the canopy, but from her best guess, she was alongside the dirt track. She ran again, ignoring broken branches and twigs stabbing her naked feet, trying to make her lose this race for survival.

Her foot caught a low-lying log, wet wood camouflaged in the dark, and she sprawled. Sprawled like when she'd spun too quickly on her heel and the front of her bulky flak jacket caught the corner of a small mud home. She'd toppled to the shadowy ground of the laneway, her carbine rifle trapped between her belly and the dirt, facing the end and the cornered monster.

It hadn't known it was cornered until it turned and saw her blocking its path. But it padded forward anyway, black fur nebulous, the reflective tint of its eyes blazing red against the moonlight.

It snarled, a guttural, perforating noise Teresa felt in her chest, and back in the Arkansas bayou, a rattlesnake shivered in warning somewhere nearby.

She pushed off the damp ground to sprint again, the exposed flesh on her arm burning.

Was this how Stacey's wound had felt? Burning? No, it was probably dull, blood loss turning her cold and the roofie killing any feeling, just like they'd intended. Her eyes were glazed at her last breath and Teresa squeezed her limp body so tight she thought they would both break.

No, Stacey hadn't felt much. Even if she had, she wouldn't have spoken up. Stacey was—had been—kind but also tough. The type who didn't like beer but would still buy the sixer. The type who didn't complain when her peanut allergy flared after kissing because you had to have that PB and J. The type who played along to catfish men with fake identities, enjoying your crazy stories, though maybe she didn't believe them and attributed them to PTSD.

Tears wanted to surge with the feeling in her gut over Stacey's death. Teresa would have married her one day.

A nearby whimper echoed through the trees. Oh, Jesus, they were so close, fuck. Her body was hypersensitive to the night air, sultry and thick in the summertime, dewy on her skin. The bayou rounded, cutting back across Teresa's path, and she instinctively slowed as the trees broke for the water and the moon flooded the land. The water's edge was so picturesque it could've been a Kincaid postcard and she slowed, making herself small and light. She was glad the knife in her hand was tacky, harder to slip.

She hadn't been able to use her pistol or rifle that night. Not in a deserted town behind the forward operating base on the Afghani front. Too likely an errant gunshot would draw attention. The monster had snarled, and instead of an observer, Teresa was suddenly prey as it hunched low and stalked forward.

But she didn't run, didn't bolt like a jack rabbit the way her instincts were screaming. Wild dogs also operated on instinct. It would have chased her down and it had sharper teeth.

She'd backed away slowly, the pair turning the corner together, locked in a strange dance. Matching steps. Matching breaths, Teresa's shallow and hoarse in her ears. She couldn't use her guns but she did have her knife. Slipping inside a blackened doorway, it followed her into the abandoned and crumbling shack of mud, stone and thatch. Dried purple thistles hung in bunches from the ceiling, old and crinkly. The last owner's attempt at beauty before they fled the war.

Among the choir of swamp crickets, white bleeding heart flowers hung from vines between oak saplings, framing the pair on their haunches by the water. The full moon—a glorious, bright face—turned the night blue like a movie filter, and the man and wolf were speaking low, trying to catch their breaths. Teresa clasped a tree, pressing her face into its rough bark as she watched them downwind.

The half-naked man's skin shone white in the dark and she noted with satisfaction his left arm still hung limp. A creek of blood, more black against white, ran from the ear she'd cut off, the side of his head flat and odd looking.

The wolf beside him was laying on its side, breathing hard, white fur rising and falling rapidly, each breath earn-ing a soft whine. Good. She had never punched anything as hard as that wolf's belly, the serried shadows of its rib bones painting her target. It even cost her a cracked knuckle. She'd felt it give beneath her fist and, when it yelped, she knew the rib bone had broken, cutting into whatever organ it held beneath its soft fur.

Now, it was dying slowly as something bled internally. Giving him a bullet would be a kindness.

No, Teresa hadn't been able to fire her gun that first night, but she had her knife. And it couldn't have turned out better. A blessing. After dancing around shadows and corners, the prowling beast had finally had enough and lunged—fucking soared—through the air at her. Both of them fell, Teresa to her back, the monster on top. It hadn't even noticed, or maybe didn't care, about the black carbonite drop knife in her hand. The way it had slid in between its ribs, a hot knife in cold butter.

The monster had laid on her stomach, panting, and Teresa crushed it tight to her body like it was a lover trying to escape. Their hearts thumped against one another. Blood ran, hot and harried. Warm breath caressed her face as its maw uselessly snapped, a hair's width away, weaker and weaker. The midnight-black fur of its breast swathed her fist clutching the buried knife. It was soft and thick, the softest thing she'd felt in her short life. The most intimacy she'd ever known as their gazes stayed locked in a showdown of wills. Its chest pulsed and vibrated, until it whined.

Teresa watched the red, reflective eyes dim until they glazed, and the thrill, the high, the goddamn exhilaration of taking that from it, watching it die, of being there at that moment made her whole body shudder in ecstasy.

She had rolled it to the cold floor. White fangs against black snout caught her eye and she plucked her pliers from her flak pocket.

A bug crawled from the tree bark onto her face and she rolled her cheek to crush it. God, she wanted that feeling again. The rush of coming so close to something so wonderful, of taking an abomination for herself. She hadn't felt anything close to that excitement since the abandoned village. Maybe a fraction of it when she met Stacey, their first night together, when they'd shared secrets and dreams.

When Teresa had told her girlfriend she thought the town Romeo was a werewolf. When she said they should have a little fun and see if it was true.

She'd known it was true. She'd seen him. Anyone else would have thought it was a coyote and been glad to go unnoticed. But she hadn't felt glad. She'd been excited, nearly aroused, when she saw those same lithe movements, those same red eyes. Then he changed by the light of the July full moon, brazen asshole thinking no hunters stayed past sundown, per Fish and Game regulations.

She had been paralyzed in her tree stand, hidden in the dense thicket, disbelieving her luck. A higher power had wanted her to find him, to give her purpose.

If only she'd known he had a brother.

Teresa exhaled against the bark. The anger of Stacey's death, the excitement of a chase, and the fear of the pair escaping had died. They had been running, frightened, since she'd stood from Stacey's dying body and went berserker, cutting off Mike's ear in a rage while he was still trying to fix his arm as if he could just 'pop it back in'. But something had happened on their escape and they thought they'd lost her.

They weren't going anywhere. They weren't leaving this bayou.

Eerie calm settled over her chest, breath exhaling. Teresa left the shadow of the tree and walked confidently to the water. Mike spun in his crouch. The white wolf snarled even as it lay limp. Instead of stopping, she forked right, veering away, and set herself down on the water's edge twenty feet away.

The brothers watched her intently but did nothing besides suck painful breaths.

Teresa squatted and leaned forward, dropping to the water with cupped hands. She splashed her face. It was bath-water warm and she could smell the unique, dank, rotting quality to Arkansas still-water. Farther out, maybe forty feet, three ridge-lined logs moved, tips casting shadows on the surface. She finally spoke without looking at them, making sure they knew she was calm, unafraid. Certain.

"You can't change can you? Not when you're hurt like that."

There was silence down the bank and, after a moment, Teresa turned her head. Mike's handsome, chiseled face was set firm, lips pressed tight.

"Huh, didn't know that part," she mumbled, adding more to herself, "Have to remember that for the next one."

"We never hurt anyone! We only give them the pills

to help them loosen up, fool around a little and make them think what they saw was a dream, like a bad trip."

Teresa's eyebrows arched, her surprise visible, and she looked at her hands, caked in Stacey's guts. He understood immediately

"YOU ATTACKED US!"

Teresa blew out a breath, fortifying herself for the next stage. "Toe-may-toe, Toe-mah-toe. You roofie my girlfriend; your brother's waiting for us in the swamp and changes, fucking lunges at me; I break his insides, you break her insides, I break your outsides. Slates getting pretty full, Mike."

She stood and the bayou noticed. Teresa was formidable, an Army vet with combat and live-fire experience. The air stiffened, the crickets stopped their chorus and she gripped Mike's knife tighter. He shot to his feet, broken and dislocated arm jerking limp. They were the same height, her taller than most men. Bulkier than most women. They had been equal, but between his arm and the knife in her hand, no longer.

"You should have said it was a double date, Mike. I would have come better prepared."

She stepped forward and both man and beast snarled. The viciousness and ferocity on both faces so unusual, so surreal, unlike anything life in a backwater town had ever provided.

"God, you're both freaks. Wonderful, beautiful freaks."

"We were born like this! We didn't ask for it!"

Teresa cocked an eyebrow and stopped. Her interest was obvious and she didn't bother hiding her business-like tone. "Born? So your mother and father are like this? Your younger sister and cousins? Both sides of the family? More of you? You said your family came from across the Mississippi, down near Clarksdale, right?"

Mike's eyes widened as she listed off his pack members.

Teresa smiled, a wonderful, broad smile, full of possibility and she chuckled. "You know, Mike. I really don't mind about Stacey. Not anymore."

His working hand curled into a fist and his thighs stiffened. She ignored his defensive stance and reached for the necklace hanging between her breasts.

"I mean, shoot, I was madder than a wet hen. But no, not anymore. You've given me purpose. A future."

She peeked around his legs to the wolf and her fingers toyed with the necklace, the tooth she'd ripped from the Afghan werewolf. It was still sharp to the touch. It hadn't dulled in years of her using it to pick dirt from under her nails. She'd pried it from the red gums, its furred tongue still warm in death, and not a moment later, a great gurgle erupted from its belly. Teresa had stepped back in amazement and watched the metamorphosis of beast to man. A great, dark man, naked and shiny, skin black, features African. But the tooth remained unchanged as its owner became human again.

She looked to the brother, Beau, in his wolf form.

"Oh, he's so beautiful. That white coat. He's gonna make a great rug."

Its upper lip rose and it bared its teeth while horror crossed Mike's face. They thought she was crazy. Of course they did. But they were amazing, beautiful, wild creatures that reminded her why life was strange and cruel and wonderful. They just couldn't live.

After the highs of combat and the soul-sucking low of mundane life, she needed this too much.

Mike's voice came out as a stutter this time, realizing he was outmatched, and Teresa was kinda hoping he'd start begging. "It doesn't work like that. We change back after we die. All anyone would find is that you murdered two men."

Teresa hadn't taken her eyes off the wolf, mesmerized as the behemoth lay on its side, bathed in the same full moon that allowed its change. There was so much she wanted to know, so many questions. But she reached into the pocket of her cutoffs, and pulled its contents out, crouching and offering it like she was trying to coax a scared puppy out of a corner, voice saccharine.

"Here, Beau. I got something nice for you, boy. A little treat to eat, if you want. I bet you need some energy, huh?"

She laid her palm flat and showed Mike's bloody ear, still intact.

She had finally pushed the right button. Mike roared at the sight of the bloody lump of cartilage, right arm rising, body closing the distance between them. Teresa stepped up from her crouch, meeting him halfway, willingly taking his blow to her shoulder if it meant she could slip the knife under that raised arm.

She grunted with the hit but held the knife tight, only for the whole forest to still the moment after and there was silence.

The two figures hugged, bodies and limbs entwined.

A vacuum hung over the trio. Over the forest. Over time.

Teresa met Mike's eyes. They were dull and colorless and staring at her, stupefied, and she was disappointed this time wasn't like the first. As a human, Mike didn't have the savagery of a beast in his stare. His warm skin was too smooth. Dirt and grit clung to him, chafing against her. It wasn't the same. There wasn't the high of knowing you'd bested something so wild it needed two bodies to hold it.

Mike exhaled and finally looked down, his own blade buried in the smooth skin beneath his armpit, between the sixth and seventh rib, the largest gap. She had cut through to his heart.

He dropped to his knees like a sack of potatoes and the blade scraped between sinew-covered bones as it escaped.

He mumbled to her cutoffs, head too heavy to look up at her towering height. "You're a fuckin' monster. We don't hurt anyone. We eat deer, we don' hur' anyone... A fuckin' monster..."

She bent over, the Were's tooth dangling in his face, and grabbed Mike's chin before kissing him. Their mouths mashed together in tongue and breath and for some reason, he let her. Joined her. Like he knew this was the last kiss he would ever get and he would do it damn well.

Then he coughed and blood smeared her lips. She pulled away and spat saliva and gore before wiping the knife clean on his smooth shoulder.

"Maybe I'm a monster," she told him, eyeing the logs in

the water, drifting closer to the bank.

She rounded Mike's body, the incapacitated wolf snarling and snapping, trying to get to its feet. Frantic. With a great heave against his limp arm, she pushed Mike aside, his body tipping over the grassy ledge and falling into the water. The logs hurried in Mike's direction, his weak thrashing drawing their interest and appetite.

"But I'm a monster with a purpose."

The gators swarmed, Mike screaming as he tried to fight, and Teresa's attention turned to the wolf. Its pathetic, weak body lying in the grass. Why hadn't it changed back to a man? So many questions. Ones that would have to wait. She sighed as it attempted to stand. This wouldn't be the same, either. Not at all.

Maybe with the sister or father. Or maybe the mother would give a good fight. All that maternal instinct and rage, multiplied when she saw the pelt of her dead son hanging from the shoulders of the hunter who'd killed him.

Yeah, maybe the mother would give Teresa what she needed.

Teresa palmed the knife, looking the white wolf over as he came to all fours, a low rumble in his chest and baring his teeth. His coat was exquisite; she hoped she didn't mess up skinning him.

"So, you gotta be alive, huh?"

THE END.

TUSK AND NAIL
BY KEVIN WALSH

'Polluted' came to Fetuilelagi's mind of the dark, brackish river to his right. Little on this planet compared to the coastal blues of his homeland Samoa, but something stained these waters.

Dusk was not humble on this summer night, deep in the French Guiana jungle. The horizon gored the sun and dragged its bleeding wake across the paling blue of the sky, and every passing second drew the darkness deeper into the surrounding jungle. A lively darkness of yellow, feline eyes, orb weavers, and slithering reptiles.

In the dying light, he spied inky shapes bobbing in the flow. Torn clothes. Ragged boots. Soaked berets. If there were human pieces to accompany the garments, they had been pulled down by hungry river-dwellers and crocodiles upstream.

The further they traveled, so left the aromatic dampness of the jungle, replaced by the growing tang of the river's thickening refuse.

"Eyes forward. Watch your lane, Fetu," grunted an Australian voice behind him.

Fetu glanced back. Swift was tall, rangy, and similarly clad in black, patchless fatigues. Behind Swift were the remaining four operators of Gamma Squad, whom Fetu didn't recognize save for the American on rear guard, Captain Thompson.

Fetu kept his rifle—an HK-416—at a low ready as he nodded and picked up his pace. The target was just over the next hill, according to the relief map he had referenced earlier. In their briefing before the insertion, Captain Thompson had delegated Fetu to point man of Gamma Squad, an unusual change of pace.

Despite his deep affiliations with the Company, Thompson was a straight shooter in more than the literal sense. He brooked no dissent or foolhardiness from his squad. If the Company gave any grunts a hard time, Thompson had their six. Everybody implicitly trusted the captain and his 20 years of combat experience, and that was why Fetu had zero compunction over his delegation to point man, even though he suspected it was tied to him being Polynesian.

"You've been through jungle, son?" Thompson had asked him, with his Louisiana drawl.

"Not all jungles are the same, sir."

The captain had considered that and clapped a hand on Fetu's broad shoulder. "Pointman will either be you or Crocodile Dundee over there."

Fetu had straightened and nodded in the affirmative, and Swift commented from the back of the room. "I heard that. If Moana over there gets dragged away by a croc, I ain't jumping in."

Fetu grinned at the memory. He would miss the banter of his brothers, even if they were of the disgraced sort.

They were private military contractors, most notably the black ops variety. Their employer had undergone a series of name changes, in a bid to dodge liability from the result of their operations. As a result, everybody called them the Company; the ominous corporatism wasn't lost on the grunts.

Fetu had served twelve years in the Australian Defense Force. During that time, he had worked on training operations with Marine Rotational Force-Darwin. The MRF-D was an American program to train Marines in Indo-Pacific regions and forge stronger partnerships with Australia and allies. Fetu had disliked his post in the dry and arid northern reaches of Australia, but he grew fond of the Marines.

It was there he'd met Captain Thompson, and after his service in the Marines, the captain had offered Fetu a chance to earn some real money to retire early. He'd accepted and for seven years, Fetu had seen the world, albeit through the optic of his rifle. Afghanistan. Ukraine. Venezuela. Taiwan, to name a few. And now, French Guiana.

Spying the hillcrest, Fetu slowed his pace and whispered into his comm-link, "Hold position."

Fetu reached into his combat vest and withdrew a thermal monocular. The squad stayed back, out of sight from the patrols posted on the hill. Fetu carefully navigated the underbrush, knifing through the dewy broadleaves with flat palms. He raised the monocular and scanned the hillcrest. Four signatures stood out in a cluster. What should have been the red glow of combatants now waned purple. Given another day, the violet signatures would blend into the blue environment.

Fetu pocketed the thermal and toggled his mic. "On me."

Gamma Squad ascended the slope of the hill and found the remains of a guard post. The wooden picket box was nothing but snapped timbers and scattered equipment. Shreds of camouflage netting lay among the destruction, covering the four dead sentries.

Thompson assessed the scene. After a beat, he said, "We may not be the only operators on site. Stay frosty."

Thompson shouldered past Fetu and took the lead. Down the embankment, their view of the facility opened to a panorama of devastation. Ahead was the main entrance to the complex, a multi-floored affair with few windows and fewer points of egress. In the complex's rear, beyond a rutted dirt track, appeared a warren of trailers and outbuildings.

Gamma Squad stared at the wreckage of the front entrance. A checkpoint bracketed by two troop transports, barriers, and concertina wire had become a charnel floor of piecemeal security personnel. Congealed blood lathered a green jeep inside the checkpoint, where eviscerated soldiers lay in pools of human ruin and spent brass. Fetu and Thompson dared closer to the carnage while the rest of the squad kept their eyes out.

"Someone got here first?" Fetu asked, his deep basso voice losing some of its edge.

"Where's the cavalry?" Swift added.

"This is a remote installation," Thompson said and shook his head. "See those buildings? The employees lived here. Help may not arrive for another few days, depending on how often these researchers reported their findings outside the complex."

Thompson knelt by the corpse of a large soldier and rolled him over. The clamshell of his ribcage yawned wide, and what little remained of his internal organs was mush. Inspecting the corpse, Thompson touched a deep slash in the man's arm.

"Swift," Thompson called. The Australian sidled up to them.

"Oh, fuck me dead," Swift intoned, standing behind the kneeling captain.

"Animal attack?" Thompson said, while scanning the surrounding carnage for similar wounds.

"Right," Swift grunted. "Ask the Aussie; he must be Irwin's mate,"

Thompson didn't raise his voice. "Swift."

Swift stared at the body, fidgeting with the strap of his rifle as he did. "Yeah, mate. Tearing wounds."

Thompson bobbed his head. "Thought so."

Fetu grimaced and turned towards the front entrance of the facility. At their briefing, intel bespoke a disruption at the research facility and now was the optimum time for a strike to seize invaluable data. Knowledge well beyond their pay grade.

"You reckon animals did all this?" Swift winced.

Corpses clad in jungle camo and red berets littered

the fifty meters between checkpoint and entrance. Swaths of wire had been pulled across the dirt, muddied by spilled intestines and pooling blood.

Thompson stayed quiet. Between the tall Swift and the block-shaped Fetu, the captain looked rather slight. His demeanor and bearing, however, was pure steel. Grey stubble swathed his lantern jaw, the muscles to which flexed in rumination.

Thompson stood and, with a chin tilt to the complex, he had said enough.

For the first time, Fetu saw Swift's features sag at the surrounding carnage. His own hackles rose at the blood-shed, turning his stomach to a ball of ice. He grabbed the collar of his vest and adjusted it against his bulk, loathing the slickness of humidity beneath his combat layers. His stubby fingers found his lanyard, and thumbed the shark tooth threaded there.

Promise me, Fetu.

The memory of Lagi's voice drifted upon his touch of the tooth's minute serrations.

On his last trip home, he'd spent a beautiful weekend with her. Her father was a fisherman, and she was his apprentice. As Fetu returned to the island to surprise her, he'd waited on the front stoop of their beachside home. Lagi's mother had never really approved of Fetu and his so-called 'dirty deeds' as a hired gun. But that day, as he sat on the front steps, she had accompanied him and talked his ear off. She had quieted when their fishing boat drew to shore. Lagi, her father, and three more fisherman had dragged the small, dead shark across the beach.

Recognizing Fetu, Lagi had dropped her section of shark and dashed across the sand. She'd jumped into his arms and he spun her in circles as she squealed in delight.

"You reek of fish," Fetu had remarked, grinning ear to ear.

"A fisherman smelling like fish, what a concept."

Lagi's laugh was a summer breeze of its own. Excitedly, she had dismounted from Fetu's arms and pulled him towards their quarry. Lagi explained they hadn't seen a shark that close to the reef in ages. That night, as they butchered and quartered the catch at the family roast, she'd said it was no coincidence a shark had appeared the day of his arrival. Lagi was just like her mother, devout in omens and portents and nature's omnipotence. Again, she warned him of his dark profession.

Then, under the stars and the tidal moon, she had told him the truth. In six months, he'd be a father. Fetu embraced her tightly, relishing her wavy hair on his shoulder. They cuddled in the sand, watching the moonlight galvanize the water into a pan of seamless steel.

"In six months, I'll be done with the company. I'll work double time and save every penny."

"Would you join us to fish?" Lagi asked, and her green eyes bore on him with more intensity than a combatant's muzzle ever could.

"Can I shoot fish?"

"No." She giggled and kissed him under the full moon. "Lean over."

Fetu obliged and she threw the lanyard around his neck.

"I worried I didn't have enough thread for that fat neck."

Fetu chuckled and eyed the shark tooth hanging by his chest.

Lagi's soft hand cupped his cheek. "Don't return a monster, Fetuilelagi."

Fetu rolled the shark tooth in his fingers. One more mission and he would retire the irons.

He tucked the tooth under the lip of his plate carrier, wanting to feel her close to his heart for his final foray into danger. Marshaling his wits, he cracked his neck and let out a long, measured breath. He followed Gamma Squad through the wreckage. Darkness chased the last of the daylight and the crew turned on the tactical lights mounted under their barrels. Before stepping through the doors, Fetu stole one last glance at the sky. The moon leered back.

Fetu followed on Swift's heels as they entered the lobby. A faint smell of antiseptic and polish greeted them, but only as an undertone to the pervasive reek of death in the building. Evidently, the power had ceased, with only the red glow at the end of the labyrinthine hallways to mark their path. Strangely enough, a generator hummed faintly from the complex's depths.

Thompson pumped a quick hand signal down the nearest hall. Gamma fell in step. A musk of sweat, feces, and wet hair cloyed the air. Only their scuffing boots and the odd jostle of gear echoed around them.

Two more corridors and the scent grew more sour, clawing into their olfactory senses.

Thompson panned his flashlight into a new passage on their right.

"Remain where you are," Thompson said suddenly, snapping the silence with his stern demand.

Fetu wheeled into the hall, bringing his rifle to bear and adding a second cone of light. Something darted into a nearby doorway. He only caught the faint image of a muddy foot retreating into the shadowy recess.

Thompson wasted little time and charged ahead.

Fetu followed, weapon tight to his shoulder as the captain panned his light into the room. He stood off to the right of the threshold, angling his beam for wider coverage.

His light settled on a naked man, trembling hands shielding his eyes from the brightness.

Fetu wavered, then his view of the man was blocked by the captain.

"Hands up!" Thompson ordered, voice like thunder in the quiet.

As per his training, Fetu stormed the room with the other four operators in tow. Their lights danced across the office, showcasing various men and women in similar states of dishevelment. A woman shied from the light and scuttled back into the corner, smearing her muddy calf against the tiled floor.

Fetu shone his light on the wall above her body, to avoid further blinding her. His hardened demeanor sagged at the sight. Scars and old wounds marred her leg, puckered rents that had healed all wrong. Their skin held a greasy sheen, pocked and contused.

What bothered Fetu was that the cowering people all bore the same deformities. Most worrisome, a thick pouch of scar tissue at the edges of their cracked, bleeding mouths. Many of them gibbered to themselves, rubbing and scraping at their own marred flesh. Whatever shell shock or catatonia had seized these people, it drove an icicle deep into Fetu's spine.

Thompson stepped back and let out a sharp breath through his nose. "Michaels, Frederick, secure this room while we reach the objective. Men, mount up."

Frederick and Michaels stayed to watch over what appeared to be the facility's only survivors.

Fetu followed the captain and the others into the hall.

"What the flying fuck is going on?" Swift grunted ahead of him.

"I don't care to find out. Move."

Thompson resumed their journey deeper into the facility.

It was a labyrinth of narrow hallways flanked by labs and file rooms. The only sign of progress was the growing hum of the generator and the thickening chemical tang.

"The river," Fetu whispered. "This is what the river smelled like."

Nobody responded to his comment.

Heel-to-toe, they proceeded into another junction when a scattered sound echoed behind them. Yells fragmented by the turns of the hall, followed closely by the echoing prattle of close-in gunfire.

Thompson keyed his radio. "Sitrep."

Gunfire drummed from the passage in short bursts. Between the shots came something throaty and glottal.

"It's the survivors. They're—"

Michaels' voice was shredded through radio distortion, in tandem with three more rapid booms from deep in the facility.

"Michaels?" Thompson hailed.

Nothing.

The gunfire ceased, replaced by rhythmic patter.

"Gamma, let's move." Thompson turned and jogged down the next corridor. "Haul ass, gentlemen."

Nobody needed to be told twice as the squad jogged deeper into the facility. Another junction yawned before them and, as they stood there, trying to discern their location, echoes funneled all around them.

Fetu heard a sound that tumbled ice into his gut. The unmistakable clomp of hooves.

He wheeled his tactical light into the nearby hallway, in time to catch a fleeting image of someone stepping away into a further junction. An afterimage stuck out in his mind, a single detail that made him wonder if he was losing it.

A hairy shoulder.

All Fetu could hear was his own labored breathing. He tried to deceive himself that it was from the jog, but as his fear spiked, he knew it was his rising fright. Grunts had a phrase for that: Pucker Factor.

His nerves felt like barbs under his skin.

A close-by rifle report momentarily deafened him. Swift had stepped into a hallway and fired three rapid shots. Through the whine of his recovering eardrums, a keening wail sounded off down the hall. The shrill wail devolved into a throaty grunt, then a deranged squeal that couldn't be produced by human vocal chords.

Fetu stepped back to assist Swift, but the hair on his neck stood up. His instincts demanded his attention. He snapped up the light and illuminated a burly figure down the hall. Its eyes squinted against his light and then slid out of view down an adjoining corridor.

Now it was Thompson's turn to pipe three rounds at an attacker. The fourth in their squad, Harker, followed suit, but his shots were far less measured.

"Harker, controlled bursts!" Thompson shouted over the din of Harker's rifle. From down Harker's hallway came a squalor of grunts and squeals.

Harker's HK-416 clicked. Fetu heard his spent magazine hit the deck while he fumbled to reload.

Hooves closed in.

Fetu bolted into action, pivoting to cover Harker's reload. He snapped up his rifle and didn't hesitate as he banged out five rounds into the running figures. The muzzle flashes revealed the attackers in snapshots. Big, impossibly proportioned, bipedal creatures. Rust-colored, bristly hair covering their hides, charging with an unnatural gait between a trot and a dash. Impossible, snarling faces staggering closer in flashing frames of light. Broad lacrimal bones dominating their features, broadening the space between dark, porcine eyes. The broad expanse of bone ended in upturned snouts and unmistakably human maws, save for two jutting, cracked tusks that oozed saliva and blood.

Fetu's rounds punched into the lead attacker's thick hide. Despite the stopping power of his rounds, it had picked up too great a head of steam. The creature let out a hellish, pained squeal as it charged through the storm of lead and bowled into him.

As a teenager, Fetu had played rugby competitively. Standing at a respectable six feet and 250 pounds of stocky, low-center gravity, he truly was an immovable object. A wall.

The thing was a freight train and, for the first time, Fetu ragdolled to the floor.

Fetu thudded hard against the floor and the breath ejected from his lungs. Wincing, he rolled to his side up against the wall. Catching his breath was a battle, and his head was lost in a dazed vortex. Fortunately, the creature had focused its efforts on Harker.

The other man had reloaded his weapon and fired a burst into the creature, but it was too late. The boar thing shoved Harker against the wall and speared a hand—tipped with a jagged hoof—into his stomach. Thompson and Swift swiveled and hammered round after round into the thing's broad, thick hide. Its agonized squeal echoed across the junction, fragmenting down every hall.

In response, the halls returned a chorus of enraged squeals and snuffling grunts. Hooves thundered from every direction.

Thompson and Swift fired and fired. Muzzle flashes

strobed the scene, fracturing the violence into a slideshow of horrors. Two boar things set upon Swift, bearing him against the wall, stabbing and rending with sharpened tusks. A gruel of blood oozed from the man's lips as he was disemboweled.

Another pack of three emerged from a hall and pulled Thompson into the dark. His screams were drowned in delighted, phlegmy squeals. With their weapons scattered every which way, Fetu lay in the dark to gaze upon two boar things feasting on Swift, lit only by the red emergency lights above. A pair of red-limned faces stopped their feast to lift their snouts from Swift's stomach cavity. One of them snorted out a gob of entrails from its nostril, stringy mucus chasing the ejected offal. Swine eyes locked on Fetu.

Their tusks dripped blood.

He now understood the strange, puckered scars around the mouths of the survivors.

They squealed and lunged.

Blackness took him.

Flittering images and sounds came to him in the dark as they dragged him through the complex by the ankles. Lumbering figures snuffled to one another, others responded with low squeals in their throats. Cloven hands gripped the thin skin of his ankles. If his faculties were in order, he'd hash out how their disfigured hands could have both hooves and fingers. Fetu winked in and out of consciousness. The heady reek of sweat and swine was nearly too much to bear before it was replaced by the eye-watering stench of chemicals.

He opened his bleary eyes and regarded the room into which he'd been dragged. He felt his gear snag and twang against a grate as they dragged him into an open industrial space. Glancing down through the grated floor, he saw a reservoir that stank of chemical refuse. To his right was a laboratory, complete with lab benches, tables proliferated with pipettes, centrifuges, beakers and trays of surgical gear.

To his left…

Fetu couldn't register what he was seeing, its contrast so stark to the opposing clean lab equipment.

Tribal masks hung on a peg wall, accompanied by tables of mortars and flasks containing unknown pastes. Idols and figurines carved from ancient wood watched the boar men drag him across the grated floor. Suspended by meat hooks were jungle critters, river panthers, canines, and boars. Their blood drained into bowls, the use of which became clear as a boar-thing pulled him closer to the room's epicenter.

Fetu didn't have the strength to fight back. His skull throbbed and his vision danced and whirled.

The boar men dropped his ankles. Fetu yelped as those disfigured hands—tipped by jagged, cloven claws—grabbed him and hoisted him to his feet. He winced at their stench and the sensation of coarse, fibrous hair against his skin.

Center stage to this marriage of mad science and ritualism lay a metal tub. Hoses sprouted from the sides of the basin, snaking into the room's dark corners. The hoses thrummed and trembled, telling Fetu where the generator had reserved its power. Sigils painted in animal blood decorated the sides in a bloody mosaic. A piss-colored liquid filled the basin, a bubbling pool of luminescent stew. Dark snakes of blood floated in patches atop the mysterious fluid, separated like oil on water.

A boar man issued a moist squeal.

It shoved Fetu into the tub.

Fetu plunged and immediately bucked against the caustic fluid. It singed his eyes but didn't blind him. Before he knew it, darkness enshrouded him as the boar men dropped a stone lid on the basin, interring him.

Fetu thrashed and bucked as he swallowed and inhaled the pungent fluid. Panic overrode all his senses. Flashes of Lagi and their unborn child were his only sane refuge in the spiraling agony. Fetu fished for the shark tooth against his skin, but it was all wrong. The tooth was a jagged firebrand, burrowing into his flesh and disappearing. The molten stake penetrated his chest bone and soon radiated through the tributaries and river ways of his veins and arteries. His entire body was a torture rack of anguish, skin bubbling and bones shifting and bending. His teeth uprooted and jagged, serrated enamel blades scissoring up through his gums.

The lid had a window, perfectly aligned to a skylight in the lab's ceiling.

Fetu's last image was of the final piece to this shamanic mayhem of science—the bright silver of the night's chancellor.

The full moon watched the creation in making.

Unsatisfied with the failed creation, the boar things pulled up a grate and dumped Fetu's maligned body into the reservoir below. It ejected into the river outside the facility, to float with the rest of the stinking refuse.

Under the guise of the full moon, a new predator swam the serpentine rivers of French Guiana, terrorizing locals and animals alike. Pieces of crocodile and the occasional boar littered the rivers in its wake. As suddenly as it arrived, the thing disappeared. Scattered reports surfaced of a mutant shark travelling the South Atlantic, and more sightings across the South Pacific.

For seven months, Samoans witnessed a large, misshapen shark at night, patrolling the shores of Upolu in the low shallows. By day, the fishermen canvassed the waters for the great, finned beast, knowing not of the scarred man living in the shadows of the forest's edge. He watched one particular fisherman come and go.

And wept for his forever broken promise.

THE END.

Thank you so much for purchasing this copy of *Monsters & Mayhem,* by Eerie River Publishing. We hoped you enjoyed the stories that were featured and the horrors that were captured within them. Please consider taking a few moments and reviewing this story wherever you obtained your copy. Reviews and recommendations are the cornerstone of small press publishing. Without you, there is no us.

OUR AUTHORS

CHRISTOPHER BOND

Christopher Bond writes dark fiction with hints of the macabre and the fantastical. He has spent most of his adult life living between Hawaii and the Midwest. He currently lives in Ohio with his wife and three kids, at least until the harsh winter drives them back to a beach somewhere.

His work has been included in anthologies from Eerie River Publishing, Fahrenheit Press, and Creative James Media, among others.

You can find him on Twitter @CbondWrites
Amazon Author Page:
https://www.amazon.com/kindle-dbs/author

ERICA CIKO CAMPBELL

Erica Ciko Campbell is an Active Member of both the SFWA and the HWA. Her stories have appeared in many eerie and enchanting venues, most recently Mythic, Cosmic Horror Monthly and Tales to Terrify. She's the Editor-in-Chief of Starward Shadows Quarterly and a First Reader at Cosmic Roots and Eldritch Shores. If you're still craving the whispers of war-torn, dead galaxies, check out her website: http://starless-imperium.com/.

You can also find her on Twitter @ECikoCampbell
Starward Shadows eZine: https://starwardshadows.com/

JESSICA CASEY

Jessica Casey is a new author just starting to get her works out there. She currently resides in New Hampshire, and is working on a collection of noir crime novellas. She loves writing older adult fiction and dabbles in horror and suspense as well. She has recently started an Instagram account to document her journey from writer to author, so feel free to follow her along in her journey at:

https://www.instagram.com/jessicacasey_writings/

GEORGIA COOK

Georgia Cook is an illustrator and writer from London. You can find her work published in such places as Baffling Magazine, Luna Station Quarterly, and Vastarien Lit, and shortlisted for various awards, including the Bridport Prize and Reflex Fiction Award, among others.

She has also written and narrated for the horror anthology podcasts *'Creepy'*, *'The Other Stories'*, and *'The Night's End'*

She can be found on twitter at @georgiacooked and on her website at https://www.georgiacookwriter.com/

RADAR DEBOARD

Radar is a horror movie and novel enthusiast who resides in Wichita, Kansas. When he's not living in his own nightmares, he's writing horrifying tales to help others find theirs. He's had stories published by Gypsum Sound Tales, Eerie Lake Publications, Macabre Ladies Publishing, Black Hare Press, Black Ink Fiction, and Little Demon Publishing. He is also a regular contributor to HorrorTree and Siren's Call Publications.

https://www.facebook.com/WriterRadarDeBoard/

J.M. FAULKNER

J.M. Faulkner is a British English teacher residing in the Czech Republic. It is the perfect place for him to steep himself in the architecture and tumultuous history that fuels his curiosity. Outside of work, you can find him hiking in splendid, Bohemian forests with his Czech partner Kat, son Jasper, and beagle Lola.

His writing has been published by Allegory, Cosmic Horror Monthly, Silverblade, Eerie River, Black Hare Press, and more.

Find out more on jmfaulkner.com

RJ FULLER

R.J. Fuller is a thinker, a writer, a world-builder, and a believer in all things magic.

DAVID GREEN

David Green is a writer of the epic and the urban, the fantastical and the mysterious.

With his character-driven dark fantasy series empire of ruin, or urban fantasy noir nick holleran, david takes readers on emotional, action-packed thrill rides.

Hailing from the north-west of england, david now lives in County Galway on the west coast of Ireland with his wife and train-obsessed son.

When not writing, david can be found wondering why he chooses to live in places where it constantly rains.

Newsletter: https://tinyurl.com/y6ah8brp
www.twitter.com/davidgreenwrite
www.davidgreenwriter.com
https://www.facebook.com/davidgreenwriter

CHRIS HEWITT

Chris Hewitt lives in the beautiful garden of England and in the odd moment he's not walking the dog, he pursues his passion for writing fiction. With horror, fantasy, and science-fiction stories published in several anthologies from Eerie River amongst others.

Facebook:www.facebook.com/chris.hewitt.writer
Twitter: @i_mused_blog
Blog: http://mused.blog
Amazon: http://mused.blog/author

ROWAN HILL

Rowan Hill is an Australian/American author of science-fiction/horror and currently lives on a volcano in Italy, but that will probably change soon. She loves travel horror stories set in the countryside, final girls, a good creature feature, and would describe herself as a child of the 80s- synth soundtrack included. She can be found on social media (but isn't terribly good at it) or visit her website for her short stories and other propaganda.

Writerrowanhill.com
https://www.facebook.com/WriterRowanHill
https://twitter.com/WriterRowanHill

HUNTER LACROSS

Hunter LaCross is an up and coming writer with works published in anthologies such as *A Cure for Chaos* by Haunted House Publishing, *Monsternomicon* by *Haunted House Publishing, Wrong Roads* by Suicide House Publishing, and *Forgotten Ones* by Eerie River Publishing. He looks forward to getting more of his writing out into the world.

NiKKi R. LEiGH

Nikki R. Leigh is a queer forever-90s-kid wallowing in all things horror. When not writing horror fiction and poetry, she can be found creating custom horror-inspired toys, making comics, and hunting vintage paperbacks. She reads her stories to her partner and her cat, one of which gets scared very easily.

Instagram - @spinetinglers
Twitter - @fivexxfive
Website - spinetinglershorror.com
Email – spinetinglersmedia@gmail.com

RONALD LINSON

Born and raised in western Connecticut, Ronald now lives in New York City. He writes mainly science fiction, fantasy, and horror, but has been known to dabble in other genres as well. In 2019, he co-founded Mannison Press, LLC with friend and critique partner Deidre J Owen where he holds the position of editor-in-chief. In addition to his work as an editor -- both freelance and as editor-in-chief -- he has published a number of short stories. These include *"Chthulhu Chicks"* (from Lovecraftiana: Lammas Eve 2019, Rogue Planet Press), *Time Served* (Mannison Press, 2020), *Agent of Change* (Mannison Press, 2019), and *"The True Nature of Swimming Holes"* (from Little Girl Lost: Thirteen Tales of Youth Disrupted, Mannison Press, 2019). His latest publication, *To Be A Dark Mother*, is a cosmic horror shared experience anthology (Mannison Press, 2021; with authors Owen, Mendees, Greene, and Giles).

Time Served:
http://getbook.at/TimeServed
Agent of Change:
http://getbook.at/AgentOfChange
To Be a Dark Mother:
http://getbook.at/DarkMother

TIM MENDEES

Tim Mendees is a horror writer from Macclesfield in the North-West of England that specialises in cosmic horror and weird fiction. A lifelong fan of classic weird tales, Tim set out to bring the pulp horror of yesteryear into the 21st Century and give it a distinctly British flavour. His work has been described as the love-child of H.P. Lovecraft and P.G. Wodehouse and is often peppered with a wry sense of humour that acts as a counterpoint to the unnerving, and often disturbing, narratives.

Tim has had over eighty published short stories and novelettes along with five stand-alone novellas and a short story collection.

When he is not arguing with the spellchecker, Tim is a goth DJ, crustacean and cephalopod enthusiast, and the presenter of a popular web series of live video readings of his material and interviews with fellow authors. Tim is also a co-host of the Innsmouth Book Club podcast. He currently lives in Brighton & Hove with his pet crab, Gerald, and an army of stuffed octopods.

https://timmendeeswriter.wordpress.com/
https://tinyurl.com/timmendeesyoutube

E.N. NEELY

E.N. Neely is an award-winning journalist and author living in the Washington D.C. area. Neely is also an accomplished fencer, has gone hunting for lost Spanish gold in the Rockies, and loves stories about things that go bump in the night. @Writer.E.N.Neely

ETHAN SABATELLA

Ethan Sabatella is a writer of sword and sorcery fantasy, historical fiction, and cosmic horror. Celtic and Norse sagas, languages, and mythology are the primary inspiration for most of his stories. The plots of his stories often focus on warriors overcoming martial challenges or encounters with hidden ancient, primordial forces. Ethan's other stories have appeared in the modern pulp magazine *"Broadswords and Blasters,"* the Lovecraftian anthology *"City in the Ice"* by Hiraeth Publishing, and the amateur sword and sorcery magazine *"Whetstone."* When Ethan is not writing, he practices Historical European Martial Arts and creates content for tabletop roleplaying games.

Facebook Page: https://www.facebook.com/ethansabatella

JOSH SIPPIE

Josh Sippie is a writer at Grim & Mild's Cabinet of Curiosities and creator of the webinar series *Inside Writing*. His work has appeared in numerous magazines and anthologies, including *Hobart, Stone of Madness, McSweeney's Internet Tendency,* and more. He is the founding editor of The Razor magazine.

More at https://joshsippie.com/
Twitter @sippenator101.

WiLLiAM STERLiNG

William Sterling is an independent author from OTP Georgia and an affiliate member of the Horror Writers Association.

He is especially focused on horror and thrillers with a soft spot for unexpected endings. He has two self-published books currently, titled *THROUGH FROZEN VEINS* and *THROUGH WITHERED ROOTS,* with more stories on the way to include Serial Killers, Zombies, Pirates, Zombie Pirates, Demon Puppets, and everything in between.

I'd love to be friends! Follow me on
Twitter @Spooky_Sterling, or send me an email at
TheWilliamSterling@gmail.com

SHELBY SUDERMAN

Shelby has been writing stories down for almost twenty years, and telling stories even longer.

Besides *Monsters & Mayhem,* she will be featured in the upcoming anthology *It Calls From the Veil* from Eerie River Publishing.

Find her on Twitter and Instagram as @ShelbySuderman

RACHEL L. TILLEY

Rachel L. Tilley, who lives in the UK, writes short stories in the fantasy and horror genres – whenever she has spare time between looking after her two little ones, her day job as an accountant, and her addictive hobby of reading lots of books.

www.facebook.com/RachelLTilleybooks
www.instagram.com/rachel_l_tilley

KEVIN WALSH

Kevin Walsh lives in Cornwall, Ontario with his pregnant wife and stepson. When he's not reading about the end of the world, he's writing about it. If you like one of his stories, you can email him at KevinWalsh-author@outlook.com for more info about upcoming releases or kindly leave a review. If you hate his work, be gentle, he's one bad review away from running off into the woods as a feral squirrel-man.

ANN WUEHLER

Ann Wuehler has four novels out, Oregon Gothic and House on Clark Boulevard, Aftermath: Boise, Idaho and The Remarkable Women of Brokenheart Lane. A short story, *Man and Mouse*, appears in the April 2020 issue of Sun magazine. Her play, *Bluegrass of God*, is in Santa Ana River Review. Her short story, *Jimmy's Jar Collection*, appeared in the Ghastling's 13. She has five stories placed with Whistle Pig, Maybelle, Bunny Slipper, Pearlie at the Gates of Dawn, Greenhorn and Elbow and Bean. *City Full of Rain* was just accepted by Litmag. *Gladys,* a short story, will appear in Agony Opera. The short story, the *Elephant Girl,* will appear in the September 2021's the Bosphorus Review. Glady, also a short story, appears in September's Agony Opera. *Pig Bait* has been included in Gore, an anthology by Poe Boy Publishing, out in October2021. *The Witch of the Highway,* a short story, appears in the World of Myth in October as well. *Blood and Bread* will appear in Hellbound Books's Toilet Zone 3, the *Royal Flush,* due out in 2022. Her Sefi and Des will be included in Brigid Gate's Musings of the Muses, due out in 2022.

https://annwuehler.wordpress.com

More from Eerie River

Eerie River Publishing, is a small independant publishing house that is devoted to releasing quality dark fiction books and anthologies.

To stay up to date with all our new releases and upcoming giveaways, follow us on Facebook, Twitter, Instagram and YouTube. Sign up for our monthly newsletter and receive a free ebook Darkness Reclaimed, as our thank you gift.

https://mailchi.mp/71e45b6d5880/welcomebook

Interested in more ways to support?
Consider becoming a Patreon member. Our patreon membership gives you exclusive sneak peeks at upcoming books, early chapter releases, covers art as well as free ebooks and discounts on paperbacks.

https://www.patreon.com/EerieRiverPub.

ALSO AVAILABLE FROM
EERIE RIVER PUBLISHING

NOVELS
Miracle Growth
Storming Area 51: Horror At the Gate
In Solitudes Shadow
Dead Man Walking
Devil Walks in Blood
SENTINEL
A Sword Named Sorrow

ANTHOLOGIES
Monsters & Mayhem
AFTER: A Post-Apocalyptic Survivor Series
Last Stop
It Calls From The Forest: Volume I
It Calls From The Forest: Volume II
It Calls From The Sky
It Calls From the Sea
It Calls Fromt he Doors
Darkness Reclaimed
With Blood and Ash
With Bone and Iron
Forgotten Ones: Drabbles of Myth and Legend
Dark Magic: Drabbles of Magic and Lore

COMING SOON
It Calls From the Veil
Path of War
Last Stop

www.EerieRiverPublishing.com

It Calls From the Sea

After: A Post-Apocalyptic Survivor Series

Sentinel by Drew Starling